Tortured

Dreams

Hadena James

- UDHR
- imagery
- setting
- characterization
- mood
- questions
- conflict
- theme / motif
- irony
- foreshadowing
- metaphor / simile
- symbolism
- personification
- suspense
- stereotypes
- personal reactions & connections

Acknowledgments

For my mother, my father, Beth and Jason, the people that believed in me and convinced me to pursue my dreams.

Also by Hadena James

Dreams & Reality Novels
Tortured Dreams
Elysium Dreams
Mercurial Dreams
Explosive Dreams
Cannibal Dreams
Butchered Dreams
Summoned Dreams
Battered Dreams

The Brenna Strachan Series
Dark Cotillion
Dark Illumination
Dark Resurrections
Dark Legacies

The Dysfunctional Chronicles
The Dysfunctional Affair
The Dysfunctional Valentine
The Dysfunctional Honeymoon
The Dysfunctional Proposal
The Dysfunctional Holiday

Short Story Collection
Tales to Read Before the End of the World

Prologue

People love a good horror story, especially when it is real. I have a Ph.D. in History. I wrote my thesis on the evolution of torture as a crime deterrent in the Middle Ages. I didn't set out to write that as my thesis, but like everything else, a thesis evolves. It went over well and I am currently turning it into a book for the layman. My name is Aislinn Cain and my life is a horror story.

Currently, I live in Washington State. I attended the University of Washington for grad school and haven't returned to my roots yet. Those are firmly planted in the Mid-West. Missouri, to be exact, and to be more exact, Columbia, Missouri, home of the Tigers, Shakespeare's Pizza and Sub Shop.

I do intend to return. My studio apartment is too small and there are way too many people in Seattle for my taste. I don't go out much, but then I never really have. I don't like crowds. I don't like being forced to meet new people.

Physically speaking, I'm healthy as a horse. I am 5 foot, 3 inches tall, I weigh 130 pounds; I have a kickboxing rig set up in the studio apartment as well as a Tread-Climber. I work out for an hour every day.

Mentally, I'm slightly broken. I suffer from a severe anxiety disorder that almost kept me from getting any

1

degrees, let alone my Ph.D. Then, there is the pesky personality disorder that lies somewhere in my fractured psyche. They call it A-Typical Sociopathic Tendencies. I lack the ability to feel empathy or sympathy. I am hard to get angry, but once there, it is an almost uncontrollable rage. I ignore most of what society considers "reasonable," replacing it instead with a set of morals and values that I can understand. I do this because if I don't, I have no morals or values.

But my mental condition is something to be understood later, when everything has been explained. To try to understand it now is to try to do a jigsaw puzzle without half the pieces.

My skin is too dark to be considered fair, somewhere in my Scottish ancestry there must have been an Italian or someone else of Mediterranean descent. My hair is brown, unless dyed burgundy. My eyes are brown, like the color of good coffee. I chew my fingernails and I smoke too much. I like caffeine and I drink a ton of soda, hence the exercise routine. You never know when you'll need to run a mile, so to work off the soda and cigarettes, I exercise every day.

Currently, I have a black eye, a chipped tooth and am recovering from my shoulder being out of socket. This explains why there are three other people in my normally vacant apartment. My best friend, Nyleena Clachan, who doubles as my cousin, is fretting in the kitchen, cleaning it like the Queen of England might drop by for a visit. The other two are men.

If Adonis was built like a body builder, this guy would have been the model. The man could probably wrestle a dragon to the ground bare handed. He is at least 6 foot, 5 inches tall, with tanned skin, close cut blonde hair that is so blonde it looks white. His shoulders are probably the same width as I am tall. His legs could crush a cinder block. He has blue eyes that seem kind and belie the overly accentuated body. The bones on his face seem hard and sculpted. I knew women that would kill for cheekbones like his.

The other is his exact opposite. He might be 6 foot. He has dark hair, almost black, but not quite. He has eyes darker than mine. Skin a shade or two lighter and about two days worth of stubble growth. He is wearing a T-Shirt announcing some brand name beer. He is in faded blue jeans with spots that are getting thin enough they will be holes the next time he washes them. His tennis shoes look as old as me. He is thin; there is muscle, but not as large or as defined as his companion. To be honest, he looks like he has just cleaned up after a six week bender. His shirt is even wrinkled.

I had been introduced to them both three days earlier, while I lay in a hospital bed. I had been recovering from a violent attack after someone had broken into my apartment. They had explained to me then that his fingerprints had matched those involved with a number of rapes in the area. I was willing to bet money, that it was all going to be past tense.

I am not a good victim. I look like I should be. Quiet, petite, alone, but looks can be deceiving. My would-be rapist had figured that out pretty quickly. A cleaning company had been through the house and removed all the blood. I was sleeping on the couch since my bed hadn't been replaced yet. Most people would not be able to stay in the place where they were attacked, but I had no emotional qualms about it.

However, we'll come back to all of this. This is not where my story begins. It begins eighteen years earlier, when I am eight years old.

One

It was four days before Halloween. I had my
costume picked out. I was going to be Sherlock Holmes
that year. I was in sixth grade. Not because I wanted to
be, but because everyone else wanted me to be. Being an
eight year old in sixth grade points out that you might be
a bit of a freak. Or at least that was my thought at the
time.

I lived only six blocks from the elementary school I
attended. I walked to and from school every day. I
carried a lunch box and a backpack. Over the summer, I
had read a book called "*The Jungle*" by Upton Sinclair
and had decided to become a vegetarian. Actually, the
thought of eating meat conjured up images from the book
that made my stomach churn.

That was why I was in the sixth grade. I had read,
digested and understood books like "*The Jungle*" long
before I had finished the third grade. It had been
discovered when I read Stephen King's "*The Stand*"
during my third grade year. My teacher had grilled me
over it and found that I had understood it. Lots of special
tests were done and instead of enrolling in 4th grade, I
enrolled in 6th and I was exempt from English classes.
I was wearing a heavy jacket. Missouri weather is
unpredictable all the time, but especially so in Spring and
Fall. There is no telling what the day might bring. It has
happened many times before, that you wake up to 70
degree weather one Tuesday in October and by the time
afternoon comes, it is 50 and still dropping. The next day,
there might be snow or it might be 70 degrees again.

5

They found my jacket, my lunchbox and my backpack on the sidewalk, a mere half-block from my house. The spot my abductor had dropped them when he snatched me up. *suspense, unexpected*

Thinking back, I wonder if my mind wasn't already a little fractured. How does an eight year old survive? I've never had an answer, just the knowledge that I did. *who was it?*

My abductor was a man in his forties. He was pudgy with sallow skin and sunken eyes. They seemed to have constant rings around them, making him look a bit like Wednesday on the Addams' Family. *always tired* *simile*

He had pristine teeth. He didn't smell bad. He looked like anybody else. He also lived on my street. I knew him as Mr. Callow. *don't judge by the cover*

Dinner that night consisted of a peanut butter and jelly sandwich. I ate it. It wasn't drugged or anything, there was actually nothing interesting or useful about it, just something to eat.

The following morning, I heard police come into Mr. Callow's house. He answered all their questions and left with them. He was going to join the search.

I have never understood why I didn't cry out when the police were there. I'm sure they would have heard me. Fear perhaps? Perhaps it was something else. Some survival instinct that kept my mouth shut. Whatever it was, I didn't cry out for help while the police questioned him. *why did he do it?*

I searched my cell while he was gone. I came up with nothing. There were no windows, no furniture. The entire room might have been 4 foot by 6 foot. There was a door, but it seemed to have come from Wonderland. It was just big enough to toss me inside the room. I heard a slide lock every time it opened. *metaphor*

That day was boring. I had nothing to do but sit on a mattress on the floor. There were no books, nothing

6

[handwritten: UDHR freedom of thought]

to entertain me except my imagination and blank walls. I was bored as could be by the time Mr. Callow returned.

Mr. Callow made noises in another room. By the sounds of it, I guessed dinner. Metal was clinking against metal, the sound grated on my nerves, it irritated me to no end.

That night for dinner, he brought me a slice of *[handwritten: why is he being nice?]* cherry pie. It made me sick. Not because he had tampered with it, but because my stomach doesn't handle *[handwritten: why is he keeping him hostage]* sweets without solid food. I threw up sometime during the night.

The following morning, Mr. Callow cleaned up the mess. He fed me cereal and a glass of milk. My stomach settled. He left. I got no lunch. *[handwritten: same day repeated]*

I don't know what time he returned. The migraine beating a rapid tempo in my brain proved that I had missed lunch. His incessant banging in the kitchen did more than just irritate me this time. It enraged me. I was so angry by the time he brought me dinner that I snapped. *[handwritten: his bubble finally bursted]*

The events that happened in those ten minutes or so happened very fast. Faster than one would think. I remember all of it.

He brought me a plastic spoon to eat corn and meatloaf. I have never liked meatloaf. I've had migraines since I could walk. There are certain foods that make migraines worse, pork and ground hamburger are among them, making meatloaf one of the things not on my "approved food list".

One doctor told me it was the migraine that made me snap. The lack of food and the excruciating pain were too much. I went into a rage because I was in so much pain, like a wounded animal. *[handwritten: simile]*

Another doctor told me that it was probably the sight of the meatloaf. He was sure that reading "*The*

Jungle" at such a young age had damaged my psyche. If it did, I recovered; I am not a vegetarian now.

Either way, I snapped and went into a rage. I grabbed the plastic spoon from the tray and shoved it into his eye, handle first. I pushed until the spoon head snapped off in my hand. He howled and grabbed at me. But it was too little too late for him. I grabbed his head and slammed it into the floor.

He didn't move after that. I climbed out the small door. It entered into a closet. I shut the doors of the closet; actually, I shut every door behind me as I made my escape.

I slammed his front door as I entered into the street. The sight of the darkened street, front windows and porch lights burning, broke whatever trance had kept me quiet. I stood on his porch and screamed for help.

Help came. The neighbor, Mrs. Henry and her son, who was a few years older than me, were the first to come out of their houses. I didn't stop screaming though until sirens could be heard in the distance and my parents could be seen running down the street.

I went to therapy for a couple of years. I was labeled "damaged" and sent to another therapist. They didn't do any better and by the time I was 13, it had been labeled as Post-Traumatic Stress Disorder along with an anxiety disorder. This was, of course, incorrect. They didn't have a better diagnosis; they were only working with part of the picture.

Two

There was something I never told the therapists. When I shoved the spoon handle into Mr. Callow, I was hoping that he died. It was the only thing I could think of at the time. I wanted him dead more than anything else in the world. *revenge for what he did*

No one would have understood it then. I'm not sure they would today. But I knew about Mr. Callow. Or at least, I had read about it in the papers. I didn't have a name to place on the serial killer at the time. I knew what a serial killer was though and I knew the moment Mr. Callow snatched me from the street that he was the one in the papers.

At that moment, even as he was shoving me in the trunk of his car, I was already plotting how to escape. I was already plotting how to kill him. *thinking ahead, so did he plan to* I believed he deserved it. He might have. Mr. Callow had a pattern. He kept his victims for two weeks. He molested them. Raped them. Tortured them. Then, only after they had endured as much as their small little bodies could endure, did he release them with death. *to stop him? so young)*

A few years later, when I realized what serial killers and other criminals did to child molesters in prison, I started to think Mr. Callow had gotten off too light. He should have lived, faced the hell of his own making in a small cell with violent men. I still believe that. *UDHR no torture*

I gave up on therapy by the time I was fourteen. There was no point. They had labeled me "damaged goods", but I was probably damaged before Mr. Callow *so young)*

9

had taken me. It wasn't something they could fix. I had to fix it.

I did. I built my own code of conduct. Thou shalt not kill was not among them. Thou shalt not kill for no reason and without provocation was.

Mr. Callow was just the beginning. I said I should be an easy victim, but I'm not. This is because I am not a victim, I am a volunteer. I invite the evil monsters into my house hoping for the best and preparing for the worst. Mr. Callow was just the first, not the last.

I finished my bachelor's degree from the University of Michigan when I was only nineteen. I held degrees in history, anthropology and sociology at that point.

I had been accepted to the University of Washington and was preparing for the move when the second one struck.

I was out with a few friends; I didn't have more than a few friends, celebrating graduation and acceptance to the graduate program. I was not old enough to drink, but my college friends were. I noticed him. They did not.

He followed us out of the bar. My stomach flopped only once. There was something about him, something indefinable. I knew that he was like Mr. Callow. He was dangerous.

One of my sociology professors had done a series of lectures on how violence begets violence and how violent people are attracted to other violent people. I understood it in ways that most of my fellow students had not. I had been attracting violent people since I was eight years old. Violent people just naturally gravitated to me. To them, I was someone who needed to be dominated, someone that needed to be taught a lesson.

I don't think violent people understand it on that level or any level. I understand it. But I have been aware of it for 18 years.

10

I ensured my girlfriends all got back to their
apartment. I even convinced one of the guys in the group
that he should stay with them. They were too drunk to be
left alone. He agreed, although, he can't say why he
agreed. He couldn't tell the police why he agreed.

I took the lone stalker back towards my own
apartment. I locked the front door. I locked the windows.
If he got in, I'd deal with it. If he didn't, then I would
sleep until morning and then go back to packing.

His name was Gerard Hawkins. He did manage to
break into my apartment. It turned out I was his prey all
along. I looked like his ex-girlfriend, a woman who had
cuckolded him and worse. His goal was to slit my throat,
it was unrealized.

I took my own knife from the bedside table and
plunged it deep into his ear canal. I was told he didn't die
immediately. He lived for a couple of seconds.

I didn't tell the university police or the local police
that I already knew that. I had watched the life drain
from him. I had watched his body twitch. I knew exactly
what had happened as he had died.

I told them it was all a blank. The knife was a
decorative piece, not a weapon of self-defense. I had
awoken when he had clamped his hand over my mouth. I
had just reacted, possibly badly.

They agreed that I had done what I needed to do.
Gerard Hawkins turned out to be my second serial killer.
He had killed six others in the Cleveland, Ohio area and
moved to Michigan when he thought they were getting on
to him.

The FBI had been brought in then too. A serial
killer crossing state lines was a big deal. By then, I knew
that I was a sociopath. During a lecture on affect in
relation to abnormal psychological conditions, specifically
Anti-Social Personality Disorder, my professor had
noticed something that all the other doctors had missed.

11

I lacked affect a great deal of the time and I was quite capable of being charming, even charismatic at times. He also noticed that I could be cold, calculating and completely void of any affect. He asked me to stay after class, pretending to want to talk to me about a paper I had written. After entering his office, he sat me down and began talking about my past. My professor was aware that I was in his class because of my previous encounters. He was the first to tell me that I was a sociopath.

After several meetings, we agreed that it would be wrong to give me an official diagnosis that would result in society stigmatizing me. Instead, he gave me some coping techniques. They were great. He also told me that I did have an anxiety disorder, but none of it was Post-Traumatic Stress Disorder. That would have required me to feel guilty.

Since guilt is also not among my emotional abilities, I have never felt guilty for defending myself. Besides, it keeps them from hurting others.

Which brings me back to my current situation and the two men sitting in my living room.

Three

My current situation had started some three weeks earlier, possibly more, but unlikely. I had noticed my follower coming home from the coffee shop one afternoon. I don't normally go to coffee shops, but I had a peculiar craving for hot chocolate and a blackberry muffin.

The coffee shop hadn't had a blackberry muffin, but they did have poppy seed muffins. So I got one of those and a hot chocolate, despite the fact that it was September. I sat in the coffee shop long enough to eat the muffin. I threw away the napkins and what not and carried my hot chocolate out to the street.

That was when I noticed him. He was leaning against a building. He had been leaning in the same spot when I arrived at the coffee shop. Even though the weather hadn't dropped to the negatives yet, it wasn't exactly outdoor weather. It was raining.

The rain was a misting, cold rain that seemed to blow in around raincoats and soak into the bones. I had a few that creaked already from being broken or dislocated, so I didn't dawdle in the street. I upped my pace, head down, coat closed to the rain and headed back home.

That was part of my routine. I left my house once a day, at the same time every day, either to get lunch or to get a snack. If I didn't force myself outside, I wouldn't leave for weeks since I didn't have classes or a job.

Tucked away in my apartment, I looked out the window and found the man standing at the building across the street. Seeing as how I try to avoid problems, I did report it to my local police. They came out, took a

13

statement and went away. One episode does not a stalker make.

Except, he was there the following morning. I waited another week and reported him again. He was turning up in restaurants where I ate and standing outside the building where I lived. The police were just as uninterested with the second report.

I called Nyleena that night. There are moments when I wonder if I have actually fallen down the rabbit hole. I told her that I thought I had a stalker, but that the police disagreed. Would she come out and see if I was going mad?

Nyleena is a lawyer in Kansas City, Missouri. A federal prosecutor to be exact. I find her job tedious and boring and necessary. She finds my lifestyle tedious, dangerous and unnecessary. She never flinches when she gets those phone calls and she always comes to stand by my side.

She jumped on a plane the next day. I wasn't hallucinating, he existed, Nyleena saw him as well. She stayed about a week and then went home, disgruntled with the third police report and I'm sure, calling in whatever favors she could.

Two days after she returned home, I had awoken with the knowledge that I wasn't alone in my small apartment. I couldn't see him. But I knew he was there.

His shoes made some noise on the floor and I immediately found his location. He was creeping through the dark. He was slinking towards me.

I did what any normal woman would do. I flipped on the lights. My bedside lamp caused him to freeze in place for a moment.

He almost had me. The fight that ensued was like no other I had ever been in. He was strong and I guess I was not properly pissed. He got a good clip at my face

14

with a blunt object. It had blackened my eye and chipped my tooth. *imagery*

The din had awoken a neighbor. They called the police while I struggled with my intruder. They responded rather fast. But not fast enough. *foreshadow*

He wrenched my arm around my back; put his knee into the shoulder blade. I felt and heard it pop out of place. I screamed wordlessly when it did. It was what I needed. The blood surged and I went to a quiet, dark place inside myself. *situational irony* *UDHR no torture*

This place is calm. Always still and calm, I never feel anything when I am in it except calm. It is a place where no light gets in. It is a place I worry one day I will enter and never leave. My only other true friend in the world, Malachi Blake, says this nothingness is the only true emotion we have. He lives there. *compares her inside as a place — metaphor*

Once I entered that calm state, the world slowed down for me. Despite his hold on me and my non-working shoulder, I grabbed at him. I caught hold of his hair and pulled his face down towards me. I was stronger than him suddenly. His twisting and turning in my grasp only pulled out his hair in chunks. *shows how hard she pulled*

I grabbed hold firmer, closer to the scalp. I could feel his blood running through my fingers. He let go of my dislocated shoulder.

When he let go, I stood up, still holding his hair. I turned on him, made sure we were face to face. I slammed my forehead into his nose. He made a gurgling noise and dropped to the ground. *she had to be calm to get*

He wasn't dead, just stunned. He rolled over. I lashed out, grabbing his head again and slamming it into the floor. I don't know how many times. Eventually, the noises stopped and the police came in. *mad again*

Once again, I was diagnosed with post-traumatic stress disorder. My life had been a real bitch. Two serial

imagery   *tru*   *metaphor*

killers and one serial rapist, none of them had survived. I have good survival instincts. ~what?. metaphor

Then I met the blonde-mountain and bender-man. I was recovering in the hospital, dreading what they would say to me when I got home.

Four

"Dr. Cain," the mountain began to talk. His voice was not as deep as one expected. It did not reverberate through the body, shaking the lungs as the sound rung in your ears. It was a bit higher pitched than my mind had told me it would sound.

"We met in the hospital, I am US Marshal Lucas McMichaels and this is Marshal Xavier Reece. Do you remember us?" He continued. *characterization*

"Vaguely," I told him, honestly. "I remember you being there, I don't remember what we talked about or anything." *tone- calm, dull*

Nyleena came in and sat down with me. She had turned on lawyer mode. Her eyes were cold and unreadable. She would tell me what questions to answer and what ones to ignore.

"Yes, sorry about the circumstances," Marshal Reece, bender-man, said. "We would have preferred to meet under different circumstances. Your essay a few years ago about torture used by the Catholic Church was fascinating."

"I'm sorry, have I missed something?" I asked both of them. *she doesn't remember*

"You really don't remember why we are here," McMichaels gave a sigh.

"You aren't here to arrest me or question me about this attack?" I decided to go with blunt. *tone - blunt*

This got me a smile from both men and a stern look from Nyleena.

"No, ma'am," McMichaels seemed to relax a little. "Unless there is something you'd like to confess. I mean, we know all about you and frankly..."

The large man spread his arms wide. I understood what he was getting at. I rolled my eyes.

"In the United States, one out of every two people will meet a serial killer in their life, of those, only about 2% of the 400 million people will ever be a victim. I have been picked by two serial killers and a serial rapist. The odds are astronomically against it being a coincidence."

"They are, but then, most people don't survive an attack at eight years old," Reece grinned at me. "But this recent encounter with a serial rapist or your previous encounters with serial killers aren't why we are here. They are just why we know you exist and might be an expert on them. We do know you're an expert on torture and that is why we are here."

"You want to torture someone using medieval means?" I frowned at them.

"No, we want your opinion on someone that does," McMichaels pulled out a folder.

"Ms. Clachan," he turned to Nyleena. "These photos are graphic."

"Try being friends with my cousin and a prosecutor for the federal government," Nyleena kept his gaze for a couple of seconds.

"All right," McMichaels opened the folder.

Several photos were on top. I took hold of the photos carefully. For a moment, my mind didn't make sense of the first image. Suddenly, it came into view, crystal clear. My stomach flopped. Nyleena gasped and looked away.

I was looking at people. They had been impaled on stakes, roughly fifteen foot tall. There were ten people total. Each had about a foot of the stake sticking out of their mouths.

18

In the foreground was the most disturbing part. There was a large, wooden table with chairs. Empty plates decorated the center of the table and one place setting was left. It had obviously been used.

I frowned harder. Nyleena excused herself from the room. I understood her need to run away. I wanted to run away. However, I recognized the scene.

"It is from a book," I handed the folder back to him. "It is a drawing from an obscure book on torture; this particular scene is about the infamous Vlad Tepes or Dracula. It is said that he impaled all the peasants who owed him money and dined while they died. It could be an old wives' tale or it could be real, Tepes was a cruel man brought up in cruel circumstances."

I got up and went to my bookcase. I pulled out a book. It was bound in leather with tape along the spine. The language was German. I opened it to the page with the drawing and handed it to McMichaels.

"Very obscure, I found the book when I was young. It was in a garage sale that a neighbor from Germany had. He was a history professor at the University in my home town. I kept in touch with him until he died a few years ago. He taught me German."

"What is it?" Reece asked.

"Literally, it means *Book of Torture*. It was written by a sociologist when the term didn't exist. It explores the reasons behind torture and why it was accepted. However, this version hasn't been in print for at least 70 years, possibly a hell of a lot longer. The Nazis banned it. I'm not even sure how many copies exist in the modern day. You can't check it out from any library that I've ever been to. However, I'm sure that is not the only time that scene has been depicted. As I said earlier, it is a well-known story about Tepes. My only concern with that picture you have and the one in that book is the exact number of people. Your picture has ten, that

19

somehow related

drawing has ten. Every other one I've seen has lots or it has only a few."

I sat back down, something nagging at the back of my brain. I waited for it to form. When it did, I cringed.

"I hate to ask, but the impaling, was it done properly?" I closed my eyes. It was not something I wanted to think about.

"Explain properly?"

"They are all female in the photo and the drawing. The other thing I find disturbing. However, in the book, it talks about Tepes impaling males through the anus and females through the vagina. Ropes were tied to their ankles; they were pulled down upon the stake. It was painful and not an immediate death. Once the impaling was started, they would stop and let gravity do the rest. Gravity would find the path of least resistance, hence the stake coming out the mouth. If they were impaled properly, they were put on the stake, alive, through the vagina, and pulled down until only about a foot to a foot and half of the stake had disappeared. Gravity would have done the rest."

motis

"Yes, it was done properly," Reece masked his face. "Why bring this to me?"

"You're an expert on historic torture and you've survived two serial killers, which might make you an expert on them as well," McMichaels told me. "This isn't the first."

"He's impaled more people?" The thought was horrifying.

"No, we found a group of ten women stuffed into five Iron Maidens about three months ago. Six months ago, we found a group of ten women, drawn and quartered."

hyperbole

My blood ran cold and my heart nearly stopped beating. I licked my lips and took the book back from

20

Reece. I turned to the first drawing and handed it back to him.

"Your killer has a copy of this book," I pointed to the first drawing. It contained the remains of ten women, tossed in a heap, all drawn and quartered.

"What on..." McMichaels took it from Reece.

"This book was written before sociology or psychology was a science, they were just philosophies. A few bright people tossing around ideas really, the author hired an artist to do the drawings in the book. One of the other members of his group noticed a disturbing pattern. All the drawings pictured women, ten of them to be exact. He also noticed that it appeared to be the same ten women in each picture. He got onto the local police. The local police got onto the artist and found the remains of ten women in his basement. He was tried, convicted and sentenced to death for cannibalism. The book was never printed again. In 1934, it was suggested that it be printed without the pictures, but the thought so repulsed the Nazi party, that they refused. They began collecting all the copies they could of it. They were among the first books burnt. To think of a German cannibal was too much even for Hitler. So they tried to erase him from the German histories. Did a pretty good job. You won't find his paintings anywhere and there are very few surviving copies of this book. About ten years ago, it was reprinted finally, but without the pictures and it had been reworked enough to get a different name stamped on the cover. However, if I'm right, the killer has an original."

I opened to another page. There was a picture of five Iron Maidens, doors open. Each held the bodies of two women, blood visible as it dripped down their bodies and made puddles on the floors.

[handwritten annotations: "why doesn't she become an investigator"; "how did they know it was him?"; "your right to life"; "situational irony"; "imagery"]

21

Five

"You think our killer has a copy of this book and there is no way to track it because it isn't likely to be a library book," McMichaels turned the page.

"That would be correct. Worse though, the obscurity of the book, the fact it isn't in English, the complexity of the German; your killer is probably brilliant." *usually they are*

"All of them are anymore. That's why we came to you," Reece opened the folder back up. He took out another picture and handed it to me.

foreshadow

It was a close-up shot of a hand. On the hand, drawn in blood, was a hieroglyphic. I frowned at it.

"It isn't Egyptian or Sumerian." I pulled the picture closer to my nose. McMichaels handed me a small magnifying glass. I held it over the photo.

"Oh, that's bad," I looked at it closer. It wasn't a hieroglyph, it was a pictograph.

"Why is it bad?"

"It is the symbol for death, not death as a state of existence, but Death the being." *like a person?*

"You recognize it?"

"Vaguely, I have seen it only a few times in my studies. It was used by a Germanic tribe. They sacked Rome, you might have heard of them, the Vandals. For the most part, Vandals didn't give a shit about reading or writing, so pictographs are pretty rare. Sorry, that was bitchy sounding, even to me."

"It is a lot to take in, Doctor," McMichaels dismissed it with a wave of his hand.

very forward / characterization

"It is, but that doesn't give me the right to treat you like a child who isn't paying attention to a lecture," I frowned hard at the pictograph.

[handwritten: simile]

"Shock will do that to you," Reece assured me.

"Anymore of these symbols?" I put the photo down.

"Loads. He seems to be sending a message. A few have been translated, most haven't. He is gloating about how smart he is with them."

[handwritten: vocab]

"Sure it's a man? Women are quite capable of torture and more likely to have a flare for the dramatic."

[handwritten: gender neutral]

"Sexual assault on the females that were found drawn and quartered says it is a man."

[handwritten: can be funny]

"Semen found?"

"No, but something very odd was." Reece looked at me with a strange look. "Are you sure you want to hear?"

[handwritten: in a serious situation]

"It can't be any worse than the impaled photo." I told him.

[handwritten: could still be a girl]

"We found excess amounts of yeast. We are guessing he has a yeast infection."

[handwritten: characterization]

"Or not," I gave a twisted smile as I said it. "The ancient Greeks created dildos out of bread."

[handwritten: characterization]

"Not this type of yeast," Reece smiled back. There was a moment of connection, I suddenly felt very comfortable with both of them. Since this never happened, it struck me as odd.

[handwritten: she's weird]

"Ok, then. So the guy has a problem and needs a doctor," I said.

[handwritten: had a satisfaction in saying that]

"Unlikely he even knows he has it. Men can carry it without knowing they have one," Reece told me.

"Really?" I looked at him again and adjusted my opinion. I had known that, but it wasn't exactly something most guys knew.

"I have a medical degree," Reece answered the unasked question. "I do most of the autopsies."

situational irony

"I wouldn't have guessed, Doctor," I continued to smile despite the horror and death in front of me.

"No one ever does," McMichaels rolled his eyes. "He always looks like he is coming off a drunk. Several days of drunken debauchery to be exact." mood- annoyed

vocab "That is exactly what I thought when I met him today," I told them.

"Back to the photos and less on my attire and appearance," Reece chimed in. "Want to see the other symbols?"

"It is unlikely I will know any of them. This one I know only because of my studies in Medieval Europe. The Vandals helped shape history when they sacked Rome."

vocab Undeterred, Xavier Reece handed me a stack of photos. All of them were close up shots of different symbols on different body parts. When compartmentalized like they were, you didn't even realize that you were looking at dead body parts.

"Egyptian," I tossed a photo to him.

"Very good," he said.

"I almost became an anthropologist. When I decided that would be boring, I considered becoming an Egyptologist," I told him.

"Sumerian or Assyrian would be my guess on that one," I handed him another photo.

"This one is Celt," I frowned at it. "Or rather, Pict. There aren't many experts on the Picts."

"We found one in England," McMichaels told me.

"Good, because my translation would be rough," I looked at a different photo and my frown deepened.

suspense "What?" Reece asked.

"This one is not from a language or at least not a real language. It has been described a few times." I got up and went to another book shelf. I selected the book I wanted and flopped back into my worn out spot on the couch.

"I don't remember the page," I handed it to them. "But Lovecraft goes into great detail about the Mark of Cthulu. An educated guess tells me that's the mark."

"We'd been having trouble with that one," McMichaels said.

"That's because you've been asking anthropologists, archeologists and historians. You'd need a lit professor for it," I told him. "They'd be more capable of giving you all the details. I've read Lovecraft many times, but Cthulu is either the Devil or some sort of Demon. I've never really figured that out."

"Latin?" I asked looking at the word that was scrawled on another arm.

"Yes, there is some Old Greek, some very Old Russian, but the weirdest one is in Aramaic."

"Aramaic? Are you sure?" I took a deep breath and held it. _is that a bad thing?._

"Yes, we found someone to translate it, sort of. We are still looking for an expert, but it seems to be about the deadest language on the planet." _personification? hyperbole_

"Check the Vatican," I let out the breath. "In theory, Christ spoke Aramaic and as far as I know, the experts in the language are all priests. It isn't spoken or written any more. I have no idea where your killer came up with it." _that'd had be to be at least 5 secs_

"I don't think the Vatican will let us in to question a priest," Reece smiled at me.

"True, but one of the big Archdioceses might and they might have an Aramaic scholar. I'd check the East Coast for it, maybe Boston or New York." _why?._

"Irish Catholics? Isn't that a bit stereotypical of you?" McMichaels asked.

"Perhaps, but I don't consider Irish Catholics to be a bad thing. Besides, an Italian Catholic would work. After all, Vatican City is in Rome."

"What else do you see?" Reece asked.

"I see some more archaic German, but I'm no help there. I learned German from a former East Berliner. I speak High German with an Eastern flare. I can give you insight into Vandals, Visigoths, Franks, Norse, and other Germanic tribes, but most of them were not real literate or concerned with it. So it isn't like there is a Rosetta Stone."

When I got to the last picture, I stopped and stared at it. In plain English, written on a leg was "Revelations 22:22 – And mankind came unto the Lord and begged his forgiveness. And the Lord heard them. He sent forth a Defender of Mankind. And then mankind began to question the Defender and went back unto the Lord and asked 'why have you sent him. He is evil, we dream of him.' And the Lord said to them 'he is wicked, defending mankind is his punishment'. And mankind said 'take this evil thing from us. He cannot help us.' And the Lord said 'nothing can help you.'"

Bible

wonder what that means

Six

"Dr. Cain?" Reece asked.

"Sorry, I just don't know what I find the most disturbing about that passage."

"We've checked..." McMichaels started.

"There is no Revelations 22:22. Revelations ends with chapter 22, verse 21. Making your own bible passage is a bit off. Making it sound authentic is creepy. And I'm tired and might be reading too much into it. *[handwritten: mood – creepy]* Mind if I keep a copy of the Revelations passage?"

"Not at all," Reece handed me a photocopy of it typed out.

"Now, Dr. Cain," McMichaels started talking again, "what we really want, is your help. There should be another murder soon, within a week or so. When it happens, we'd like you to look at the scene while it's still fresh, see what you can see." *[handwritten: why don't they prevent it?]*

[handwritten: used to it] "Sure," I put the passage on the table.

"You might pack an overnight bag and have it ready to go the moment the call comes in. At this time, we don't have enough to stop him; we don't have enough to even pick up his trail. He isn't striking in the same locations."

"So he could pop up just about anywhere," I nodded once.

"Pretty much, we'll come by tomorrow," Reece got up.

I stood with them, waved good bye at the door and came back to my couch with a sense of relief. Nyleena also joined me, her face still hard set. Her eyes were no longer cold.

"You have a bad habit of killing people who attack you," she said after a couple of seconds. "Do you think working with the police is a good idea?"

"I'm not a serial killer Nyleena, just a survivalist and sociopath. Besides, maybe if I help, a few of them will leave me alone."

looking out for her friend "Or you'll attract more when your face suddenly appears in the USA Today and New York Times."

"There is that," I met her eyes for a second, "somehow, I know this is right."

"I know, you seemed to connect to those two. You don't do that very often," she sighed in resignation.

"What was the big deal with the Revelations passage?" We had been silent for a long time when Nyleena asked.

"It's coherent, well planned, authentic sounding," I told her.

"But I know you and that isn't why you asked for a copy."

"It was his subject choice and words. Dreams, Evil, Defender of Mankind, that seems odd."

"Holy…" Nyleena took a deep breath through her nose and frowned at me, "maybe you should wait for the next one."

"The next what Nyleena? The next serial killer who comes knocking on my door to sell me satellite TV and then realizes I'd be fun to cut up? Despite what you *sarcasm* think, it isn't a life I picked. They're moths and I'm the flame. If I do this, if I see it from the inside, maybe there *metaphor* won't be a next time. Maybe the light will be extinguished."

"Unlikely," Nyleena gave me a long hard look, "ok, do this. But I'm guessing this is a recruitment and this case is your trial by fire. I've heard of these guys. They are a bit reckless and they are stationed in Missouri, near the Fortress. They live in that fancy, secured, all police neighborhood. They are the bogeymen of serial killers. A bit loose and on the fringe. Malachi would fit in perfect with them."

My only two real friends in the world did not get along. Malachi thought that Nyleena didn't understand the way the world worked and Nyleena thought it was wrong for a psychopath to work for the FBI. Of course, they had been feuding long before that. It was just their newest reason to fight.

"You think it is aimed at you?" Nyleena asked.

"No, I think we are just jittery because my life is what it is," I shrugged at her.

Nyleena took a strand of her long, raven colored hair and began to twirl it. It was graying in streaks, but she had managed to avoid grabbing any of the gray. I never knew how she managed.

"Ok, we'll go with that for now," she returned the shrug and stood up.

"What now?"

"Now, we have dinner, if I can remove that image from my brain."

"You've seen worse."

"That's true. I keep considering becoming a vegetarian as a result."

"You'd be a terrible vegetarian," I smiled at her and relaxed a bit. The storm was over. Her anger and fear were still there, but they weren't going to surface now. Since it hadn't happened, everything seemed right with the world again.

"Where are we ordering from?" I asked.

"I found a pan and made pasta." Nyleena informed me.

"Oh," I thought for a moment. "You found a pan where?"

"Under the sink."

"Toss out the pasta, we'll order out."

"Why?" Nyleena asked.

"I only have two pans and they were both in the dish drainer when I was attacked. Since blood made it to the counter, both of them should have been pitched. So, why was there a pan under the sink?"

"Think someone brought it?"

"I could have bought it and forgot, but why take that chance," I was paranoid out of habit.

"As paranoid as you are, I'm surprised you let others fix your food."

"Well, I tried eating at home, every meal, every day and found I had to do a lot of dishes. Besides, it would be just as easy to poison bottles of spaghetti sauce at the store as it would be to poison a pizza from the place down the road. The difference is that if it is from the place down the road, they are more likely to get caught than if they just randomly hit bottles of spaghetti sauce at the store."

"Why does your paranoid logic make sense?"

"Because you've known me for a long, long time," I told her. "And because some, including you, would say that my paranoia is somewhat justified."

"Stop, that freaks me out. Crazy people should not sound that rational. Ever," she gave me a wicked grin that made her gray eyes light up.

"Since I fixed pasta, I'm ordering pasta," she grabbed her cell phone and speed dialed a place down the road. It was amazing that she had those numbers programmed into her phone.

"If it had something to do with me, Reece and McMichaels would have figured it out, they seem smart and capable. They have my file, I'm sure it has my full name."

"Not many men know that most mothers' pick names for their meanings as well as the lyrical sounds of them and their uniqueness," Nyleena gave me look, "even

30

if you spelled it all out for them, I still am not sure they would get it."

"You think it was actually meant for me?"

"No, I think you are right, we read too much into it because we are jittery and jumping at shadows."

"Should I tell them I have plans to move back to Missouri at the end of the month?" for what

"Yes, they should know. If this thing drags on, if you don't catch him this time, they will need to know where you are."

"Think they can catch him?"

I think she will

Seven

At ten in the morning, there was a knock on the door. I hadn't slept well the night before, but I hadn't slept well in almost twenty years. It is a side effect of my life. tragic life

McMichaels and Reece came into the apartment. They returned to the seats they had vacated the day before. Nyleena sat down next to me on the couch. She took hold of my hand.

"There's something I should tell you, before I get involved in this case," I took a deep breath. "I have a 'fan' for lack of a better word, although, 'creepy stalker' might work. I don't know who it is or where he is or much about him. He sends me letters on my birthday, a Christmas card at Christmas and once or twice a year, I get an extra letter from him. He signs his letters 'The Butcher' and describes his latest kill in graphic detail. It started right before I left for college. There was an incident that local reporters found newsworthy. I got the first letter about two weeks after that incident. By then though, I had moved to Michigan, so I don't know how he got my new address. He always seems to have my address. I reported it to the FBI, but they didn't have any victims matching his description, so they wrote it off as a hoax. My friend, Malachi Blake, works for the FBI and he now collects the stuff The Butcher sends me. Malachi has been trying to get a fix on him since the FBI wrote it off. It's a spare-time thing. Nyleena sees the letters and works on them from her end. So far, nothing has popped up on him."

"How many people know about it?" Reece asked.

32

"Including the people in this room?"

"Yes," Reece answered.

"Seven. The four of us, the original FBI agent, Malachi Blake and the guy who sends the letters."

"Are they threatening?" McMichaels asked.

"No, just twisted," I frowned. "I'd give you copies, but I don't keep the originals or any copies. I hand them all over."

"We will talk to someone and have them look more thoroughly into the matter," McMichaels answered.

"Ok, not sure it will do any good, but feel free to dig."

"How many victims would he be up to if he really is killing them?"

"It's been ten years, so ten birthdays, ten Christmases and a handful of others..." I shrugged. "At least twenty-one, but some years, I get two letters besides the usual." *this is normal for her*

"This year?" He asked.

"I've had only one besides the one on my birthday."

"I see," McMichaels seemed to think for a while. "Any connection to this case?"

"Only me, I just thought you should be aware of it."

"Well, I don't see that it will hinder anything," Reece joined back in.

"What now?"

"Now, we officially make you a consultant. Our unit is a trial unit; we've been together about three years. None of us could pass a psych test, so they didn't bother with that. There are four of us total, you will be working mostly with Xavier and myself, simply because Alejandro doesn't like consultants. He's a bit of an ass, but he's good at what he does. We have a geek, his name is Michael Giovanni. He does all our roving tech support. Xavier is our on scene medical examiner. I'm the

character introduction   33   *characterization*

pyschologist. I have a degree from Yale in psychology. Xavier and I both served as SEALS, not sure how we slipped in, but we did. Alejandro has a last name, he refuses to use it. We won't bother to tell you what it is because he'll yell loudly if you use it."

"An entire unit of head cases?" Nyleena raised an eyebrow.

"Yes, who better to track serial killers than functional monsters just one step away from being one themselves?" McMichaels looked at her. "Hence the word 'trial'. We've had good success so far, almost 100% on cases we've worked. Usually, two months is the average time we work a case. This one isn't average and isn't making us look very good."

"I understand," I lied through my teeth.

"Lucas has a compensation problem, hence the enormous girth. I have PTSD that manifests into violent rages. Alejandro is his own special breed. Michael is about as social as a plank of wood. And now we have a sociopathic consultant. It should be a good case."

"You know I'm a sociopath?"

"There isn't much we don't know about you. We know Malachi Blake is smart enough to fake being normal, hence how he became an FBI agent. He also suffers from a dissociative disorder, but he is a full-blown psychopath. Nyleena Clachan, cousin and best friend, defender of Kansas City, has an outstanding prosecution rate, specializes in serial crimes, no doubt because of your past. Your father is deceased. Shot and killed in the line of duty while investigating a domestic disturbance. Your mother is a librarian and worrier. You have one older brother who is currently serving a life sentence in The Fortress. You have one sister, also deceased, from the same domestic violence call that claimed your father. Your mother has four sisters and two brothers. Your father has two brothers and one sister. You are mostly estranged from your family. There is no history of abuse in your family. There is some history of mental instability, on both sides. You changed your name shortly before you turned sixteen because you didn't want to be known as the 'child that survived' on your driver's license. You are very close to your mother, Malachi Blake and Nyleena, but you don't seem to be close to anyone else. You haven't been on a date in over a year and it has probably been seven years since you bothered with a relationship," McMichaels told me. *well, they did their research*

"You're good and for the record, I haven't been on a date in over three years. My last date died in a random, freak accident." *her life seems to be constant tragedies*

"Maybe not so random or freak or accident," Xavier tilted his head to the side and looked at me. "That would be one Thomas Barter. He was killed in a hit and run."

"That would be correct," I answered.

"Hit while waiting to retrieve his car from valet parking, the car turned out to be stolen. Nothing on the inside. Case never solved."

"Pretty much. I stopped dating after that."

"Possible your 'fan' did it?"

"Anything is possible in my world," I lit a cigarette. *symbolism – relieving stress*

"Could you not..." Reece started to say. *against smoking*

"I could not light it up, sure, but since my choices seem to be death by serial killer or death by bad habits..." I lit the cigarette again, stupid safety cigarettes always burn out when they are in your hand and then start ashtray fires because they won't go out if you aren't holding them.

"Point taken, enjoy," McMichaels shot Reece a look that said many things, if you were on the inside. I wasn't.

"So, does she get paid for consulting?" Nyleena asked, always the practical one.

"Yes, standard rates apply to consultants," McMichaels assured her.

"Good, because she is running through her trust fund; she could use a little cash infusion."

"Ah the trust fund," McMichaels smiled.

"Started when you were eight years old by your maternal grandparents. They started it while you were missing. Several people chipped in at the time. Now your family still adds money to it every so often."

"Everyone was pretty sure I wouldn't function if I was found, so they built a trust fund," I shrugged. "Nyleena continues to contribute because she knows I do not function well in society." just looking out

"Malachi Blake has also contributed in the past," McMichaels added.

"He also knows I don't function well. I have no student loans, but I sure made a lot of college kid's cry," I stubbed out the cigarette.

"College paid for with scholarships, tutoring in English and paper writing. Grad school was partially paid for by tutoring in German, English and paper writing, the other by working for the college as an assistant. And you're fluent in German," Reece added.

"And enough about me. What about you guys? Why did you pick me? I know there are other experts out there."

"Because they don't deal with serial killers, you do." McMichaels answered.

tone - sarcastic "So I win the creepy prize," I shook my soda can and found it empty. I got up, walked the ten feet and got a refill.

"Maybe you should lay off the caffeine," Reece looked at the full can of Coca-Cola.

"I don't sleep. I exercise every day. I have a possible serial killer who sends me letters. I don't eat junk food. I don't live extravagantly. I think letting me have a cigarette and a soda is allowed." *very reasonable*

"Why don't you sleep?" McMichaels showed concern.

"If people broke into your house twice in seven years, would you sleep?" I asked him.

"Yes," He answered. *tone - sharp*

"That isn't why she doesn't sleep. If you were kidnapped at the age of eight, then killed two serial killers and had a creepy fan, would you sleep?" Nyleena corrected.

"Probably not," Reece answered. *probably from her experiences*

"I find my dreams to be very vivid and very bad, so I have trouble sleeping through the night," I told them. "My childhood may have had something to do with it, but I was having them long before I was kidnapped."

"Interesting and on that note, we leave you again. When are your movers scheduled to arrive?" Reece asked.

"In a couple of weeks," I frowned. "How'd you know?" *now they sound like stalkers... hmmm?*

"The FBI isn't the only agency that can keep tabs on people. We singled you out because of your uniqueness, so we keep track of you. Have for several years now. How many eight year olds survive a serial killer?" McMichaels asked. *why would he lie?*

"He's lying, we've known about you since you were kidnapped. My dad was a bureau man and worked your case. He brought his work home all the time. It was interesting back then. Now, it is downright mind boggling," Reece said. *situational irony*

"So, you've been stalking me for nearly 20 years?"

"My dad kept track of you after you survived. When he died, I got all his paperwork. By then Lucas and I were both Marshals. My dad had copies of your essays and things that shouldn't have been in your file. It finally

dawned on me that my dad thought you were special. So
we looked into it and we agree."

They left.

So   sudden

Eight

"I'm a bit disturbed that the US Marshals have been keeping tabs on me. I'm even more disturbed that the FBI did it before them."

[handwritten: situational irony]

"But you're not surprised," Nyleena finished the thought. *[handwritten: isn't it easier to not be?]*

"No, no I'm not. I wish I was," I lit another cigarette. *[handwritten: stress reliever]*

"What movers do you have coming?" She asked after a minute or two.

"You and me. I am taking my clothes, my books, and my computer equipment. Everything else is going away," I answered.

"That's what I thought," Nyleena looked around. "Why don't we pack up your car with your clothes and books? Pack up your book bag and computer gear and just go?"

"I don't have anywhere to live," I reminded her.

"That is an easy problem. You stay with me for a month while you look for a place."

"I thought you were going to stop contributing to the trust fund?" *[handwritten: foreshadow]*

"I am, as soon as your book gets published and you have some sort of income," she walked over to my closet, dug out all the clothes and tossed them onto the floor.

"Ready?" She asked.

"Not in the least," I told her.

"Fine," she picked up something from the coffee table.

39

"Yeah, hi, it's Nyleena Clachan. Could you come back to the apartment for a minute?" She said a few more things then hung up.

"Who was that?" *Foreshadow*

"That was McMichaels and Reece. I want out of this crazy town. A mattress on the floor doesn't count as a bed. I'm tired of sleeping on it."

"How'd you get their numbers?"

"They gave both of us cards when you were in the hospital."

"Great," I hung my head in resignation. I could dominate anyone but Nyleena. It was a personal choice.

She's just trying to help

It took less than five minutes for my two new acquaintances to get turned around and back to my apartment. McMichaels scanned the room, noticed the clothes on the floor and raised an eyebrow.

"I always leave my stuff," I told him in response.

"Well, the good news is we have you an apartment already. The bad news is there isn't any furniture," Reece told me. *It's like they knew, now? mood - weird*

fore-unsure "You have an apartment for me?" I frowned.

"Yes, the Marshals will pay for it for six months. It's in a secure building. You'll have to be let in by a doorman. The key code changes every six hours."

"Sounds like my building," Nyleena randomly picked some clothes up and tossed them into a suitcase.

"That's because it is your building. Twentieth floor, apartment 2020. It isn't furnished though," Reece continued.

"Really? Why my building?" Nyleena asked.

"Because it is one of the few Federal Guard Apartment buildings in KC. Since KC has the Federal Guard Neighborhood, they didn't build very many FGAs."

"I hadn't realized that," Nyleena nodded once.

"They are expanding the FG Neighborhood, going to give it an official name even. Got your name on the list for a house in it, yet?" Reece asked her.

"Nope, I like my condo."

The Federal Guard buildings were housing for law enforcement, judges, lawyers, anyone involved in the criminal justice system. They were the result of one mass murderer twenty years earlier. He had managed to kill seven judges, including a supreme justice and a still unknown number of lawyers and police officers. They were sure that the number was well over two hundred, but how well over, they weren't sure. Secure housing had been constructed and encouraged. With serial killers and mass murderers on the rise, it didn't pay well to be a member of the justice system. The secure housing was part of the package. Nyleena had gotten her condo the day she had signed on to work for the prosecutor's office.

"We'll be neighbors," I commented dryly.

"We will and with a little luck, I won't come home one day and find a serial killer in your apartment," she stuffed the last of my clothes into a second suitcase. "What about your books?"

I scanned the two bookshelves. I had well over a thousand books on them. I shrugged at her.

"We'll pack them for now and when you decide to get furniture, you can put them on new shelves," she told me.

"Why don't you take your furniture?" Reece asked, eyes narrowed.

"I killed someone here. I'd like to leave behind everything possible. I may be a sociopath, but I'm also a touch superstitious. Killing people brings about bad mojo."

"Bad mojo that gets trapped in your furniture?" Reece pressed.

"Honestly, if I could burn down the apartment building and everything in it, I would. Since that is unreasonable, I take my clothes, my books and my electronics. Everything else goes to Goodwill."

"How many times have you done this?" He asked.

"Well, let's see, she's moved twice since getting here, there were five moves in Michigan, plus moving to Michigan and now moving to KC. How many is that?" Nyleena grinned.

"And you always leave your furniture?" McMichaels asked.

"I buy cheap furniture, usually from the nearest thrift shop. It's a thing. I don't know how to explain it. I just can't stand the thought of moving the furniture," I rolled my eyes and lit up a cigarette. *relieving stress*

"The FGA is non-smoking, you know that right?" Nyleena asked me.

"Think my smoking is what they should be concerned about?" I cocked my head sideways at her.

"I really like the doormen, they are all trained federal officers," she cleared off a shelf from the bookcase into a very large Rubbermaid container.

"You act like she is certain to bring doom and gloom to the building," McMichaels said, mimicking Nyleena with a different bookshelf. *she's her cousin*

"When you've been around my cousin for a while, you'll understand. We once went to a movie and when we left, someone tossed a soda at her. She didn't retaliate until they cornered us in the parking lot. The woman cornered us and blamed us for talking during the movie. The psycho bitch broke two of the car windows. Aislinn just attracts violent people like cheese grows mold. You think its fine and then suddenly, you're being mobbed by hoards of violent people."

"Can we do something about the 'Aislinn' thing?" Reece asked.

Smile

"Huh?" I frowned at him.

"I'm officially renaming you 'Ace.' You can call me Xavier and him, Lucas. Just seems like a good idea to get that out of the way. I hate formalities." characterization

"I've never had a nickname," I mused.

"Well, you do now," Lucas wiped another shelf clean. He seemed to be enjoying himself.

Nine

My plane landed in Kansas City. Everything I owned was packed into seven large containers and three suitcases, the containers were mostly books. The suitcases were clothes, computer equipment, CDs and DVDs. Lucas had called Goodwill to have my furniture picked up.

Lucas and Xavier had flown most of my belongings back. It turned out the Serial Crimes Tracking Unit had their own plane. We had not flown back with them. I had a suitcase, Nyleena, an ID card and a set of keys.

In theory, I had a job to do before I went to my new apartment. I had to go furniture shopping. This was an easy fix. Nyleena stopped at a furniture outlet store on the way.

I ordered a bed, a couch, a two person dining room table and two chairs, a recliner, an end table and three book cases. Nyleena frowned at me as I handed them my debit card. I understood her frustration. But my somewhat odd and compulsive behavior triumphed over her disapproval. They made arrangements for delivery.

That was going to be a nightmare and a half. Nyleena called the apartment building to tell them about the delivery while I drove. We had one more stop to make.

"Aislinn! Nyleena! Thank god, you are both ok!" My mother squealed as we entered her living room.

"Hi mom," we both said in unison. It didn't seem to matter that she was actually Nyleena's aunt. She was "mom" to everyone. She was the mother that everyone loved and adored.

44

"What are you doing here?" My mom asked. Nyleena had moved her to KC when I had gone off to college. My father had a good pension and an even better life insurance policy. She worked two days a week now as a librarian at a local municipal library.

"I came to get my car," I told her.

"Your car?" She frowned for a second.

"Yep, I'm moving, no, moved back?" I made it a question. *tone - unsure*

"Where are you staying? Do you want your room?" She was suddenly in motion.

"Nope, I'm doing some consultant work for the Marshals mom, so I have an apartment in Nyleena's building for the next six months. That will give me plenty of time to find a place."

"Are you sure?" She asked.

"Yep, I'm sure. If I don't find a place at the end of the six months, I may come back for a while, but..." I shrugged at her. *probably from her experiences*

"Always so independent," my mother gave me a smile. "So, I heard about your latest adventure."

"Yeah, I'm sure you did," I told her.

"Malachi came and told me everything, including that you were all right and that the Marshal Service wanted to use you for a case."

"How's he treating you?" I asked her.

"Same ol' Malachi," even Malachi called my mom "Mom". I wasn't sure anyone except me knew her first name. *hyperbole*

My mom disappeared into the kitchen and came out with a glass of tea, a glass of milk and two pieces of pie. She set the tray down in front of us. I got the glass of milk; Nyleena the tea. We both took them and the small plates of pie.

"Secure housing is probably a good idea for you," mom said as I forked in another chunk of the apple pie.

45

"That's what I think," Nyleena agreed.

"It will be interesting." I said.

"You aren't happy to be back?" Mom asked.

"Oh, I am. Washington wasn't working out either, but..." I shrugged.

I had this enormous sense of impending doom when I lived close to my mother. She knew it. I had told her many times that if anyone with a gun ever showed up on her front door, she was to shoot first and ask questions later. My family was stuck in a pattern of violence. I couldn't imagine anyone gunning down the 63 year old woman who baked pies, had grandchildren and loved SyFy Original Movies, but weirder things happened all the time.

"Aislinn," my mother pursed her lips together. "I'm a big girl, capable of taking care of myself. Sometimes, more so than you. I may not be as quick with a knife or eager to retaliate in self-defense, but I'm not an idiot and I'm not feeble."

"I know, I know," I finished off my pie. "But I feel I put you in unnecessary danger."

"Non-sense. My family has never put me in unnecessary danger." That was a point that could be argued either way. I dropped it.

"Anyway, since I'm going to be living in the area, I figured I might as well get my car," I said.

"Do you need help with furniture or clothing or anything?" Mom asked.

"Yeah, she needs cookware; we've gotten the rest of it." Nyleena quipped.

"I'll put it on my to-do list tomorrow. I have to go to the store anyway." Mom said.

"Thanks, mom," I said to her. My mother always made me feel sad. "How are the kids?"

"Growing like weeds, you will hardly recognize any of them." She grinned and got up. She grabbed a couple

simile

of pictures and showed them to me. <u>My nieces and nephews were indeed growing like</u> weeds. It had been a few years since I had seen them. They had gotten to be teens in that time.

My sister was 18 years older than me. <u>She was 31 with a husband and three kids when she died.</u> <u>Her best friend was in an abusive relationship and had just found out she was pregnant.</u> My sister had slipped over while the boyfriend was at work. They were leaving when he returned home early. He emptied an entire clip from a .45 into her. <u>She died instantly.</u> *she and her fam seem to have really bad luck*

My father was dispatched to a shots fired domestic disturbance. When he arrived, he and his partner were both gunned down by a semi-automatic as they made their way to the building. <u>The gunman shot my sister's friend with the semi-automatic too.</u> *UDHR right to life*

Four years later, he was released. Not because he wasn't guilty, but because he had been high on cocaine and found a loop-hole. <u>My brother, seeing the pain my mother went through over that release, took a sniper's rifle up to the roof of a building and shot him in the head.</u> At the time, my brother had been 33. He had been married with four children and a fifth on the way. *couldn't endure the pain anymore*

That should have been the end of the story. But it isn't. Feeling empowered and half-mad with grief, my brother took <u>vigilantism</u> to the extreme and started popping off prisoners inside the fence. He was convicted under the then new "Mass and Serial Killer Law" as a mass murder and sentenced to life without parole inside The Fortress. *vocab*

Their exes still make sure that my mother and I have contact with the children. Hell, my sister-in-law refuses to divorce my brother and is now an advocate for wrongful imprisonment due to severe emotional distress. <u>Which is ironically, what got the murderer released in the first place.</u> *irony*

47

My mother stopped visiting my brother at The Fortress because he asked her to. I have never been. I'm not on his approved visitor's list. He wouldn't add my name. I was seventeen when he went to jail.

My parents didn't raise us wrong. We were just touched by lots of tragedy. It happens.

My mother was still chattering away about the grandkids, when I snapped back into the conversation. She stopped and frowned at me.

"I hate when you turn off like that," she scolded me.

"Sorry, I try not to, sometimes, it just happens."

"We really need to get going anyway. Thanks for the pie and I'll make sure that Aislinn visits you now that she's home. Also, here's her address." Nyleena scribbled down my apartment number. "I'll put you on the security list for her as well as me."

"Thank you, Nyleena. You two girls stay safe and keep your heads down," my mom stood up, hugged us both and handed me the keys to my car.

"In the garage?" I asked her.

"Yes," she answered. One tear formed, slipped from her eye and was deftly wiped away. If you hadn't been staring at her, you wouldn't have noticed. It was a trick she had perfected.

I entered the garage, alone. There were two cars. One was a Nissan Pathfinder, newer model, painted black. The other was a 1969 Dodge Charger. The Charger was mine. It got about 12 miles to the gallon, made lots of noise and wasn't exactly inconspicuous. However, my dad had started building the car for me when I was eight. When he died, my brother finished it for me. It was built with their blood and sweat. I had fond memories of handing both of them wrenches, nut drivers, oil, whatever they needed.

48

personification

It took a couple of turns before the motor cranked. It whined before settling into a deep, bass rumble that could be felt in your body. I listened to the rumble and sighed. I loved being home; I just wasn't sure about the circumstances.

Ten

I arrived at the apartment building to find a comedy of errors in progress. Nyleena, Lucas, Xavier, a tall man with long black hair and several uniformed police officers were arguing with men in delivery uniforms. My furniture was all sitting on the sidewalk. My suitcases and Rubbermaid containers were with them.

It was a secure building, with secure parking. I had been in the parking garage before, but this was the first time I had an actual parking space instead of just putting my car in the generic visitor's spots. The gate man took my ID and looked over it. While he checked out a list, my ID still in his hands, another walked around my car.

Bomb search complete, I continued into the garage and heard the heavy iron bars that kept out unwanted visitors close. The mechanisms whined and whirred and then clanked as they slid into place. To exit the garage, I had to either enter the building or have one of the guards open the secure pedestrian door. The guard gave me a tight smile as he opened the secure door.

It opened onto the street. I took a moment to take in the sights and sounds of Kansas City. It wasn't Seattle. It wasn't as damp. It also wasn't as climate controlled, but I was used to screwy Missouri weather. I returned to the group on the street. They were still arguing.

"Problems?" I asked as I walked up.

The man with black hair turned to look at me, "yes, these fucking idiots don't get that they can't go up

50

and deliver the furniture themselves. It has to be delivered by someone with clearance. And they don't have it." *I wouldn't be arguing w/ him if I were them*

The man was well over seven foot tall. He had dark skin, dark eyes, hair at least a foot and a half in length. If I had to guess, I'd say he was pure Native American. His voice was deep and rich. He had a slight draw to it like he grew up in the southwest. *characterization*

"Great," I rolled my eyes. "So how do you intend to get the furniture inside if the furniture movers don't do it?"

"Listen, we got a couple of strong backed guys here, we'll get it up. Go visit whoever you came to visit and let us get on our way."

"Well, I would, but that's my furniture," I told the guy.

"You're Aislinn Cain, PhD?" He said the last like it left a bitter taste in his mouth. *Simile*

"I am and you are?" I asked.

"Your boss, Alejandro Gui."

"Gui?" I frowned.

"It was either that or Running Wolf and that just doesn't work on federal forms very well. You may call me Alejandro."

"All right, Alejandro. Grab a bookcase and let's get this show on the road. I don't have all day and it looks like rain." *simile*

There wasn't a cloud in the sky, but my knee felt like someone had shoved a dagger into it. Good sign it was going to rain. I didn't limp, but I wanted to as I grabbed a suitcase. *like a dog*

"Go, shoo, we got it from here," I handed the delivery guys a twenty a piece and motioned them off. They grumbled at me, but kept the money and left.

"Problem solved," I turned to the doorman, who was really a trained Navy SEAL who had gotten stuck with this job for two years. I had met him once before. I showed him my new ID badge. He frowned and let me in.

I didn't wait around to see if the others were following. It was one of those things. I knew they would, furniture in hand. I was that sort of person.

Nyleena pulled a Rubbermaid container into the elevator. The doors swooshed closed and we started upwards. *onamonapia*

"Bossing around your boss on the day you meet him is probably not a good idea," she said as the numbers moved by. *situational irony*

"He isn't my boss for very long. I have every intention of helping them out and then getting a job at a university or something."

"So you can attract nut jobs in college. Good plan."

"It's good to have goals," I told her. The elevator opened as she snickered. I found the door labeled 2020 and opened it with the keys. Each door had a microchip in it that disabled an alarm system as well as worked an electronic deadbolt.

The door opened with the slightest touch once all the safety locks had been disabled. The apartment had a kitchen, a dining room, a living room, a bathroom and two bedrooms. I didn't know what I would do with the extra bedroom. I didn't own a TV; my books would be in the living room instead.

"Damn," I looked at Nyleena who put the Rubbermaid container on the floor, out of the way.

"What?" She asked.

"I forgot to buy a dresser."

"I have an extra one upstairs you can borrow for now. I have no desire to go through the delivery man routine again."

"Ok," I put the suitcases in the extra bedroom.

"How long will it take you to unpack once everything is here?"

"Six, seven weeks," I told her.

"How about we do it all today and then go to dinner?"

"Where?" I asked. yummm

"Somewhere with Thai food," she suggested.

"Ok," I was going to say something else, but my couch suddenly arrived. Lucas and Alejandro were carrying it. Behind them, a uniformed officer was helping Xavier with part of the bed.

"Bed in there. Couch there," I pointed at the places I wanted them to go.

I ordered the men to and fro with my furniture. It was all carried up, piece by piece, using the freight elevator. It only took an hour and a half to get it all upstairs.

As the last piece was set, everyone excused themselves except Alejandro. He sat on the couch and stared at me. I took a spot in a recliner.

"What?" I asked after a moment.

"I'm guessing Lucas and Xavier filled you in on the details of the case." dramatic irony   saw it coming

"Yes."

"Good, now I'll fill you in on the rest of it. If we find you useful in the field, you'll be offered a job. We need a woman who can take care of herself. More importantly, we need a woman who isn't going to flinch when she sees a serial killer at his worst. I think you will do nicely. Your name has already been put on the list to get into the FG Neighborhood. With your new credentials, you have full access to any prisoner in The Fortress. You'll be expected to do some research on it and the prisoners inside. Knowledge is power. You will have access to your brother. He's been helpful in the past theme when we've come up against mass murderers that don't fit the psychological profile of someone who kills for fun or

stereotyping

sexual gratification. You'll be required to pass a fire arms test."

"Can do, my friend Malachi has taught me to use a gun. So this consulting thing is a trial run?"

"Trial by fire," Alejandro stood up. "You'll get your badge in a few days. Tomorrow, you'll report for your first fire arms training. We have a nondescript building in the warehouse district. Here's the address."

He handed me a business card with an address and nothing else on it. He left. Nyleena came back about 10 minutes later.

"Were you watching?" I asked.

"Something like that. Now, we unpack your books and clothes and go to dinner."

Eleven

That night, I lay awake, tossing and turning. I had been pretty quiet after Alejandro had left. Nyleena had known something was bothering me, but hadn't asked me what. I wasn't sure I could explain it.

It wasn't the apartment or the weird job offer or the sudden move. It was that in my position, I would have access to my brother. I hadn't seen him in ten years. He hadn't wanted me to visit. I wasn't on his approved visitor's list. He couldn't even get my mail.

Now though, now I had complete access. He could turn me away once I got there, but not before. I wasn't entirely sure what I thought of that. It bothered me in a way that I couldn't explain.

I was terrified at the thought of the new job; it was nothing like I had done before. Before, my life and work had always revolved around a college campus, for the first time, it didn't.

I tossed and turned as the digital clock next to the bed continued to count off the hours. I hadn't slept the night before either. I didn't feel exhausted, but I would by the afternoon. I was used to sleepless nights. With my stomach in knots, I finally gave up on sleep. It wouldn't come now, no matter what I tried. Sleep had escaped me.

Today though, I had something to do. A task. I had to get approved to carry a firearm.

I had never owned a gun. I had never felt the need to own one. An argument could be made that I was exactly the sort of person that needed one, but not by me.

I showered until I ran out of hot water. My skin had turned a dark red from the heat. I toweled off, got dressed and exited my apartment. I heard the bolts slide into place as I turned the key in the deadbolt to lock it. A small beep signaled that the alarm had been set as well.

I waved to the two guys at the security desk. They smiled and nodded back. The doorman had changed, I was unfamiliar with him. He said good morning. I agreed with him and went to the garage.

Once at the garage, I had to show my ID again. An attendant let me in. I found my parking space and my car.

Darkness was still upon the city. For an hour or so, I drove around aimlessly. I may not have been born in Kansas City, but I had been here often as a kid and knew my way around. Eventually, I found my way to the address on the card.

I knocked and showed my ID badge to the camera. Someone buzzed me in. A skinny guy with black hair and a goatee that was well trimmed met me at the door.

He smiled and showed me to my office. He was the night security guard. No one else was in yet.

My office was drab and sparse. A utility desk, a high-backed office chair, a laptop with docking station, an empty bookcase and a second, less comfortable looking chair was all it held. The night guard told me to make myself at home. He gave me a temporary password and told me to change it immediately or "The Geek" would be all over my ass.

I did what I was told. I logged onto the laptop that appeared to be brand new. I changed my password to a long passphrase that was half Russian, half German and then stared out the window.

At least it had a window. It looked out onto a field. The field was a wasteland. Tall weeds were fighting with prairie grass to see which would win the plot of land. Not a single tree could be seen. Dirt could though, in spots, particularly when the eye moved closer to the asphalt.

"Around here, we give out nickels for your thoughts," a new guy entered the office.

My first impression was not a good one. He seemed out of place. His shirt had a Doctor Who reference that I got only because Nyleena was in love with Doctor Who. His glasses had tape on them. Not on the ear pieces, but a sliver of it on the lens. His hair was strawberry blonde and unkempt. His jeans were faded, but not showing their thread count. And he was wearing Doc Martin boots. I have nothing against Doc Martin's. I happened to love mine, but they didn't seem to fit with the surroundings.

His hand had a nearly invisible stamp on it. Remnants of eyeliner could be seen where he hadn't washed his face well before going to bed or coming to work. I didn't know who he was.

"Aislinn Cain," I said, not standing up.

"Michael Giovanni." He came in and sat down in the chair across from the desk.

"Ah, pleasure to meet you, you missed some eyeliner." I handed him a tissue from the box on my desk. Since I didn't normally keep things like tissues around, they seemed just as out of place as Michael Giovanni.

"I know, it never washes off entirely. I need new eye-makeup remover or something."

"Rave?" I asked, pointing to the stamp.

"Never too old to get down and party," he smiled and it made him look older. Deep lines creased his face. Too many late nights and who knew what else.

"What can I do for you?"

"I'm here to show you all the cool little toys that we've built."

"Ok," I flipped the laptop around to him and scooted my chair out from behind the desk.

"You've changed your password?"

"Oh yeah," I nodded.

"Great, it isn't some combination of your name, birthday and address is it?"

"Give me some credit." I rolled my eyes.

"You'd be amazed what people do here," he closed the lid. He opened it back up.

For fifteen minutes, we sat with him trying to crack the password. When it didn't happen, he smiled at me.

"Ok, log on and we'll be on our adventure."

I logged on.

"The first program I'm going to show you is a database of all violent murders in the US that are unsolved. It has a fancy name; we just call it 'Victims' around here."

He opened a program that looked like a mix between FoxPro and something I had never seen before.

"Every murder that goes unsolved for more than two months comes here. I enter the information and make it searchable. I'm hoping you'll be able to help; the others are useless at it. So, say you are searching for murders that match our current serial killer. Type in something like 'women', 'torture' and 'medieval' in the query boxes and hit search."

A list of victims came up. I recognized a face here and there from the photos that had been shown to me. He double clicked on a name. Suddenly, I was being bombarded by information.

There was at least 30 pictures and three pages of information on the victim and how they died. He had picked a victim that had been drawn and quartered. The pictures were pretty gruesome. I thought about looking away, but this was my job now.

58

"Ok, as you can see, we have all her information right here. Autopsy photos, crime scene photos, information gathered about her, information from Xavier's autopsy, etc." He closed the screen.

"Now let's say, you don't know if there's a pattern or not. We'll type in 'men', '30-40' and throat slashed." He punched it all in. *crazy how much you can find on*

Three hits came up. I looked at them and frowned. They were all in KC. *the*

"We have ourselves a serial killer." I answered. *internet*

"Actually, thanks to this program, we've identified five serial killers currently active in Kansas City, Missouri or Kansas City, Kansas. It is part of the reason we are stationed here. Not only is it pretty centrally located, but Missouri has the highest serial killer per capita rate in the country. Even worse though, when you look at the number of serial killers in the state, it also ranks the highest. The only state even close to us is California, but they aren't that close."

"Nice to know I live in a safe state." I quipped.

"Exactly," he looked at me. "Think you understand the database?"

"Got it." I told him. I didn't tell him that I had been working with computers for years and could use a query function and a database.

"The next is the Serial Killers and Mass Murderers Database. It is a catalog of all captured serial killers and mass murderers. It includes their MO's, stats, everything. The two can be used together, but it is very technical and we won't get to it right now. However, it is a good way to find copy-cats. Next to each offender are a couple of important things. This check box here means they talk to the police. This check box here means they are in The Fortress. If this one is checked, it's a bad idea for women to talk to them. If this one is checked, it's a bad idea for men to talk to them." *if what was checked?*

"Got it," I told him and did a quick search. My brother came up. It called him "docile", "cooperative" and "easy-going". Strange words to use about a mass murderer. situational irony

"He's a mass murderer with a cause. Went after the man that killed half his family. When he finished with him, he started putting rounds into convicts that were in the yard." defending him

"I know," I told Michael. "He's my brother."

"Oh, well then you should be familiar with the story. Any questions?"

"Not really," I looked at the screen.

"Good because you have got a ton of things to learn today. This is just the beginning. I believe Alejandro wants to start training you on firearms. I'm going to teach you to enter victim profiles. Lucas is going to make you sit through a psych interview with a serial killer and Xavier is going to force you into an autopsy room. He even procured a cadaver for it." demanding words

"That sounds like a barrel of laughs," I frowned at him. I wasn't so sure about the autopsy thing. I might throw up. simile

"Most of us threw up." Lucas said, entering my office, suddenly it felt very small. I was betting he could read my mind by the look on his face.

"Good to know," I heard more feet enter the office. Alejandro loomed over us.

"Ready for your first firearms lesson?" He turned and left.

"He's a man of few words," Michael said.

"I'm getting that." I answered. I followed Alejandro out of the room. Michael and Lucas at my heels.

Twelve

After walking down a narrow flight of stairs that I hadn't seen earlier, I found Alejandro. They had their own shooting range. Xavier was already there and had his ear protection on. Michael and Lucas each grabbed a pair and slipped them on.

"This is a .9mm Beretta. Lucas suggested trying it before trying to make you hold a Glock. You seem to have issues with guns," Xavier said, setting the gun down on the range counter. *I gotta Glock in my rari*

"I do have issues with guns." I slipped on my own pair of protective headgear. I ignored the fact that they had picked out pink for me. At least I knew I wouldn't be wearing other people's ear protection. *stereotype*

"Now, take a steady breath and then we'll see what you can do." Lucas said calmly. *basically girls aren't*

I was feeling a bit insulted. I had issues with *fit to* guns, but they weren't big issues, it was mostly the *do what* thought that if I had one, I'd use it. Malachi had spent *guys do* years teaching me to use a gun, a knife, and a sword. I wasn't sure I would ever need to know how to use a sword, but better safe than sorry. *she won't miss*

I fired nine shots into the paper hanging up at the back of the range. Alejandro hit a button and pulled it forward. All nine shots were in the head. He frowned at me. *foreshadow*

"I know how to fire a gun," I reminded him.

"OK, we'll go back further. This time, empty the clip in less than 15 seconds. I'll keep time." *they don't think*

"Ok," the paper target was replaced with a new *she* one. Alejandro moved it back. It went further this time. *can do it.*

I used a second lining up the sight. I emptied the clip. Alejandro let out a quiet growl. Lucas had a coughing fit.

"13.7 seconds, not bad Cain, that's faster than either Lucas or Xavier by a second and Michael didn't finish it. Now let's see how many you hit."

There was a whir and the paper moved forward. I could already tell that all of them had been in the head. Most of it was gone. Not a single bullet seemed to have hit outside the black outline.

"Do you like the Beretta or do you want a different gun?" Alejandro asked.

"I kind of like this one." I switched it to the other hand. "Send another one back."

Alejandro hung up a third target. It whirred to the back. I fired left handed. He pulled it forward. Nine rounds to the head. I had only fired nine rounds again.

"You pass and it would appear you are ambidextrous." Alejandro sighed.

"You never know when you won't be able to use your dominant hand. Does this mean I get to carry two guns?"

"Can you fire two guns simultaneously?" He asked.

"Yes," I answered.

"I want to see that." He handed me a second Beretta. The target was once again whirred backwards. I took another second and started firing. I emptied both clips.

"Damn," Alejandro looked at it. "You missed with only three shots."

"That seems like a bad average," I frowned at my lack of skills.

"Most people can't really fire two guns simultaneously and hit their target with any of the rounds," Lucas told me.

"Really?" Malachi had trained me that way. He could do it.

"Really." Alejandro said as he signed a piece of paper.

"What now?" I asked.

"Firearms training passed. You may now legally carry two guns in a shoulder holster. You might consider getting a double holster made. We don't have any."

"Do I get to keep the Berettas?" I asked as he walked away.

"They're yours." He shouted back. he salty

"Interesting," I murmured at his back.

"Don't take it personally, you did better than him. He's going to go sulk for a while. Congrats on the firearms training," Lucas smiled at me.

"What now?" I asked, looking around.

"Now, we go to autopsy. If you decide to throw up, please do it away from the body." Xavier removed his ear protection, grabbed my hand and dragged me into another room. demanding

It was cooler in the next room. Hospital clean and smelling of disinfectant. The smell alone would be enough to make a person throw up.

"Ok, I have to do this autopsy anyway. It's pretty standard and routine. It's for the ATF. It appears he shot himself in the head, so it will be messy."

I didn't say anything, just prepared myself for the removal of the sheet. I didn't gag. I didn't throw up. I was slightly perturbed by the fact that the guy looked dead and had a large hole in his head that Xavier ran a stick through. vocab he's prob used to it

He was talking into a recorder, leaving notes for himself. His hands worked swiftly. I stayed just to the side, out of the way and watched. I felt the calm come over me. I didn't toss my cookies. The urge didn't even hit. personification

When Xavier finished, he turned off the recorder, pulled the sheet back over the guy and looked at me. He removed his visor and gloves. I did the same.

metaphor

"You must have a cast iron stomach. I was even trying to get you..." Xavier stopped talking and looked at me. "If I could even begin to imagine what you were thinking about at this exact moment, I would be a millionaire."

"What?" I asked him, feeling the calm recede.

"What is that?" He asked.

"What is what?" I asked back.

metaphor

"That mask. I looked at you and you were completely blank. Even your eyes. I've seen guys on this slab with more alive looking eyes than yours. It's gone now though."

I shrugged. I didn't have an answer. It wasn't a new question either. Others had asked it before.

When will she have an answer?

Thirteen

The Fortress is probably the most intimidating prison ever built. Even Alcatraz is a cake-walk next to it. It houses only the worst of the worst. There are no shared cells; it drops the population too quickly. The *like hell* doors are built out of steel, like an old-fashioned asylum.

However, getting there is mind blowing. It looks like a dirt road to nowhere. We have lots of them in *simile* Missouri. Even in areas of high populations.

About two miles down the road, there is suddenly a large sign. It reads "DO NOT PICK UP *could be people* HITCHHIKERS FOR THE NEXT TEN MILES". This *that* sign seems out of place. The roadside is littered with *escaped* trees, there doesn't seem to be anything interesting. Five miles later, the road suddenly changes back to pavement. At the road change, there is another sign. It reads "THE USE OF LETHAL FORCE IS AUTHORIZED FOR THE NEXT FIVE MILES. PLEASE HAVE IDENTIFICATION READY." *mood – anxious, jitty*

At this point, all the trees disappear. With the vanishing trees, the structure becomes a dominating feature, despite looking small. The car is still five miles from the entrance. *for keeping things in/out*

Here you can see the barbed wire fence with razor wire on the top. There are also two guard towers that loom over the road on each side. The guard towers mark the beginning of the free-fire range.

The surprises don't stop there though. The closer the car moves to The Fortress, the more apparent it becomes on how it got its name.

65

Sturdy

The building is made of cinderblocks. It is ten stories tall. Behind it, is a cliff that borders The Fortress on three sides. The cliff is dizzyingly taller than the cinderblock building.

More barbed wire fences topped with razor wire. More guard towers are visible in the distance. The guard towers have machine gun turrets on them.

My heart was pounding rapidly as we finally reached the gates. Lucas handed both our ID badges to the guard on the outside of the gate. He looked at them, did something on a screen and handed them back. The first set of gates slid open.

They rattled as they closed behind us. The bolts latched into place. The gates in front of us opened. We moved forward about thirty feet. A buzzer sounded. We stopped. The gates closed behind us. We waited.

Another guard walked up to us. Lucas opened the door. I followed suit. We both got out of the SUV. A dog was brought in. Our SUV was searched inside and out. We were motioned back into the car. We got in. The gates in front of us opened. Lucas continued forward.

He stopped again. There was a final set of gates in front of us. The metal clinked and clanked behind us. Once the gate behind us was closed and secure, the gate in front of us opened.

Very secure building

setting

Lucas waited for it to open completely. He drove through, found a parking spot, parked and got out. He smiled at me.

"Well?" He asked.

"Ask me when we have left," I told him, finding my breath again.

"It is something."

"I've seen it before. Never up close, but I have seen it before."

"Your brother?"

"Yes."

66

"Don't worry; we won't be interviewing him today. We have a serial killer on the menu, not a mass murderer." *reassuring and sad at the same time*

Getting inside The Fortress was just as harrowing. We entered through a heavy steel door. Once inside, we surrendered our guns, keys and anything else that could be considered a weapon. We were wanded, sent through a metal detector that went off because Lucas's boots were steel-toed and then wanded again. *like at an airport*

It took about thirty minutes before we were led into a conference room. There were two chairs on one side of the table, one on the other side. All three were bolted to the floor. *why?. can be used as a weapon?*

The single chair was occupied. Lucas and I took the two that were together. Three guards were in the room with us. One had his hand on his Taser. *mood -*

"Hello again, Brent," Lucas smiled amiably. *intimidating*

"Agent McMichaels." He looked at me. "Who's the chick?" *vocab*

"Agent Cain," he introduced me. "Agent Cain this is Brent Timmons, better known as the Tallahassee Terror." *intimidating name*

I racked my brain quickly and came up with a few headlines. I didn't remember much about the case, just that he had been important enough to make national headlines. That took a lot of bodies or some really extreme methods anymore.

"Mr. Timmons," I nodded at him. *characterization*

"I'm offended," Brent Timmons answered. "I know who you are, but you don't seem to know who I am."

"I don't know why you would know who I am." I countered. *very straight forward*

"Eight year old kills serial killer and escapes. Funny though, most of us in here would have bet money that you would end up on this side of the table, being

67

prodded by Dr. McMichaels and not by his side, prodding us." He smiled at me.

"My last name is Cain," I told him. When I was eight, it was Clachan, I thought.

"That may be, but your picture was in the paper and while you've aged since then, you still look much like that picture. Then there was the picture of you in the paper again when you were 19, I believe. Different picture, different last name, but that first name and the fact that you haven't changed much in looks despite your aging; it doesn't take a rocket scientist to figure it out. So you changed your name. You're still the same Aislinn Clachan that escaped the clutches of a child killer at the age of eight."

I thought for a minute and smiled back.

"And I'm sure all those press reports and pictures of me and my family in the newspapers nine years ago also help connect the dots. Plus, I'm sure you've heard of my brother, this place may not cater to inmate interaction, but it still allows some."

He laughed, loudly. It sounded brittle and hollow in my ears.

"Yes, the fact that Alex Clachan is an inmate might have something to do with it. He seems quite proud of you."

"Now, we can cut through the pleasantries, and get on with it," I continued to smile at him.

"Do you miss him?" Brent Timmons asked.

"Every day, but I think that is neither here nor there. I miss the members of my family that were avenged by him as well. In some ways, you could say I was proud of him as well."

"Proud to have a mass murderer in the family? That is twisted. McMichaels is going to have a ball analyzing you."

Sarcastic asshole characterization

Can't then why see him + Cain?

68

"Probably, but again, neither here nor there. Today, I'm here to learn how to analyze you."

"Learning are we? And McMichaels thought of me. Do you know why?" proper

"You made national headlines. Impressive in a country where serial killers are being argued to be the next step in our evolutionary chain. Even more impressive when you are competing with serial killers that eat their victims or kill two or three hundred people. You're obviously very intelligent. Not mentally ill in the usual sense of the word. I'm guessing it is because you are the new breed of serial killer, not the Son of Sam version." VDHR no torture

"You learn quickly, obviously you are not an idiot yourself. Do you know why I made national headlines?"

"I was eleven when you were grabbing the press's attention. I don't remember the circumstances of what you did."

"I would sneak into the home of a family and kill them all via decapitation. I would subdue them with gas, tie them up, put their heads on the kitchen table and severe it with a single blow. After they had woken up of course. Do you know how hard it is to severe the human head with a single blow?" I will never understand people

"Yes." I did know. Most of the time it took three or four. like this

"Do you know why I did it?"

"To see if it really takes twelve seconds for the brain to die after it has been severed from the body?" I didn't know if this was the real reason or not, but it sounded good.

"Good guess and in some ways, yes, that is why I chose that method. It was interesting to see the eyes blink and the mouths move. But I really did it because I enjoyed it. Nothing makes you feel more like god than killing people." simile - daanggg

69

He suddenly attempted a lunge. It was theatrical, intended to startle me. It didn't. It did bring on the calm. He sat back down, cocked his head to one side and stared at me.

mood - creepy

"She's an interesting one indeed," Timmons continued. "She didn't startle; I'm not sure what that is though."

"What what is?" I asked him, to prove that I hadn't fainted like a goat.

simile

"That look. I've seen it before, but usually it's a permanent state. Some of the other inmates here have it." He turned his attention to Lucas. "Where did you dig her up from and is she really as out of it as some of the other inmates or is it rehearsed to rattle me?"

"It's not rehearsed." Lucas told him. I could feel him staring at me. "But she is not the subject of the interview, you are."

"That look could send children running for cover. It might send a few serial killers running for it as well. I can see where she would be an asset to you. It makes the blood run cold, goose bumps form and your feet freeze to the ground."

hyperbole

"My mental state aside," I dismissed their conversation. "I'm here to learn how to interview a serial killer."

"And you are learning." Timmons informed me. "See, most of the killers in this place are like me. They had day jobs, they were skilled, they are smart, they took a long time to get caught and they appreciate a little banter. Interviewing us isn't like interviewing some gang banger or drug dealer. We like respect and give it in return. We have some of the same idiosyncrasies as the other criminals, but not many. Child molesters aren't allowed in our sections, they don't live long. Killing children is fine, but to molest them before hand, well, that's just evil and unspeakable. You were brought to me

Characterization

please clarify??

70

vocab

because there are rules and I know them. Most of us will cooperate with the Marshals Serial Crimes Unit because they are nearly as crazy as us. They respect us. In return, we respect them and are willing to help."

"I see. So, because you get respect for your work from the Marshals unit, you respect them in return and help where they need help. It is a symbiotic relationship based upon respect." *what they want*

"Yes and helping them to learn about each *metophor* monster so that they can catch the next monster is also good for us. When you leave today, I'll get dessert with dinner or I'll get an extra half-hour out of my cell or I'll get a new puzzle book or some other reward. We have few luxuries here and a puzzle book is a thing of wonder. It gives us something to whittle away the hours. It is harder since we aren't allowed anything but crayons, but we take what we can get."

"Worried about uprisings if you have a pencil?" I mused.

"Something like that. Completely unfounded, mind you, but still. Most of us are comfortable here. The urge to kill hasn't left us though. We wouldn't rise up, but one of us might take some of that pent up frustration out on a guard or another inmate should we be given something like a pencil."

"And crayons are harmless?"

"They are in this place." He pulled one from his breast pocket. "They are too soft to do much damage. Might make a mark, but wouldn't break the skin. Hell, it's hard to get them to write most of the time. But as I said, a luxury is a luxury no matter how small or dysfunctional."

"I see. Why beheading?" I asked.

"Because it was a show of force. To cleave the spine and severe the head takes a great deal of strength.

Plus there is a 'wow' factor to using a sword to take off a head."

"What sort of sword?" I asked.

"An English broad sword. I made it myself."

"What did you do before you were caught?"

"My day job?" He smiled at me. "I was an astrophysicist." *vocab*

"Impressive."

"It was, but there are astrophysicists everywhere anymore. Only some of them are good at it, but they still exist. Mediocrity of the intelligent class."

"Unlike the Marshals unit." I smiled.

"What do you mean?" *theme*

"We are all damaged. We are all accomplished and have well above average intelligence. There is no mediocrity in our unit. Mediocrity wouldn't cut it."

smartest people can turn out to be the worst kind

theme

He smiled at me. His eyes wide and laughing. His cheeks flushed.

"Very good, yes, besides respect, there is the level of intelligence we are dealing with. It is much easier for me to talk to someone with an IQ near my own than it is for me to talk to someone who is average. They don't understand what I'm talking about. Dr. McMichaels here is near enough my own. You though, I think you might be smarter."

"I would guarantee it," Lucas answered.

"Really? Is that why you are training her? Get her to talk to some of the killers who find you beneath them?"

"Possibly," Lucas answered. *he's offended*

"Clever. But the fact that she's a woman..."

stereotyping

"A woman who survived a serial killer at eight and another at nineteen. A woman who graduated with a Ph.D. by the time she was 26 and has seven other degrees which is why it took her until she was 26 to get her Ph.D. I think they will forgive her being a woman."

72

"You may be right, Agent McMichaels. Actually, I'd go so far as to say after you two leave, the prison will be buzzing with the news of her entering the unit. You might have killers clamoring to talk to her. So why did you pick me and not one of the smarter ones?" He narrowed his eyes.

"You beheaded your victims," I answered for Lucas, finally getting it. "I have a degree in Medieval history when beheading was at its finest."

"That would explain why you said you knew it took a lot to cleave the spine."

"Most beheadings take three or four whacks. To do it in a single blow was the perfect beheading, he was the executioner you wanted if that was your sentence back then." I smiled again. *intimidating*

"That is the smile of a person who has found your weakness and is ready to pounce upon you." He commented.

"I've heard worse."

"I imagine. I imagine that on those rare occasions your friends have seen it, they have screamed and ran for cover." *who?*

"A few have," I admitted.

"What have you learned today, Agent Cain?"

"That serial killers of above average intelligence work with the Marshals because of mutual respect and the intellectual challenge of it. Luxuries should not be taken for granted. And that serial killers like company."

"Why do you say that?" He asked.

"Because helping us, helps catch other serial killers, therefore creating more inmates and more company for the rest of you stuck in this place."

"She is good," Timmons smiled. "Did you get what you came for then?"

"Yes," Lucas answered. *can she relate?*

characterization

symbolism
enjoyment, their work

"Good, I wonder what my prize will be," Timmons'
eyes sparkled just a bit. Lucas reached down into a bag
they had allowed him to carry in. He fished out a logic
problems magazine. It was rated extremely hard.

He slid it across the table to Timmons. Timmons
clapped enthusiastically. *like a child*

"They never get the good ones," his fingers
caressed the front of the book.

"Hence why I brought you one myself," Lucas stood
up. I followed.

We didn't talk until we were well away from the
prison and back on the interstate, headed towards
civilization. *gathering overwhelmed thoughts*

"Well?" He finally asked.

"I think I understand why my brother didn't put
me on his visitor's list."

"You do have a following in there. I probably
should have warned you."

"Why do I have a following?" I asked.

"You're smart, pretty and dangerous. It attracts
all the wrong attention."

"Humph," I grunted in response. I wasn't sure
what else to say. *seems to already know that*

"Indeed. You must remember that they have
nothing to do but read newspapers and books. They will
latch onto anything they see that suits their interests and
you do. They follow all of our cases. They'll enjoy having
you as an addition." *foreshadow*

"That's creepy."

"Speaking of creepy, what do you feel when you
detach?"

why does she?

"Nothing, just a dark calm or stillness. There is no
emotion involved. I don't think there are any emotions
available in that place. And it just happens. It's some
sort of defense mechanism."

74

"Your sociopathic tendencies are a defense mechanism?"

"Seems to be, although, it happens at other times too. I can't predict it or do anything about it when it comes over me. It just happens and I go with it. Sometimes, it lasts only a few minutes, sometimes for days."

"How often?"

"I don't know. It might happen twice in one week and then not happen again for three or four weeks."

"And do you realize you look different when it happens?" diffrent how?

"Yes, Nyleena has pointed it out many times."

"We'll be exploring it more as it happens. I couldn't prod it in there; just admit that it had happened." vocab

"Why do you reward the killers?"

"Because most of us are just one stressor away from being them. Every being is capable of murder in one form or another. They give into their impulses and urges, most of us don't."

"How do I fit into that then?"

"You don't kill idiots just because you can't deal with their stupidity. Even though I am sure you have thought about it a time or two. You have killed three times, all were dire circumstances. Most people would be victims, you aren't. You still fit in with the rest of us and not them."

"I see."

"You say that often."

"I say it when I understand what is being said, but have yet to decide if I agree or disagree."

"I'll remember that for future reference."

We drove the rest of the way in silence. He dropped me at my car as the sun was going down.

Michael met me at the door. He had a binder and my laptop.

"Take this home and study it." He told me, handing me both as he walked out the door.

"Ok," I said to the air as he walked away.

"Don't worry; it isn't always about sitting around. Our killer should strike in the next seven days. We have no clues, no leads, nothing to go on except his time table. That doesn't give us much to go on. As bad as it sounds, we have to wait for him to do it again."

I nodded and took my stuff. My car roared to life. In the confines of my car, engine whirring, I took a moment. Brent Timmons hadn't unnerved me. The fact that serial killers kept track of me, had. It meant The Butcher could indeed be everything he claimed to be. Suddenly, I knew exactly what I was going to do when I got home.

Fourteen

My searches that night were unhelpful. I couldn't find anything that matched what The Butcher had described exactly. But then I wasn't sure I could remember every detail he had written. It was a catch-22 situation.

I had ordered in dinner that night. One of the security guards had brought it up. His comment as I had taken the food was that I was just like my cousin. *they're practically sisters*

With that reminder, I wandered up to her apartment. It was five floors above mine. I found her eating Chinese take-out. I plopped into a dining chair with my Mexican take-out.

"How was the first day?"

"Uneventful. I'm not sure I can do this job. Today, Lucas told me that we would just have to wait for him to kill again before we could make any progress. I'm not sure I'll be very good at that." *What progress would that make?*

"Unfortunately, that's how it goes sometimes." She shrugged and forked in a mouthful of beef with broccoli.

"Is it easier for you? Easier because you only deal with the aftermath?"

"If you think my job is at all easy, you must have checked out the day you did job shadowing in high school." Nyleena, like most of the members of my family, should have belonged to a different generation. She was twelve years my senior.

"That isn't what I meant. I meant that because you don't have the waiting and the worrying about what is going to happen next, is it somehow more fulfilling?"

"Some people are born to capture the monsters, others, like me, are born to put them away. None of our jobs are easy, but we can't imagine doing anything else. You know I was offered a corporate gig several years ago. I would have been making a million dollars a year. I'm still here; I don't make that in ten years."

"You think I was born for this?"

"I do, you have been doing it all your life and just didn't know it. Now, you'll get paid for it."

"You are my own personal, twisted Jiminy Cricket."

"I know, are you going to eat that?" She pointed to the guacamole.

"Not in this lifetime."

"Good, give it here, I'll keep it for lunch tomorrow. There's a Mexican place that delivers to our office and they never remember the guac."

"Ok. Doing anything tonight?"

"I have a date in a couple of hours. Why?"

"Just wondering. Here or there?"

"There. He doesn't live in secure housing."

"Ok, be safe." I left Nyleena's apartment.

Nyleena still maintained relationships of a sort. She didn't get serious, but she had "friends" that she hooked up with when time and interest allowed. I didn't have that. I had shut off that part of my life a long time ago. I didn't even have the urge or drive or desire to be with another person anymore.

Mine had become a solitary life, with occasional interruptions by my mother, Malachi or Nyleena. I had had acquaintances in Washington, but they would disappear within the year. Most would disappear immediately, since my apartment had been broken into and I had killed someone as a result. But I was used to that too.

My apartment was quiet. The computer making the only noise. I loaded up some of my favorite TV shows and sat back to watch the reruns.

I awoke sometime in the wee morning hours. There was a scratching noise outside my apartment. I grabbed one of the new guns from the table and walked to the door. I saw nothing through the peep hole, so I opened it.

Nyleena was curled up on the floor, snoring. She smelled of wine. I smiled, dragged her inside and put her in my bed. She was built like me; it was the only thing that denoted us as family.

I went back to the couch, turned on another episode of *Waiting for God* and fell back asleep.

"My head," Nyleena's voice came to me from the other room. It wasn't dawn yet. The room was still dark.

"Shouldn't drink so much."

"Oh my, did I get drunk? Aislinn? What the hell?"

"Confused are you?"

"A bit."

"You showed up on my doorstep instead of your own last night. So I put you in my bed. You snored the entire time I was moving you. How much did you have to drink and how did you get home?"

"Oh dear, he's in my apartment." She moaned.

"I thought you were going out?"

"I was and then decided I'd just have him come over. I had a very nice bottle of pinot and I knew I couldn't drink it and drive." She closed her eyes.

"He fell asleep in my bed, so I left and came here. I remember getting in the elevator. I don't remember getting out."

"Did you drink the entire bottle?"

"No, we drank the entire case." She rubbed her eyes. "Tell me it's Saturday."

"You're lucky, it's Saturday. So, your date is still in your apartment and you're in mine."

"I hate when they sleep over."

"I know you do. Here," I handed her some Pamprin and a glass of water. I had discovered in college it was great for hangovers. "Take these, drink this and go back to bed."

Nyleena popped the Pamprin, drank the water and stopped. She looked at herself.

"I have extra PJs in my closet. I hung them all up since I don't have a dresser yet."

"Thanks," she went into my room.

"Do you want me to go roust your date out of bed?"

"No, he'll wake up and leave when he realizes I'm not there. He always does."

"Ok, nighty night."

"Night, Aislinn." Her snoring was almost instant.

There were moments I envied Nyleena. She could have frivolous relationships and human contact without worrying about them being a serial killer. I had gotten to the point where I was almost suspicious of everyone I met.

Sleep came quickly, but didn't stay long. My phone began vibrating on the coffee table. It vibrated itself off onto the carpet. I fumbled for it in the dark.

The display had a number I didn't recognize, but at 5 a.m., it was unlikely to be a telemarketer. I hit the button to answer it.

"Hello?"

"Bags packed? We roll out as soon as you get to the airport. Lucas and Xavier are on their way to get you." Alejandro came over the speaker.

"He's struck again then."

"He has." The line disconnected. I scribbled a note for Nyleena. I had done as I was told and packed a bag for three or four days and sat it near the door.

The intercom buzzed, "Ms. Cain, your ride is here."

"I'll be right down," I said, locking the apartment behind me. Nyleena had a set of keys. It had come with two sets.

Fifteen

The plane ride was uneventful. Alejandro was silent, brooding. He smelled of whiskey and coffee. Lucas looked bright eyed, busying himself in a book. Xavier went back to sleep the moment we boarded. Michael sat playing video games.

We landed about an hour later in a small airport just outside of Chicago, Illinois. Alejandro barked orders at the pilots as we exited the plane. Outside was a small army. I counted four local police cars and an SUV. We were herded into the SUV.

Alejandro and the driver of the SUV made small talk about the case, but nothing important seemed to be said. I didn't tune them out, but I wasn't sure how they could be talking so calmly. I felt like I was about to crawl out of my skin. — anxious

Lucas gave me a wink. I gave him the best smile I could manage. I was going to the first crime scene where I wasn't involved. It was different to be sure.

The car stopped. The driver looked at me as we stepped out of the car.

"It's not pleasant," he said to Alejandro.

"She's our torture expert." He responded. The driver shrugged and we began trekking through the woods.

Light was beginning to brighten the sky, which seemed to make it darker on the ground. Even without their leaves, the trees cast extensive shadows on the undergrowth. Xavier walked right next to me, a flashlight on the ground. Silently I thanked him from keeping me from tripping over a stick and making myself look like an idiot.

We entered a clearing. There was a small, wood cabin that looked at least a hundred years old. Planks were missing out of it.

"Some bow hunters found it. They are at the hospital and can be interviewed there. Although, I think it might take a while before the sedatives wear off." The driver said to us.

He opened the door. I was let into the cabin second. They had set up flood lights. It made the scene even more gruesome and surreal. There was nothing in the room that looked like a torture device. There were ten bodies though. *so what did the killer use?*

Each seemed twisted and broken. Several were in a fetal position. There was a bruise visible on one of them across the back. It seemed about two inches in width.

"Xavier?" I motioned him over.

"What?" He asked, kneeling down. *what's that?*

"I think it's a Scavenger's Daughter," I pointed to the band. "But I won't know for sure until the autopsies. I need a catalogue of every broken bone. If I'm right, there will be lots of them."

Xavier picked up a hand. The arm flopped wrong as he did it. He dropped it. *like jelly*

"I'd say there's at least four fractures to that arm," he looked at me.

"What are you two whispering about?" Alejandro asked.

"I think I know what did this. It's called a Scavenger's Daughter. Basically, it's a hoop. You put the victim inside and a screw on top allows the hoop to tighten. It was rarely fatal, but when it was, they died of either trauma to the spine or suffocation. Everywhere the band touches, it breaks. So victims have multiple fractures."

UDHR
no torture

"Why would a hoop cause multiple fractures?" Xavier asked.

"Oh, it isn't a hoop like you are thinking. It's like an upright hula hoop. The victim was forced to kneel in it; the bottom of the hoop would be just below the knees. The arms were tucked in at the sides. And the top of the hoop went over their backs. It was common to dislocate the knees, break the tibia and fibula, break the arms in multiple places and break the spine. In some cases, it would cause multiple spine fractures because once it broke a vertebra; the stress on the spine could be increased. The increased pressure caused more damage to the spine."

imagery

"You said it was rarely fatal." Alejandro pointed out.

"Rarely because it was torture and dead people don't endure public humiliation. It wasn't meant to kill people, just injure them severely and it was used in public. Most of the time, it was tightened just enough to keep the person from moving. It would break the arms or legs and be done. It also wasn't a tool meant to be endured. Fifteen or twenty minutes, not longer. However, you tighten it enough and your knees are in your lungs, your bones are breaking and eventually you suffocate."

"How long it took to suffocate would depend on the tightness of the hoop," Xavier clarified.

"Here, look at this," Michael had his laptop out. There was a picture on the screen.

"That's the Scavenger's Daughter," I said, looking at the picture. "If I'm wrong, we'll have to figure out what made that bruise. But based on it and the boneless flopping of the victim's arm..."

"You got all that from a mark on the back and a broken arm?" The anonymous man sneered.

Smart alec

84

"Do you know the exact number of hours it requires before you can be considered an expert on any subject? 10,000 hours. That means that I have spent over 10,000 hours looking at torture devices and their aftermath. I have read medical reports, seen drawings and pictures and read accounts of things that you can't even begin to imagine. So, yes, I can pretty accurately say that the device involved is a Scavenger's Daughter. If I'm wrong, I have another theory or two, but they don't work as neatly and means he is torturing them by hand, as well." *confident in her work*

"What else could it have been?" Alejandro asked.

"A wheel possibly, but that wouldn't account for the fetal position or their death and it isn't exactly portable. And they should have other injuries, external injuries from fire or spikes. I don't see that here. A rack might account for the broken bones or dislocations, but a rack is less fatal than a Scavenger's Daughter. It can kill, but that's pretty extreme and normally means that the limbs have become detached or the abdomen split open. Again though, a rack isn't all that portable. A Hanging Coffin might do it, but that would be weird and there should be marks on the feet, the face, and scavengers should have attacked." *Same*

"She lost me," Michael said.

"Me too." Alejandro looked at me for a second. "Is that your expert opinion?"

"Yes, my expert opinion is that while we could find other devices that would cause the mark on the back or the break on the arms, it is unlikely that they would cause both. A Scavenger's Daughter would cause both and is very portable. If tight enough, I imagine he could have killed all ten of them in the space of two hours."

"How does he subdue them all? Especially the tenth one who is watching the others die?" Alejandro asked. *why is it called that?*

85

"That I don't know. That sounds like a medical and psychological question. Not a torture question."

"Any ideas how he manages to impale ten women, draw and quarter ten other women, put ten women in Iron Maidens and then use this scavenger thing on ten more without them fighting back or retaliating?"

"Wait." I frowned at him. "He used five Iron Maidens."

she got an idea
foreshadow

"So?"

"So why didn't I think of it before? Iron Maidens were thought to be a myth until the 1800's when one was found in a castle in Germany. Since then we've found others, but they aren't plentiful. You certainly can't buy them from any place or steal five of them without it making international news. You'd have to have them made. Iron Maidens have very specific specifications. Most iron workers couldn't do it. And with the spikes, that would be an odd order indeed. Someone had to make them. Someone who knows how to make them. I need to see the Iron Maidens." *What is that anyway?*

it's like she knows exactly what the killer does

"What about the hoop thing?" Xavier asked.

"Would be fairly easy to make, except the precision device that tightens it. Another custom order from a blacksmith that has a clue about medieval blacksmithing. I imagine the killer didn't do it, they were ordered. Specialty shops will make all sorts of things; some specialize in the darker side of life. The steel items probably have a maker's mark. That kind of work, it would be a shame not to sign it."

"We didn't find a maker's mark on the Iron Maidens." Alejandro frowned at me.

"Then either you didn't look in the right spot or our killer is a blacksmith, possibly in his spare time and probably dealing with renaissance period items."

"Huh?" The driver, who still hadn't introduced himself to me said.

it's a work of art, simile

"You don't create works of art like Iron Maidens and Scavenger's Daughters without signing them. It would be like creating the Mona Lisa and not signing it. There is a renaissance subculture in the world, along with a vampire subculture and a werewolf subculture and who knows what else. These subcultures still collect and make things from their respective periods. I once met a man who had hand-carved a Torture Wheel. He did it to see if he could. He sold it for several hundreds of thousands of dollars."

"Could he or the buyer be our killer?" Lucas asked.

"Seems unlikely. The carver was a woodcrafter, not a blacksmith. The buyer, maybe, but he bought it for a museum display piece. They were getting ready to open a medieval exhibit. It would seem weird for a museum curator to buy a Torture Wheel and then use other torture devices to kill."

"Is the Scavenger's Daughter in the book?" Lucas asked.

"Yes, but not with a picture plate. The *Book of Torture* covers almost 200 different methods of torture. There are only 11 plates in it. The Scavenger's Daughter does not have a plate."

"What's on the plates?" Alejandro asked.

"Impaling, drawing and quartering, rats in a head box, a Skull Crusher, a Pear of Anguish, the Torture Wheel, the Breast Ripper, Iron Maidens, a Hanging Coffin with spikes, burning at the stake, and possibly the worst ever, a Yoke." *the least intimidating word, situational irony*

"Like the thing they put on oxen?" Xavier asked.

"Sort of, same principle, but the Yoke had a blade in the back of the harness. It would slowly sever the head of the wearer."

"Why not just take it off?" The driver asked.

tone - fed up

"Who are you and why do you keep asking dumb questions?" I finally snapped.

"I'm Special Agent Gabriel Henders with the FBI and it isn't dumb if I don't know the answer."

true

"You would have your hands bound behind your back when you were yoked or broken at the elbows. It weighed a little over 100 pounds. If you fell, there were safe-guards to keep it from slipping from your neck. Medieval torturers took their jobs very seriously. And to them, every device they built was a work of art."

"Yeah, but didn't most of that come from…"

tone - annoyed

"If you say Spanish Inquisition I am liable to leave the room. Torture was an art long before the Inquisition. It was an art long after the Inquisition."

"I was going to say that," I got my first smile from Agent Gabriel Henders.

"Torture has been around as long as human civilization." I told him.

"And you can tell the method by the marks?"

"You can when you've seen as much of it as I have," I answered.

"Cain, you've earned yourself a trip to the morgue with Reece. You can watch him do the autopsies and see if they match what you expect." Alejandro said.

"Yes sir." I looked at Xavier. He smiled back at me. It seemed wrong in a room full of death.

situational irony

Sixteen

I stepped outside as men with gurneys filled the small, overly cramped cabin. Morning was in full bloom, light had blossomed over the clearing of death. The sun only seemed to provide light, not heat. My breathing was clearly visible in the cold morning air. *winter*

My attention was directed at the ground. Hundreds of footprints, frozen in time, littered the mostly dirt clearing around the cabin. Some lead into the woods, some lead out of the woods. There were pairs, groups, and individuals. They circled the cabin. They lead down a narrow path that ended at a small shed like building.

Their presence seemed as grotesque and out of place as ours. This was a forest, not a murderer's lair. I could only identify a few sets of animal prints. They had either been lost under the human prints or they didn't dare venture here.

There were dozens of people milling around outside. They were chatting quietly or not speaking at all. Several held insulated cups that steamed in the harsh Illinois air. They watched the woods, not each other. They seemed prepared to divert anyone that came their direction.

Lucas joined me on the porch. His breath steamed just as mine did. His breathing was steadier, deeper than my own and it was noticeable in the cold.

He didn't speak. His eyes followed the tracks on the ground. He traced their movements to and from, as I had done upon seeing them. I would have given anything to be able to read his mind at that moment.

Personification

Why?

89

"One set of these tracks belongs to our killer," he finally spoke. His voice was quiet and hushed, almost as if we were in a museum or a cathedral.

"Why do you say that?" I asked in the same muted voice.

"Because it has rained here for most of the last week. Last night, it suddenly froze. That means the tracks of every person who stepped in this mud-riddled wasteland has been preserved."

I nodded. His analysis seemed to be correct. It was a wasteland. At least, it was now. Two weeks ago it was probably just a cabin in the woods that local teenagers made out in and hunters caught in the weather sought refuge in. Now, it would be stigmatized, demonized. It would be infamous.

"Not only our killer, but our victims' as well. Their final steps have been immortalized, at least until the thaw."

"Very dark and gothic." I told him.

"Perhaps," he nodded, "sometimes I can't help it. I see the victims or what is left of them and unlike Xavier and Alejandro; I don't have an off button. I'd like to think of them as just victims, but I see their lives too. It always touches me with a bit of sadness and melancholy. Life cut down, but something of them always remains. In this case, their last walk. Somewhere among these hundreds of prints are the prints of ten women who walked to their deaths. I think it is worth a little darkness and drama. Their killer had a touch of humanity. They weren't barefoot in this terrible weather when they walked to their deaths. There aren't any barefooted prints. Everyone who stepped in the mud had on shoes. So our victims must have had their shoes on when they walked here. This means they were given the grace and dignity of not being paraded here naked and barefoot."

90

does she agree?

I had nothing to say to that. His thoughts were too deep for me at that moment. I couldn't sympathize with the victims. He could. I appreciated that someone could feel their horror and pain.

"Our monster has a human streak, a redeeming quality, that can be seen in something as tiny as footprints," Alejandro joined us on the porch.

"I am not sure I find that reassuring." I admitted.

"You shouldn't," Lucas told me. "Having a touch of humanity does not make up for what he did to them once he got them here. It just proves that he is human."

"Are you going to take casts of all the prints?" I asked. *theme*

"What for?" Alejandro turned his dark eyes to me.

"To compare." *can tell he's still jealous*

"To what, Cain? We have no elimination prints. The ground was frozen this morning when our hunters found the bodies. It rained steadily for five days. There is no telling how many different sets of prints there are or who they belong to. I'm sure there are tracks from hunters and nature walkers and teenagers and our killer and his victims, but we will never figure out which prints belong to which person." Alejandro left the porch.

"Come here," he was kneeling on the ground.

I followed and knelt with him.

"This is a smallish print, probably a woman, but it walks into the woods, not out of them. Furthermore, she was alone and she wasn't here recently because her prints disappear under the prints of this one." He pointed to another set of tracks.

These tracks came out of the woods about half-way. They stopped. The prints where they stopped were deep. Then they turned and went back into the woods. The female prints Alejandro had just shown me disappeared under them. *suspense*

"This is probably a park ranger, judging by the boot. Male. These deep prints are where he stood, probably for several minutes, then he turned and went back towards the road."

"We'll probably cast them, as many as we can, but they will go nowhere." Lucas said joining us. "There are just too many of them and we have nothing to compare it to. If we had an idea of our killer's shoe size, it would help. We can find our victim's tracks, but we have the victims'."

Again I was left speechless. I stood and examined the scene. Alejandro continued to look at the tracks.

"Here Cain," he yelled to me.

"What?" I asked, joining him.

"Here are our victims' footprints." He stood, I knelt.

I didn't touch them. I could see a handful of smallish prints, frozen in the ground. Coming from a different direction and walking over top of them were another set of prints. They were much bigger, with deeper treads and a pattern that was meant for grip.

"Hunters," Alejandro said, pointing to a nearby tree.

I followed the prints to where Alejandro stood. On the ground was some blood. Not much, but enough to know that something had died there.

"What is it?" I asked.

"My guess, it's what scared our killer out of that cabin and it's part of the reason the tracks are useless." He pointed to the tree.

There was a small bullet hole in it. The bark had been ripped away. Blood was spattered on the tree. The difference between the bark and the living wood underneath was evident.

"Analyze this," Alejandro shouted to a crime scene tech.

The tech came over. He put the blood on the end of a cotton swab and stuck it in some solution. A couple of seconds later, the solution turned green. *foreshadow*

"Not human," the tech told us as he began digging the bullet out of the tree.

"But it's bow season," I frowned.

"Yes, but poaching knows no season." Alejandro walked away from me.

I watched him walk away from me again. This time, he went back into the cabin and began shouting at people. I had no desire to be in the crosshairs, so I stayed outside in the cold.

"Our own master hunter there," Lucas nodded towards the cabin. "Before he became part of this team, he worked on a reservation as something. He tracked people lost in the desert or the woods or wherever. He's hunted just about everything and he has the heads on his wall to prove it. He doesn't like poachers anymore than he likes serial killers." *vocab*

I frowned at Lucas. Lucas frowned back.

"He doesn't seem to care about the tracks." I told him.

"No, I imagine he doesn't. They aren't that helpful. We can isolate the victims', that's about it. And there aren't that many of them. They give us the direction they marched from, but that's about it. Finding our killer's tracks will be much harder. He probably lead them here, tied together with rope or something else. His tracks probably walk parallel to theirs, but as you can see, there's another party here." Lucas pointed at some tracks. *How does he know?*

"And another here," Lucas pointed at a different set, "and here." *group of people*

Each "party" seemed to have different tread patterns. They moved in random directions. None of them seemed to move directly with the victims'.

their strategy   93

"What do you see?" Lucas asked.

"Different treads." I commented dryly.

"These were made by a heavier man; see how they are deeper than the others in his group? These were made by someone with a limp." He pointed to two sets.

"I don't see it; I'll have to take your word for it."

"Then take my word for it." Lucas smiled at me, "I can give you that information, but Alejandro could give you even more."

Before we could continue the conversation, Xavier came out of the cabin. He was helping with a gurney. They were moving the bodies. It was time to leave the cold wasteland.

very observant

Seventeen

"The first victim is a brunette based on her roots, although it is dyed much darker at this time, roughly 5 feet and six inches tall. Good teeth, blue eyes, Caucasian, with a recent pedicure and manicure," Xavier was speaking into his recorder again. *imagery*

"X-rays indicate she has over 200 fractures, some minor stress fractures, some major fracturing of the bones. Her spinal cord has been severed, but the skin remains unbroken. Her ribs all have multiple fractures, two have broken off completely. One pierced her liver, the other her heart. She was already dead when it happened." *UDHR no torture at least she was dead*

He looked at me, "are you sure you want to be here for this?"

"Nope, I am sure I don't. I would rather be doing a lot of other things than watching you cut her open, but I was ordered to be here." *it's her job*

"Go get a coffee or soda; I'll be out in just a minute. We have cause of death and I think we can fairly easily agree that your torture hoop is a good match. We'd need the exact hoop to know for sure, but a circular item that caused intense pressure is the only thing I can see that would make these types of fractures."

"Great, want anything?"

"Coffee, black." *eww that's gross*

I left the room and got Xavier a coffee and me a Mountain Dew from the vending machines. When I returned he was sitting outside. He looked at me.

"You're positive that the hoop thing could do that kind of damage?" *second-guessing Cain*

95

description

"The Scavenger's Daughter is a precision device. It's a giant iron ring, like you'd find on an old fashioned barrel. At the top of the ring, there is a mechanism. Like a screw that either tightens the hoop or loosens the hoop. I can't think of anything to compare the mechanism to at the moment. The hoop gets larger or smaller depending on how it is turned. As it tightens, the victim, who is kneeling in the fetal position, becomes constricted. The tighter it gets the more damage it does. Since it is mechanized and forged iron or steel, it is pretty durable. I found records of torturers taking it too far and victims spontaneously start bleeding from all their orifices *vocab* because there is just nowhere in the body for the blood to flow. So it finds an exit. There was an incident where the hoop slipped and cut off a head. It wasn't intended to be deadly, it just happened once in a while."

"Now it is being used for that," Xavier commented. "And why deviate? He's been sticking to the pictures; why not stick to the pictures?"

"Too gruesome or hard to fulfill?" I suggested.

"How do you figure?"

"I don't know. It's hard to get more gruesome than drawing and quartering or impaling. The Pear of Anguish and the Skull Crusher are both mechanized and easy to use. The torture wheel would be the only difficult one, but if you can get five Iron Maidens, you can get a torture wheel. He isn't sticking with just mechanized forms. Impaling requires wood, not metal and isn't mechanized. Drawing and quartering was done with horses, now days it could be done with cars, but it wouldn't work without more than one person. The four corners of movement are what make it really terrible."

"Stop, explain that." Xavier said.

"Ok, with drawing and quartering, you were tied to four horses or oxen, normally. Each animal was then 'encouraged' to run the direction they were pointing. This

more like forced

caused <u>massive damage and pain</u>. Being pulled in four directions at once is what really caused it. If only one horse or ox moved, the others would actually go with that one. <u>In rare cases, they'd stay stationary</u>, but that meant the victim usually only lost a limb. When all of them were moving, one would get a torso or the torso would be ripped in half as well as the limbs being pulled off. If you were tied to four cars and only one of them moved, the same thing would happen. You'd lose a limb, you wouldn't actually be quartered. If you only use two animals or cars, the victim tended to tear in half and the arms came off. The legs were so firmly attached that they often remained connected. So you need four points of motion to draw and quarter. Are we positive that they were drawn and quartered and not just hacked off?"

"Oh yeah, they were ripped apart." Xavier encouraged.

"Meaning four points of motion. <u>Horses or oxen?</u>"

"We don't know, there was no manure found at the scene."

"No manure when he would have had to use animals? <u>Oh, wait,</u>" I frowned hard. "There are two other ways. Neither was used very often. It's very messy for the person doing the drawing and quartering. One was called corralling, four horses, locked in a corral. You spook one, it begins jerking and tugging, spooks the others, however, since they are in a corral, they can only run so far. The limbs were usually wrenched off, joints dislocated as the horses attempted to bolt. Most of the time, they ended up running in a circle, but since they were joined together by the victim, it was an awkward gait that did more damage to the bodies. The second doesn't have a name. And you have to find two trees, but you tie limbs to the trees and a third to the horse, the horse takes off, the force exerted removes two of the limbs. <u>You stop the horse, retie and do it again.</u> You can

97

effectively draw and quarter someone doing it, but it takes longer and you get bloody."

"None of that makes me feel any better. If anything, it makes me feel worse. The killer would be covered in arterial spray. The only good thing is the victim would die of blood loss pretty quickly once the femoral artery was torn. Anything else?"

"You found no maker's mark on the Iron Maidens? What about the stakes?"

"Oak, looked hand cut, but the ends were sharpened with a grinder."

"That's odd. Why use a grinder on them? If you took the time to cut the stakes by hand, why not hand sharpen them?"

"I don't know, but they were all the same length or at least within an inch of being the same length. The bottoms weren't cleaned; we found axe marks on them. But it was a common hand axe. They were all within an inch of being the same diameter as well."

"So he selects and hand cuts the wood he wants to use for the stakes, but uses a grinder to sharpen them? That's the only modern thing about it."

"Think it means something?"

"I don't know. Maybe he was just tired from chopping down the trees."

"What are you thinking, Ace?"

"I'm not. I'm chasing my tail. The grinder doesn't make sense. The Scavenger's Daughter doesn't make sense. We've missed something, but I can't figure out what."

"Think it is something psychological?"

"Maybe, but it could be something historical. The Scavenger's Daughter is a very late Medieval creation, but impaling has been around since the beginning of time. It was easy and effective."

"And the others?"

"Well, as I said earlier, it was believed for a long time that the Iron Maiden was fiction. It was described as early as the 1200's, but no one had seen one until the 1800's. It went out of fashion around the 1500's, if not earlier. The Iron Maiden is a female torture device. The others are all unisex." I thought for a moment about that.

"Damn, that's it. They all have something that isn't exactly right for its use in the menagerie. The Iron Maiden was a female device. Drawing and quartering was an improvised device, they did it mostly in the rural areas, where torture devices weren't so common. Impaling had a long history, but it never became widespread except when Vlad Tepes was in power, it was his favorite. The Scavenger's Daughter was mostly about humiliation and was a late Middle Ages device created in England. It almost doesn't fit the time-line and unlike the others, it wasn't intended to be used as a death sentence."

"Think that fits?" Xavier asked.

"No, but I can't think of anything else for the randomness. We have devices that require master blacksmiths, a wooden stake that requires very little skill and horses or oxen. The only thing we can tie together are the Scavenger's Daughter and the Iron Maidens."

"You keep coming back to the Iron Maidens."

"You examined the bodies, right?"

"Yes."

"Did you see what they actually do?"

"They pierce holes in you. Most of the women died from trauma to their organs."

"Uh, no, they shouldn't have." I looked at him.

"What do you mean, they shouldn't have?"

"Iron Maidens have spikes, but not long spikes. The intention was to prick the victim all over their body and let them slowly bleed to death. The eye stakes were the most important piece; they were carefully measured to not puncture the brain."

"These punctured the brain. Front and back."

"That's wrong." I told him. "A true Iron Maiden doesn't have spikes at the back of the head. They have very small spikes that stick out the back, but it was mainly to keep the women in them from moving around. The front was two doors that closed and the spikes were positioned with pinpoint accuracy to not nick major veins or arteries, not puncture the brain and they weren't long enough to go into the body more than an inch or so. The women literally bleed to death over hours or even days. That's what the hole in the bottom was for, so that the blood could drain out. There was usually a person watching to make sure the blood wasn't draining too quickly. If it was, the maiden was opened and the spikes adjusted."

"These spikes were not adjustable, Ace. And most measured between eight and twelve inches long. The women didn't live very long in them. After all ten were dead, they were shoved into them, two at a time and sealed back up."

"You're positive that it wasn't done at the same time?"

"Positive. There were two different sets of puncture marks. One before death and one after death, the ones after death were all one-sided and much worse. There was tearing of the skin, but no bruising around them."

"Whoever built the maidens didn't have proper schematics and probably thought they were being built for show. Replicas tend to have longer spikes to make them look more terrifying because few people understand how they actually worked."

"I didn't," Xavier agreed.

"We need to find a master blacksmith who deals with replicas; high quality replicas and we need to find his maker's mark inside the maidens."

"You keep talking about a maker's mark." Alejandro's voice suddenly floated to me. I looked up and saw the rest of the unit walking down the hall.

"The Maidens were built to be show pieces, not actual torture devices. True maidens had short spikes, not long ones. They were meant to prolong death, not make it quick and brutal. However, a replica show piece would have longer spikes that were not adjustable. Our torturer would know that. But for whatever reason, doesn't have the ability to get an accurate replica. This means there has to be a maker's mark somewhere inside or outside the maiden."

"We didn't find any marks." Alejandro reiterated.

"Did you find any spots that looked like they had been ground down then? Someone who builds something like that is going to brand it as their work. It's complicated and only a master blacksmith would have the skills, even today it would have to be hand forged."

"No spots that looked ground either," Alejandro assured me.

"Well hell," I stared at him. "I still want to examine the maidens, but it can wait."

"Good because we found something else in the woods." Alejandro gave me a look.

"What?"

"Lucas, go get it." Lucas disappeared and came back with a hoop. There was a device on top that worked as a tightening mechanism. I stared at the Scavenger's Daughter. There was blood on the ring.

"You two can go over this. I'm having the maidens brought here. They should be here in the next couple of hours," Alejandro pointed to Xavier.

Lucas handed the hoop over. Xavier took it gently between gloves. I frowned at it.

"It's iron."

"Very perceptive," Alejandro frowned back at me.

"Who works with iron anymore? I was really expecting it to be steel."

"Well, it isn't." He turned and walked away.

"Don't take it personally; he doesn't like women, smart people or people who don't cower at his feet." Michael smiled at me. "You seem to fall into all three categories."

"Why are you considering hiring me to work for someone who can't stand me?" I turned to Lucas.

"Because the rest of us like you and he's just the guy who barks orders." Lucas turned to Xavier.

"What?" Xavier asked.

"I didn't see blood on any victims, but we found what appears to be blood on the thingy."

"I noticed. Doesn't mean a victim didn't vomit it up and it get cleaned up from everything but the hoop." Xavier countered.

"But if it isn't the victim's..."

"Yes, Lucas, I had already had that thought, but I am trying really hard not to get my hopes up."

"Just so long as we're clear."

"Crystal." Xavier took the hoop into the examining room we had just left.

The bodies had disappeared. I didn't know where or when they had left, but a part of me was glad. Xavier pulled over a steel table.

"What'cha think?" He asked, lying it down.

"I think it's iron and I think that for some reason that little fact is important. What do you think?"

"I think I have never seen anything like it and I'm going to need help taking it apart."

102

wants to find the maker's mark   *foreshadow*

"Sure," I found the latches and screws and began disassembling it. As I did, I put each piece carefully onto the table. Xavier labeled each with a number and a letter.

"All done," I said.

"That was much faster than I anticipated."

I shrugged in response. The hoop section was actually two pieces, hinged together at the bottom. As the screw on top was turned, the pieces moved together or apart at the top. They were oiled and moved easily, sliding over each other perfectly. It was a detail most people would have missed. *observant*

"Why do you keep playing with that?" Xavier *vocab* finally asked, as I closed the hoop for the umpteenth time.

"Because it fits so perfectly well together. It looks round, but it really isn't. See, this side here is actually just a fraction smaller than the other so that when it closes, the smaller side of the hoop slides under the band on the larger side."

"Ok and that's significant?"

"If they were the same size, it wouldn't work. Metal doesn't like to move into the same space as other metal. It's a minute detail, but the one that makes the entire thing work."

"Fascinated by the details?" *characterization*

"Yes."

"Does it tell you anything?"

"That the person that made it knew exactly what they were making and how it worked." *But who?*

"Unlike the maidens?"

"Or exactly like the maidens. Iron Maidens just don't look scary. This doesn't either, but Iron Maidens should look scary because of what they do. There's a psychological aspect to it. Just because you build a replica that isn't exact, doesn't mean you don't know what it is. It just means you know the psychology of it."

"That sounds like Lucas's department."

"It is, but all torture carries aspects of psychology. Back in the day, when these things were used, the populace knew and understood exactly what they were. Five hundred years later, give or take, and the populace doesn't understand torture the way they used to, so you have to intensify it to make it understandable. This isn't meant to be lethal; therefore, the scary factor drops. It is meant to work and be uncomfortable and break bones. I think we can see that just by looking at it."

"You must be a riot at dinner parties."

"I stopped being invited to dinner parties long before I started studying torture." I ran my fingers over a piece of the Scavenger's Daughter.

"Are we looking for something specific, other than DNA?" Xavier asked.

"I'm not looking for DNA or fingerprints. I'm searching for a maker's mark. You get to do the medically stuff."

"You're obsessed with maker's marks." Xavier smiled and rolled his eyes.

"If you were making items like this, items that required this much work and skill, wouldn't you flaunt it?"

"I see your point."

"Good, got any magnifying goggles or something?"

"Think it's that small?"

"Some are no bigger than the eraser of a pencil. They appear as flaws in the metal."

Xavier handed me a pair of glasses. I put them on and the world grew much bigger. Slowly I turned the hoop between my fingers, examining every millimeter of the band. There was nothing on it. I grabbed a piece of the handle.

104

There it was. A small imprinted stamp. It was less than a centimeter square in size and stamped on the underside of the turning handle. *tone - excited*

"Here!" I pointed excitedly. "We need pictures or something of it. What do you do with it?"

"We need a geek," Xavier drew a cell phone out of his jeans.

He spoke for a few minutes. We waited a few more minutes. Then Michael, Lucas and Alejandro all walked into the room. *simile*

"You look like one of those goldfish with the weird bubble eyes," Michael said, coming around the table.

"Thanks, look here." I pointed to the spot. "We need to somehow get a picture, blow it up and find out who made it." *very crucial finding*

"Yeah, I got it," Michael was already rummaging around in his bag. He pulled out a small camera.

"Your maidens will be here soon," Alejandro said. "Giovanni, get that photo out and find out who the hell made this thing and if they've made anything else." *tone - demanding*

With that, Alejandro whisked himself out of the room. He walked silently, but his absence was noticeable in the room. It seemed freer.

"He's like a dark brooding bear," I said, narrowing my eyes at the closed door. *simile*

"He takes a lot of getting used to," Michael took more pictures.

"Dr. Cain," Special Agent Gabriel Henders entered the room.

"Yes," I blinked at him, wondering if he had been waiting outside the door for Alejandro to leave.

"I have your maidens," he said it with a frown.

"Great! Bring them in."

tone - extatic

105

Eighteen

yes she is

"You aren't really going to examine each of them? Individually?" Lucas asked as several people carried in the Iron Maidens.

"Yep." I changed my gloves and put the goggles back on. "Just stand them up, carefully."

"Yes, ma'am," one of the men said. They stood all five up and left. Gabriel Henders remained.

Polite

"Going to watch?"

underestimating

"Not sure what you're going to find that we didn't, so yeah, I think I'll watch."

"Would you mind taking some notes then?" I asked.

"I could do that." Gabriel Henders pulled out a notebook and a pen.

"Great."

Xavier and Lucas moved the Scavenger's Daughter and took seats on the steel table. Michael shook his head, took his camera and left. I was guessing he was going to follow orders. mood - annoyed

The first maiden stood around five foot seven inches tall. Larger than most models I had seen. It was made of iron as well. The outside was bland, no special features or marks. Real ones tended to be painted, usually with the image of the Virgin Mary. why?

This one was coated to keep it protected from the elements. That was all though. I opened one side. There was still dried blood on the inside.

"Can we clean this?" I asked.

"Yes, it's been processed." Xavier got up and grabbed a steel shower head.

106

He turned it on. I carefully opened both doors. He sprayed the inside gently; the blood slowly began to run off of everything. It ran down the molded interior and into a drain on the floor. personification

"Thanks," I said when he finished.

The spikes were definitely wrong. The back spikes were at least eight inches in length. The front spikes were twelve. I closed one of the doors and shined a flashlight in around it. The spikes here didn't just touch, they overlapped. Definitely not intended to kill slowly.

The back of it even had spikes where the head would go. I stared at them. processing her thoughts

"You seem very lost in thought."

"I'm thinking of how awful this is, but how much worse a real one would be." I opened the door back up.

"Ok, very carefully, hold these doors open." I stepped into the maiden. Lucas and Xavier both grabbed a door. I let my body rest against the spikes in the back.

"That's why the doors are so heavy," I muttered.

"What?" Gabriel asked.

"The doors. They seem unnaturally heavy. Like there is more weight than just the metal. Come look from the side." why?

"Ok," Gabriel moved to stand by Xavier.

"See how much of my body is visible outside the maiden? Imagine shoving someone in against these spikes and closing the door. They are going to struggle and fight you every inch, unless they can't."

"I still don't see your point." Lucas said.

"If you closed the doors right now, the weight of them would pin me in, push me back against the spikes. It would be impossible for me to struggle against the weight of the doors, the force of a person and the spikes."

"Gotcha." Xavier smiled. "Now get the hell out of there, I have this vision of telling Nyleena that we

humorous characterization

dropped the doors of this Maiden and you bled to death before we could get you out."

"Fair enough." I climbed out. "The other problem. None of those spikes would have hit my eyes. There should be places to move the spikes. Too long, too many, not in the right places. Whoever made it had something to go off of, but it was a show piece, not a real maiden."

"The eyes are important?" Xavier asked.

"Very, if you lived, you were blinded and branded by the marks of the maiden."

might as well kill yourself

"Did anyone live?"

"No one really knows. All the stuff we actually know about Iron Maidens comes from antiquity. You have to really scour the books to find it." *vocab*

"And you have." Gabriel flashed me a grin.

"I have. I actually went to Germany for the specific purpose of seeing a real one. Real ones are incredibly rare."

"How rare?"

why does this spark her interest so much?

"I don't know, maybe thirty or so in the entire world. That might also be a gross overestimate. Most museum pieces are replicas."

"You seem obsessed with the maidens, why?" Lucas asked. *asked that before*

"Because they are so wrong." I told him. "You're the psychologist, this is scary, yes? These long spikes, knowing you are going to be shoved in and die from it."

"It looks terrifying," Lucas agreed.

"Real maidens don't. They have short spikes. The spikes screw in and out of different spots. There are two where the eyes are located, but no others are in the head of the maiden. The outside gets painted like the Virgin Mary most of the time. The spikes prick the skin, they don't stab you. They never go deep enough to puncture an organ or sever a vein. You bleed to death. It's like the Chinese 'Death of a Thousand Cuts' torture. This isn't

Simile

quick. It's slow and excruciatingly painful. There's a serious psychology to the Iron Maiden. It isn't just about death, it's about knowing you are going to die and it's going to take several hours, maybe days for it to happen."

"So the maiden is meant to kill, but it is also meant to psychologically torment you while you die."

"Exactly. They weren't 'scary' looking unless you knew what you were looking at." *It tricks you*   *torture*

"That's why you are obsessed with the maidens." Lucas answered the question. "The killer would have known they were wrong, but went with them anyway."

"Because he couldn't get anything else." I smiled at him, "because a Scavenger's Daughter doesn't raise suspicion, but an exact Iron Maiden would."

"Because it wouldn't have any psychological effects today," Lucas smiled back.

"Exactly. Hence the question of the maidens."

"Where would a maker hide his mark in a maiden?" Xavier grinned.

"My guess, one of the spikes. If it is the same maker as the other iron piece, then he would put it somewhere no one would look, because while he signs all his work, he is used to creating high quality replicas that are intended for collections."

"Why do you think that?" Gabriel asked.

"Because you don't just wake up one morning and look at a schematic and make an Iron Maiden. All the metal is coated with primer. He was expecting the maidens to be painted. He was expecting them to go to a private collection or a museum or both. Any blacksmith with a diagram could make the Scavenger's Daughter, but only the most skilled could make an Iron Maiden. And he's done it before based on how it was treated."

"So we are looking for a blacksmith that creates replicas for museums and private collectors?" Xavier frowned, "who collects replicas of torture devices?"

[margin note, top left: "why?"]

"I have a replica of a ceremonial dagger that was used to cut out the tongues of people being put in a Brazen Bull." I answered.

"I have no clue what that is," Xavier said.

"It's a torture device of the highest gruesomeness. On a scale of one to ten, it's about a fifteen. Only impaling actually seems worse and then, only sometimes."

"You seem to have gotten off topic. The maker's mark?" Gabriel reminded me.

[margin note, left: "very secret places"]

"Oh yes, so a maker's mark. Check all of them. Check each spike on each maiden. Check the ring at the bottom where the blood drains. Check the tip of the spikes. Somewhere on these, there is a maker's mark."

"The FBI went over them with a fine toothed comb." Gabriel said. *[margin note: "well not good enough"]*

"And yet, they left the blood inside." I pointed out. "Hard to see a maker's mark if it is caked with blood. And a stamped piece of iron, even with primer on it, would collect blood. Wait, don't clean all of them. Check to see abnormal blood spots. Particularly on the spikes."

"Why the spikes?" Xavier asked, opening one of the others.

"If I were the maker, I'd leave my mark on the underside of one of the spikes. It would be there, but no one would see it." *[margin note: "clever"]*

"What about this?" Lucas asked, pointing to a spike in the maiden he had just opened.

"What is it?" I asked.

"There's a weird blood pattern on the bottom of this, where the feet would be."

Carefully, I took a damp cloth from Gabriel and wiped at the spot. When it was clean, there was nothing there but a toenail. I gagged.

"Really? You can watch an autopsy but toenail clippings make you gag?"

[margin note, bottom left: "characterization"]

110

"I don't do well with snot, vomit, poop or urine either. Blood I'm fine with though," I told them.

"Not really mother material then, are you?"

"I intend to never have children. Can you imagine miniature copies of me running around the world? Good lord." I shook my head and went back to the cleaned maiden. *very independent characterication*

I began the process by searching the spikes of the maiden. That done, I searched the interior, then the exterior. I found no marks. I had just opened the doors again when Michael came in with food.

"I didn't know if you were a vegetarian or not, so there's a cheeseburger and a salad." *thoughtful of him*

"Thanks, I like both," I took the cheeseburger, *char.* picked off the tomato and turned my attention back to the maiden. One door had swung shut. I frowned at it. *mood-*

"Xavier, will you wedge those open for me?" I *creepy* asked, chewing and talking with my mouth full. *suspense*

"Gross, but yes," Xavier said, also with a mouthful of food. He got off the table, I stole his spot.

"That's why you wanted me to open the doors? So you could have my seat?" *comfortable w/ each other*

"Pretty much," I smiled and took another bite of the cheeseburger. *tone - flirty*

"And you just let her," Xavier looked at Lucas.

"She smells better than you," Lucas said.

"Yeah, you smell a bit like death," I told him.

"I did an autopsy. Do you expect me to smell like Drakkor or something?" *??*

simile "Ew, not Drakkor. Bvlgari," I suggested.

My eyes fixed on the maiden again. There it was. Plain as day. I dropped my cheeseburger in my haste to jump from the table. *foreshadow* *so sudden*

"What the hell?" Lucas asked, jumping off the table as well. *tone - suprised*

"Is it just me or does this arrangement of spikes look like an "H" with the cross-line being a sword?"

"It does, now that you mention it," Gabriel chimed in.

"Could be your mind matrixing it." Lucas moved closer.

vocab

motif "Or not," I narrowed my eyes at it.

"Or not," Lucas agreed, we were both leaning in really close to them. _suspense_

"If either of you trip, you'll both end up dead." Xavier pushed his way in to look.

"I think you found your mark," Lucas said.

"I think it matches the mark on the Scavenger's Daughter as well." I told him.

Michael and Gabriel had now stepped in to look at them. Michael took out his camera and began snapping pictures. _seems to always be right_

"Well, Cain, you were right, the answer was in the maidens." Gabriel said.

"Actually, it is just a beginning. We know who made the maidens."

"I'll call Alejandro." Lucas moved away.

"Damn, I guess I'll eat the salad." I picked the cheeseburger up off the floor.

"Yeah, I wouldn't eat that now," Xavier grinned.

Nineteen

getting late

"We should get checked into the motel." Xavier sighed as we left the morgue.

"You can sleep right now?" I asked him.

"Yes, at least for an hour or two."

"We've already been checked in; your bags are in your rooms." Alejandro was leading the way. He seemed a bit pissed that the maidens had maker's marks. *he wants to make a lead-selfish Char.*

"I need to stop by a museum." I told them.

"Why?"

"We are in Chicago and the Field has an excellent collection of torture implements. I was wondering if any were replicas and if they knew this maker. Besides, I have a thought that I want to put to a test and I'll need some professionals to help me."

"We aren't professional enough?" Alejandro sneered. *tone - annoyed*

"Sure, but not the right professionals. I need a couple of historians and maybe an archeologist. I figure the museum would be a good spot for that."

"Fine," Alejandro looked at Gabriel. "Will you ferry her to the museum after you have dropped us at the hotel." *he's so jealous of Cain*

"Can I have Xavier?" I asked.

"Sure, I'll go with you, why?"

"I'll need some medical advice as well."

Gabriel dropped off Lucas, Michael and Alejandro at the hotel. We took Lake Shore Drive to the Field Museum. I checked my watch. They would be closing soon.

"What's your thoughts?" Xavier asked.

"Something struck me while I was staring at the maiden. Maybe the devices are being used because they are recognizable."

"What do you mean?"

"Iron Maidens, impaling, and drawing and quartering are all well known torture devices. The Scavenger's Daughter is less well known, but it isn't as obscure in concept as the Pear of Anguish."

"I don't know what that is."

"You didn't know what a Scavenger's Daughter was either." I reminded him.

"True, still not sure I do." Xavier yawned.

"Don't do that," I told him.

"You're thinking of something else," Xavier said.

"I am." I took a deep breath and held it for a minute. "Ok, here goes. Aside from the obscure book, why else pick torture as a weapon? Different types of torture? Then I remembered. A couple of years ago, while I was working on my dissertation, I came to Chicago. They were having a special exhibition on torture. It was going to be traveling. On exhibit was a maiden, a rack, a Scavenger's Daughter, impaling, drawing and quartering, rats in a cage, a skull crusher and a Hanging Coffin. All of those were from the Middle Ages. There were others too, but they were not from Europe or from the Middle Ages. That's all we have here. Impaling was perfected by Vlad Tepes making it European. Drawing and quartering was used long before the Middle Ages, but it became vogue in England and some of the other northern countries during the high Middle Ages because it was quick and easy to improvise. The maiden was first discovered in modern times in Germany. The Scavenger's Daughter was invented by an Englishman. All have the European stamp on them. And all are well known as a result. The Skull Crusher, the

Pear of Anguish, less common, the pear was a favorite of the Inquisition."

"So you want to see what else they had on display and find out where it went after it left Chicago?" Xavier asked.

"Precisely. Maybe our killer saw the exhibition. Maybe that is why he picked different forms of torture. That, combined with the book, would answer why there isn't a pattern to it."

"That's thin."

"I know, but I can't think of anything else. Hence the museum trip."

"Speaking of museums, we're here." Gabriel said as the car slowed to a stop.

The Field Museum is a majestic stone structure. It is intimidating to some degree. Mostly though, I just find it breathtaking. It never fails to inspire me with awe. It was the first museum I had ever visited. It holds a special place in my heart as a result.

The architect had known how to make it as powerful as the objects inside. The entire thing was made of large pieces of white stone. It is a tribute to the glory days of the Roman Empire. Four large, imposing columns support the heavy stone ceiling covering the entrance. A wide, sweeping staircase leads up to the imposing columns and six gilded gold and glass doors.

These are not the only columns though. The entire outside of the Field is decorated with the supportive neoclassical columns. The caryatid porches have columns carved in the shape of women. Below the caryatids are reliefs that depict scenes reminiscent of any Ancient Greek or Roman structure.

All of it combines to create the impression of walking into a temple of one of the fallen gods or visiting the Oracle of Delphi, rather than a museum. It is worth stopping to stare at and taking a few pictures.

115

"Hi, I'm Marshal Xavier Reece, this is Dr. Aislinn Cain and this is Special Agent Gabriel Henders. We've come to speak to the curator please," Xavier was in professional mode as he spoke, flashing badges and identification cards.

We stood still, waiting for the curator. Xavier coughed lightly and pointed at a woman walking past us. She had neon green hair. It reminded me of younger days when Nyleena and I used to participate in the counter-cultures.

"Dr. Cain." The curator, Dr. Sam Samuels said.

"Dr. Samuels," I smiled at the rotund man.

He had left a good impression the last time I was here. He was in his sixties with no hair and wire rimmed glasses. His stature was small and round. His face creased with smile lines. He was good natured.

"I'm glad to see you came back, although," he motioned to the others.

"They are difficult circumstances," I admitted.

"Come to my office."

We followed him through the main hall and through a door marked "Authorized personnel only." His office was big with lots of furniture. It was comfortable and full of creature comforts.

"Sit, please," he motioned us into chairs.

"Dr. Samuels, I'm consulting with the US Marshals on a case. I have some questions about the torture exhibit."

"Of course, but…" He stopped and sighed.

"If I remember correctly, you had some interesting pieces."

"Which pieces exactly?" Dr. Samuels asked, cocking his head to the side.

"Specifically, I'd like to see your Iron Maiden and get the information on it."

"Our Iron Maiden?" He frowned harder.

116

"Yes, please."

"Of course, it is not on display at the moment, it is being held in storage since the exhibit stopped traveling a couple of months ago. You don't think someone used..."

"No, not in the least. We have a maiden in custody and I want to compare the details."

"Oh," Dr. Samuels stood up. We all stood up and followed him.

I had been in the storage space on my previous visit. They did have a very rare piece that Dr. Samuels had been interested in showing me. At the time, I had been just a student. I hadn't been alone; my thesis advisor had been with me and had known Dr. Samuels.

We entered one of the many storage facilities at the Field. Dr. Samuels turned on the lights. The fluorescent lights shocked my eyes, making them water for a moment. I wiped them and gave them time to adjust. *me when the teacher turns on the light*

"It's over there." Dr. Samuels pointed.

"Thank you, Doctor," I walked over to the maiden. *exact* It was a replica, but a true replica. The spikes were short and adjustable. The head space only had two spikes where the eyes would be estimated to be. The outside was painted like the Virgin Mary. I studied it for several minutes. *simile*

"Who made it, Dr. Samuels?" I asked, finally turning from it.

"I don't know. It was acquired way before my time."

"It is a replica?" I asked.

"We think so. There is no real documentation on it. If it isn't, lots of questions are going to be asked."

"And you don't know how the museum acquired it?" I frowned. *by who?*

"It was an estate donation made sometime in the 1940's. The paperwork that should have been with the

117

donation doesn't seem to exist though. We had to look into it before we could exhibit it. It was part of the reason we did the exhibit." *to make it more creepy*

"What paperwork did you have?"

"About half the stuff in the donation was documented, but all of it was real, not replicas. The replicas were all of high quality, but there was very little paperwork with them. Since they were replicas and donated during World War II, it turned out that we didn't need all the paperwork that we would have needed if it was real." He had begun to talk very fast. *is he nervous?*

"I'm not with customs," I frowned harder. "I don't actually care about the paperwork. I care about the maker if it is a replica. If it isn't, the point is moot. *vocab* Finding someone now days that could make a maiden, that would be a skill passed down from generation to generation."

"Ah, I see," Dr. Samuels visibly relaxed. "There is a maker's mark. We've never investigated it though."

"Afraid you'd find out it was real?"

"Something like that." Dr. Samuels finally smiled again. After a moment, the smile faded and something seemed to dawn on him. *suspense* *figured something out*

"Oh my... You mean someone used one?"

"Not a real one," I told him, looking at Xavier. Xavier nodded.

"A high-priced replica was used, but it wasn't a true replica. It was a..." I shrugged unsure what to call it.

"What?" Dr. Samuels asked.

"It was the scary version used by collectors and low budget museums."

"Extra long spikes, not adjustable, those sorts of things?" He asked.

"Yes." I agreed.

"Here," Dr. Samuels came over and pointed out the mark. I took out my cell phone and took pictures. It was nothing like our mark, but I hadn't expected it to be since it was well over 70 years old. *setting - present*

"Thank you; do you have a medievalist on staff?" I asked.

"Yes, although I think you are the better qualified medievalist." Dr. Samuels smiled again. *not amused*

"Maybe," I shrugged again. "Can I speak with them as well as you and maybe another historian or two?"

"Well, most of the staff will be going home about now, but I'll see who I can scrounge up. Please, don't touch anything." *vocab*

"I know." I grinned.

"I was talking to them." He hooked a finger at Gabriel who was indeed about to touch something. He jerked back. The verbal hand-slapping getting his attention. He blushed. *embarassed*

I looked around, but almost everything was sealed in something. The maiden was about the only thing in the room that was out. Gabriel and Xavier did the same. They prodded semi-opened crates to see what was inside. They snickered quietly as they read the abbreviated cards on the outsides of the crates.

I had been here before. I understood the *childish - char.* abbreviations and the cataloging system. Still, I could see where they would find it amusing. I had once been there too, snickering over the weirdly worded abbreviated *but she learned and grew up* labels. Gabriel pointed something out to Xavier.

The room wasn't dark, but shaded. The fluorescent lights were softened to protect the artifacts. The lighting wasn't intended to be gloomy. The effect though in this room was much different. It conjured up images of dungeons and the mind imagined tortured voices screaming in the distant corners. Some passage

mood - creepy

Something triggered it

from a Lovecraft novel floated through my memory, but was lost just as quickly as it had come.

About fifteen minutes later, Dr. Samuels returned with three other people. More people didn't dispel the gloom, if anything, it heightened it. I was introduced to Dr. Carin Pickerd, the medievalist and Dr.'s Adam Baker and Kim Leon, historians. *explains why it's gloomy*

"What can I do for you Dr. Cain?" Dr. Pickerd asked, not wasting time. It was obvious that she had been about to leave. *rushing but being nice Char.*

"I'm going to give you a list of four items; can you tell me if they seem to have anything other than the obvious in common?"

"I suppose I can try."

"An Iron Maiden, a Scavenger's Daughter, drawing and quartering and impaling."

"I'm guessing the obvious is torture." She frowned at me.

"Yes, that would be the obvious connection."

"Well, they are all from the Middle Ages to some degree, maybe not impaling and drawing and quartering, but the other two are definitely Middle Ages. The Scavenger's Daughter seems out of place, it was a punishment that was meant to humiliate and hurt, not kill, while the other three were definitely lethal."

"Anything else?"

"The maiden and the Scavenger would all require skilled craftsmanship, while the other two would not."

"Yeah, I thought of all that already. I was hoping to get a fresh perspective." I sighed. *tone - disappointed*

"What if you are looking at it wrong?" She suggested. *internal conflict*

"What do you mean?"

"What if you are trying to find a connection when there isn't one? What if the means of torture is exactly

120

that, a means of torture? You're a medievalist, what do you know about torturers?"

"Oh hell," I met her gaze. "You're right, the torture is just torture. What the torturer gets from it is important."

finally realizes

"Exactly. Think about them individually. Impaling is impersonal, the Iron Maiden is anonymous, drawing and quartering is very hands on and a Scavenger's Daughter is about humiliation."

"No, it's deeper than that. Drawing and quartering is hands on, but impersonal. You don't really do it, the animals do the work. Impaling is impersonal unless you are Vlad Tepes and dining while they die. The Iron Maiden is anonymous for the tortured, not the torturer. And the Scavenger's Daughter actually means you are inflicting the pain yourself."

"Does this help?" Gabriel asked.

"Yes, very much. I have one last thing. I want each of you think of a torture device from the Middle Ages that hasn't been mentioned. You have ten seconds." *pressure*

"Skull crusher," Dr. Pickerd said instantly.

"The Rack," Dr. Leon offered.

"Brazen Bull," Dr. Baker suggested.

"A Knee-capper," Dr. Samuels offered.

"Brazen Bull is too difficult. The skull crusher, not bad. The rack also too difficult. What do you think is the most recognizable among those not mentioned?"

"That's a weird sentence." Dr. Samuels said.

"Ok, of all the torture methods of the Middle Ages and ignoring the maiden, the scavenger, impaling and drawing, what is the most recognizable?"

"Rats in a head cage." Dr. Samuels answered.

"Brazen Bull," Dr. Pickerd said.

"The Rack," Dr. Leon stuck with her suggestion.

"I don't know much about torture," Dr. Baker said. "If I had to guess something, I'd say the guillotine."

I dont know what any of those are

"Not Middle Ages and not a torture device," Dr. Pickerd said.

"That's true, but it might not be a bad thought." I looked around the room. "How many items were in the exhibit?"

"Over three hundred not to mention the ones featured just in pictures or description plaques."

"Ok, thank you all, I may have someone come back in the next couple of days to ask some more questions. He's a psychologist and has a different perspective than me on the devices." I walked out, leaving Gabriel and Xavier to catch up with me.

They did, at the car. Gabriel hit the button to let me in. Xavier got in, wordlessly staring at me. Confused

"What was that about?" He asked, after the car doors had been shut.

"Just a feeling." I frowned and looked out the window.

"Care to elaborate?"

"Nope, I need to talk to Lucas," I ended the conversation. Foreshadow

Twenty

mood - dull

onomatopoeia

My room was quiet. There was the whooshing of a heating vent. Somewhere down the hall I could faintly hear a TV. Xavier, Gabriel and Lucas were all very quietly staring at me. Michael was busy comparing *that's really creepy* maker's marks. No one could find Alejandro.

We were staying at a Hilton. I found this irritating, but at least I had a balcony. The rooms were old fashioned in build. Large ceilings, lots of lights, and big furniture were the dominating features.

The men were unwilling to speak; afraid I'd *suspense* pounce on them or something. They just stared, quietly, burning holes into me. I didn't know exactly how to say what I wanted to say without sounding like an idiot, so I hadn't started yet. *woman power!* *hyperbole*

"If this is going to take a while, I'm ordering room service," Xavier finally said.

He stood up when I made no comment, went to the phone and ordered up food for the four of us. At least, I thought it was for the four of us. It might have been for eight or nine people. I had seen Lucas and Xavier eat before. They could put it away. I was guessing that was why Lucas worked out like he did.

"Lucas, I'd like you to go to the museum tomorrow and interview Doctors Samuels, Leon, Baker and Pickerd. There was something off about one of them, but I want to see what you think." *foreshadow*

"Ok," Lucas said blandly. *indimidated*

"I think I'm looking at it wrong. I know that the devices are the key to finding the clues, but I haven't thought much about the person doing the torture."

duh!

"And that's important?" Lucas asked.

"Yes," I blinked at him. "What does it take to torture someone?" *like he's an idiot*

"It used to be a sense of righteousness." Lucas said.

"Exactly. Torturers might be the first documented serial killers when you really think about it. The difference being they were supposed to do it, it was their job. Saying that though, your average person couldn't have done it, even back then. They could watch as long as they weren't directly involved. The average person could sit and watch an execution, but they couldn't partake in them. If they had been the hangman, it just wouldn't have happened." *you have to be pretty clever*

"So you think we need to figure out more about the torturer." Xavier said. *tone - unsure*

"Sort of. It dawned on me while I was talking to the others that the Iron Maidens would have had to be ordered way in advance. Probably more than a year ago. This means that the maidens were ordered long before he actually started killing. Each kill is a progression. The first was drawing and quartering. It is violent and painful, but aside from tying the victim up, you don't really do anything except get the animals moving. Impaling is much more personal, but you don't sit there and watch them die, it is too slow. That's why the maidens are so wrong. Like impaling, it can take days. However, these maidens wouldn't take more than a few minutes..."

"But he dined while they were impaled." Xavier commented.

"That's the thing, he did, but either he impaled them and then ate or he came back for the meal or it was completely staged. I don't know. I just know that he didn't sit there for two days and watch them die. That would require a special kind of crazy." *internal conflict*

124

"That would explain the tongues." Lucas said.

"What?" I asked.

"The impaling victims and the drawing and quartering victims were missing their tongues," Lucas said.

"That's kind of standard practice." I dismissed it. *not important*

"Removing the tongue is standard practice?" Gabriel frowned at me. *tone - concerned*

"Yes. If you plan on torturing someone to death, you remove the tongue. Torture victims are loud and rightly so. That was part of the beauty and horror of the Brazen Bull."

"What the hell is that? We keep hearing it, but you haven't explained it." Xavier scolded. *tone - demanding*

"Possibly the worst thing to ever happen to a human being. A large bronze bull is created with a hatch in the back. The body is hollow, but not the legs. The victim was stripped naked, their tongue was cut out and they were put inside the body of the bull. Then a fire was lit under the belly. The victim couldn't scream, but they could move. The movement of the victim would make the bull appear to be alive. But essentially, it was a way to cook a human without the spectators ever seeing the human. Again, the torturer knows. The public knows there is a human inside, but they have the distance because the bull and lack of screaming makes it surreal."

"I am so sorry that I asked," Xavier frowned. *UDHR no torture*

"It was invented in Ancient Greece. Not used much during the later Middle Ages, but it was used a few times in the early Middle Ages." I told him.

"How awful," Gabriel said.

"I don't think that even comes close to describing it. Anyway, if you knew you were going to torture someone to death and you weren't trying to get a confession or other information out of them, you cut out the tongues so they can't scream."

defensive

"Barbaric." Xavier commented.

"An art form in itself," I corrected. "That's what the marks are about. I don't know why I didn't see it earlier. We thought they were random, jumbled messages. We are wrong. They are messages, but not the sort we think. It was very popular to brand people that were sentenced to death or meant to be tortured. The branding reflected the crime and how they were supposed to die. However in some cases, the torturer would also brand them. It was to show who had done it. Torture really was an art form. That's the part we've been *now* missing. We look at it in horror, but in context, it is art. Cutting out the tongue is a good way to kill someone, they bleed to death. Our torturer knows that the knife needs to be hot, needs to sear the vessels closed with the slicing. He didn't take the tongues of the maiden or scavengers' victims. He knew they wouldn't be able to scream. The maiden was too quick. The scavenger victims didn't have the air. Their knees were in their chest and the screw tightened too fast. They couldn't scream."

"The marks on them aren't random? You think they tell a message or series of messages?" Lucas asked.

"No, I think they tell why they were chosen. I think one of the marks is particular to our killer. He will repeat it, possibly only on one body out of each group. It will be his mark, his signature."

symbolism

"Why doesn't he take trophies?" Gabriel asked.

"We think he does. Until the maidens, we thought the tongues were the trophies. After the maidens, we had to come up with something else. However, what that something else is, is beyond us. He could be taking pictures or a lock of hair or a fingernail clipping. Something from the body that is so minute, it escapes notice."

"Blood," I suggested. "It was not unheard of for torturers to keep a vial of blood from each person that they tortured."

"Why would a torturer keep blood from each of the people he tortures?" Xavier asked.

"Why would anyone keep a souvenir from someone they tortured or kill?" I returned the question.

"You think torturers are the same as serial killers?" Lucas frowned at me. *she's defending killers*

"Just because you get to legally kill doesn't mean you don't enjoy it or it doesn't give you a sexual thrill. It just means it's legal and you won't be tortured for it."

"By that reasoning..." Xavier started.

"Yes, all torturers from the Middle Ages, probably further back, were already deviants and the ability to kill as well as the ability to torture is not common." I answered. "Torturers were picked for their inhumanity. Whether they belonged to the Church or to the government didn't make much of a difference, they were still dedicated to their jobs. And yes, most enjoyed it." *How? Why?*

"Torturers are our first serial killers then?" Gabriel asked.

"Or mass murderers," I answered, "there is a difference, but not one that is distinguishable for the time period."

"If our torturer is really leaving his mark on them, what mark?" Lucas asked.

"I have to wonder if it is the death symbol." I took my laptop out. "Despite being put on the bodies in different languages, it gets repeated on almost all the bodies. I think it is his mark."

"Why the different languages then?" Xavier asked.

"To show how smart he is? Because it was rare for the peasantry to speak the same language as the government? Because different areas spoke different languages? Because he can?" I offered.

127 *tone - sassy / defensive*

"You don't know." Xavier grinned.

"If I did, then we might have another piece of the case solved." I grinned back.

"Different languages, different victims." Lucas offered.

"That could be or it could be whatever crime, real or imaginary he placed upon them. Or it could just be."

"What do you think exactly?" Gabriel asked.

"Honestly?" I frowned at him.

"Honestly."

"I think the languages are just him showing off and keeping us from realizing what is really there. Much like the verse from Revelations that doesn't exist. Most people have never read Revelations..." I stopped, remembering it.

"What?" Xavier asked.

"Oh it's just that the verse kind of makes me think of me." I told him.

"We know," Xavier cleared his throat.

"You know?"

"That was another reason for you being singled out for the consult. Not only do you have experience and the necessary background and expertise, but we think he knows you." Lucas raised an eyebrow at me.

"And you just now decided to tell me this?"

"We were waiting for you to figure it out."

"One more reason for you to go to the museum tomorrow," I stopped because there was a knock on the door.

The food was carried in and set on the small table. It filled it up. The overflow was set out on the long, low to the ground, dresser.

Everyone filled plates. Xavier took a spot on the bed I was sleeping in. I glared at him, he switched beds.

"What's in the museum exactly?" Lucas had already polished off most of his first plate of food.

"People. I'm good with torture. You're the one good with people."

"What exactly bothered you?" Lucas prodded some more.

"Let's see. What bothered me? Dr. Samuels I think is fine. Dr. Pickerd would know just about everything I know. She didn't write a thesis on torture, but she is a medievalist and no matter what you think, torture was a part of it. Dr. Leon didn't really ring any bells. She's a historian, but she's a Renaissance historian which means her area of expertise is right at the cusp of the era. She specializes in restoring documents from the Enlightenment."

vocab

"And Dr. Baker?" Xavier asked.

"In theory, his specialty is military history of the last two centuries. He gets kept on staff because he knows more about weapons than most people. But he said he didn't know much about torture. That seems to contradict his expertise. He also mentioned the Brazen Bull. It wasn't popular in the Middle Ages, it was popular before that time period, but there are a couple of infamous incidents with the Brazen Bull in the Middle Ages that instantly pop into mind when talking about torture. For someone who doesn't know much about it, why pick that? Why not pick burning at the stake? That is the illusion. Burning at the stake was supposed to be popular."

"Ah, you got a creepy vibe because he picked an actual torture device?" Xavier sighed. *got his hopes up*

"No, I got the vibe because he picked an obscure torture device all the while protesting that he didn't know much about torture and instead of picking the obvious answer. I can see why Pickerd and Samuels said other things. I can even see Leon picking something else. But why Baker? Why did he pick an obscure piece that no American museum has?" *conflict*

suspense

"Really, there isn't one in all of the US?" Lucas made a face.

"If there is, I haven't heard of it." I answered, "I'll rephrase that. If there is one, I have never heard of it being displayed. I'm sure there are some, replicas and relics alike. I'm sure there are some in private collections. But I've never actually seen one displayed in the US."

"Well, your hunches aside, is there anything else about the guy?"

"He's met me before." I pointed out.

"When?" Lucas asked.

"A couple of years ago, when I was at the Field for their exhibit. I met Dr. Samuels, Dr. Leon and Dr. Baker. Dr. Pickerd is the one they hired when I turned down the position of medievalist on their staff."

"Why did you turn it down?" why?

"Grants. I would have to do public speaking to get grants and that just isn't happening. My department would flounder and I, as well as my staff, would have been out of work pretty quickly."

"You give presentations on torture but you can't present to get a grant?" Lucas narrowed his eyes at me.

"I can talk about torture and the Middle Ages all day long. Asking people to give me money so I can talk about torture and the Middle Ages all day long is a completely different beast. It requires me to not only know my area of expertise but pretend I like people and kiss their asses." characterization

hyperbole

"Interesting." Gabriel was refilling his plate with chicken and rice.

"Well, at least I'm honest." I told him.

"Ok, I'll go tomorrow to see if I can get any information from their body language."

"Great," I finally filled a plate. I grabbed a piece of eggplant parmesan and some green beans.

"I'll tell them I want to get into the psychology of the time."

"Historians can't help but listen to themselves talk about their periods of expertise. You'll have lots to work with." I grinned again. "Look at me."

"Yes indeed," Lucas made the face again.

"No more talk about death, let's just eat." Gabriel offered as he forked a bit of lamb into his mouth.

"If we aren't going to talk about death, what are we going to talk about?" Xavier asked.

"Football?" I suggested with a giggle. We finished eating in silence.

there's nothing else thy can talk about

Twenty-One

she seems to talk the most, they're intimided by her

"Fine, you guys know a lot about me. I know nothing about you." I said, after the dinner plates had been put back onto the room service cart and shoved roughly into the hallway to wait for some poor maid to deal with them.

"Well, I'm seven days older than Lucas," Xavier started.

"We grew up next door to each other until I was nine," Lucas added.

"Then he moved in with my family." Xavier continued. *tone - sarcastic*

"That's strange, don't do that," Gabriel smiled at the two men.

"Best friends for life then," I ignored Gabriel.

"Actually, it started because our parents were best friends. My father was an FBI agent. Lucas's father was a county sheriff. However, they were roommates in college and when they got out, they were pretty much inseparable. I have three siblings, all younger than me. Two brothers and a sister, none of them went into law enforcement. One is a doctor, one is a firefighter and my sister is a school teacher, she teaches first grade." Xavier said. *that's sad, how?*

"I had one brother, a couple years older than me; he died when I was nine." Lucas grimaced.

"You don't have to talk about it." I looked down at my hands. *How does she know he was?*

"I made my peace with it a long time ago. My brother drowned during a boating trip we all took. My parents didn't handle his death very well. They sent me

probably blamed themselves

132

to live with Xavier's family. One night, my dad was supposed to go to work, he didn't show up there and he never came home. He just disappeared. My mother was eventually institutionalized. That's why I got a degree in psychology. I couldn't understand why I was never enough. Turned out not to have anything to do with me at all. But Xavier's family was good to me. I was never treated differently. I was always treated like one of their own children. I joined the navy at 18. Xavier joined with me." Lucas shrugged.

stuck together   simile

"Why the navy?" I asked.

"Why not?" Xavier asked back. "It was a chance to get away. We grew up on the East Coast. Neither of us was mature enough to go to college right out of high school. We would have flunked out. So we enlisted in the navy when a recruiter came to our high school. Served six years, most of it spent in Desert Storm. During that time, we were both approached to join the SEALS. We did. Our first mission was fine. We got back, I had a break down. They labeled it PTSD. I was honorably discharged and sent to med school. Lucas joined me six months later, enrolling in the same college."

"Also honorably discharged," Lucas added quickly. "Injured in the line of duty; got a Purple Heart for it. I started college, Xavier and I took a lot of intro classes together. When we both finished our bachelor's and began looking at med schools, we both got accepted to John Hopkins, me in psychology, Xavier in general medicine. We graduated the same year with our doctorates."

"Lucas was recruited by the FBI at that time," Xavier picked up the story. "He went to work for the Behavioral Analysis Unit at Quantico. I went to work as a coroner for the city of New York. Then the US Marshals approached us."

"We both accepted. Now we are here." Lucas shrugged.

"How old are you both?" I frowned at them.

"36," Xavier told me.

"That's a lot of accomplishments." I frowned harder.

"What about you, Gabriel?" Xavier asked.

"Small town born and raised, in Arizona. Nothing bad or tragic ever happened in my life. Hell, all my grandparents are still alive even. I have a sister, she has four kids. They live in Arizona near our parents. I've been married once, divorced once. She didn't like the lifestyle. Started at a community college, moved to Arizona State after that and got a degree in criminal justice." Gabriel paused, seeming to be lost in the memory.

"I don't really have a best friend like the rest of you. My ex wife held that job for many years. I'm 34, two kids that I almost never see. Their mother has remarried and is trying to get her new husband to adopt them. She doesn't want me to expose them to death and destruction. Last year the witch returned their Christmas and birthday gifts unopened. I keep in close contact with my sister and her kids as well as my parents. My sister's husband is out of the picture, so I send her money every month to help with the expenses. She hates it, but I do it anyway. One thing about working with serial killers and mass murderers, they pay well."

"What's Michael's story?" I asked.

"Don't know. He doesn't talk about his past. Says it's in the past, why drag it up," Xavier said.

"May I ask about how much you guys actually make in a year?"

"About two hundred grand a year. A little more by the time you figure in the houses." Lucas told me.

"Wow, that's a lot." I had never made more than thirty grand in a year.

"It is, but our life expectancy is pretty short." *why?* Lucas shrugged, "we are compensated by money that we can leave to our friends and family."

"If this works, I'll have to talk to everyone about moving my trust fund into the names of my nieces and nephews and adding more money to it."

"We all have trusts set up for family." Gabriel told me.

"What is the average life expectancy for this job?"

"Four years," Gabriel answered flatly.

"How long have you guys been doing it again?"

"Three," Xavier answered.

"Two," Gabriel said.

"I see." This brought about silence and we sat *} mood- awkward* staring at each other unable to fill the void with conversation any longer.

"Night, Ace," Xavier got up. I stood with him, welcoming the reprieve from the dreadful quiet. The others followed.

I was left alone. I went back onto the balcony to have another cigarette. *another?*

Chicago, like every other big city, never really got dark. The street lights gave off sickly glows that the shadows dared not touch. The El-Train was still running. Buildings still had windows lit. All of that light kept the city from actually being dark. There were dark places though. I could see them from where I stood. Places under the El platforms, places in darkened doorways, places that the light didn't penetrate. Places that people avoided now that they relied on those street lights and lighted windows. *personification*

I finished the cigarette while watching a drunk stumble from the El. He weaved and wobbled his way

135

down the stairs and onto the street. Even in his
inebriated state, he avoided the dark.

vocab

Twenty-Two

More tossing and turning. The source of the maidens had been figured out. It didn't seem to mean we were any closer to catching the killer though.

The source of the Scavenger's Daughter was still a mystery. It turned out the marks were similar, not the same. It was hard to tell until Michael blew up the pictures to examine them. I was hoping that Michael and Alejandro would return in the morning and give us the name of the guy who ordered the maidens. That would make things much easier. *I feel like Cain is doing most work*

However, there was still something nagging at me. Something I couldn't quite put my finger on. Something that told me while we were close, we weren't close enough. *foreshadow*

"Get up," someone yelled through the door of the hotel room. I could hear banging and shuffling outside. Xavier suddenly burst into the room. *sudden*

"What?" I jumped from bed.

"He struck again." *tone - surprised*

"He couldn't have. It hasn't been three months."

"Lucas thinks that since he didn't get to sign his work last time, he hit early. In the last two hours, ten women have gone missing."

"Oh, yeah, that sounds like our guy."

"No, that sounds like a tragedy. The fact that each was kidnapped from their bedrooms while they slept sounds like our guy. And we think we know how he is taking them. The last one put up a struggle. We found LSD in the apartment."

"The hallucinogen?"

"Yep." *How does he know?*

"That would be one very bad trip."

"Yep. We are on our way to look at a place with no dead bodies. We are hoping you can help."

"Probably not." I answered, but I was already pulling on my clothes. *hyperbole*

The apartment was flooded with lights. The blinds were all down. The bedroom door was damaged. I frowned at it all.

Things were knocked over. There had obviously been a struggle, actually a hell of a fight. There were drops of drying liquid on the floor that had proved to be the hallucinogen.

Nothing jumped out at me, but I wasn't a real investigator. I was just sort of here to round out the numbers.

"What's this?" Xavier brought something over to me.

"It's a dagger."

"Like the one you keep?"

I looked at it very closely. It wasn't like the one I kept. It was military grade.

"No, mine is a replica of a ceremonial knife. This looks like military."

"How old?"

"The past century or so. The style looks vaguely familiar."

"Why do you know so much about daggers?"

"I have a degree in History; I didn't always set out to be a medievalist. That just sort of happened. I started out wanting to be an Egyptologist. When that failed, I tried my hand at military history. I got wrapped up in the Children's Crusades and became a medievalist."

"So medieval Europe was your third choice?"

"Something like that."

"Which is why you know about daggers?" Xavier frowned.

"Some of it." I frowned back. "What are you getting at?"

"Did you touch this?"

"No, until now, I hadn't seen it. Why?"

"It has your fingerprints on it."

"Oh," I shook my head. "That's very bad."

"Yes, it is. Get out, go to the hotel, we'll come see you when we are done."

Gabriel ferried me back to the hotel. I looked at him before I got out.

"Hey, I don't believe you did it. I believe that you touched that knife at some point though."

"I don't think I have ever seen it before." I answered and headed back upstairs.

I tried to watch TV. It couldn't hold my interest. I tried to surf the internet, but had the same problem. Finally, after five hours, Lucas and Xavier came into my hotel room.

"Why do you have a key to my room?" I asked as they entered.

"Why not?" Lucas shrugged. "Better me than him."

"So, what's the story with the dagger?"

"We don't know. We just know it tested positive for blood and that we found a single fingerprint on it. It's your fingerprint."

"It isn't really mine." I told him.

"We don't think you are involved in the killings, Ace. We think someone you know is. We've got a team sitting on all the Field Museum workers you came in contact with both today and your visit a few years ago."

"Great, just great."

"What do you know about the dagger?"

"It looks old. It looks military."

139

"She was into art, not weaponry. This is the only piece we found. It was definitely out of place in her apartment." Lucas said.

"What do we do now?" I asked.

"We have to assume that you are victim number ten," Lucas said.

"I thought you said we had ten?" I countered.

"We thought we did. One of them showed up though, already dead. We think he killed her and decided to replace her with you," Lucas answered.

"Oh." I considered that for a long time. I was used to serial killers, but I normally didn't have to wait for them to strike, they just came at me. The waiting was going to be an issue.

"How do you think he will do it?" I asked, frowning hard enough that I felt a vein in my forehead suddenly pop out.

"Kill the next ten?" Xavier asked.

"I don't know. Something more horrific than the first four. That's what has been nagging me. Each one seems to be getting worse. Not by modern day standards, I'm not sure by what standards, but each seems a bit more horrific to me. The drawing and quartering was bad. Lots of blood, lots of body parts. The impaling was horrific, but then I realized he didn't sit around waiting for them to die. The maidens were quick, painful, but quick. The hoop took longer and they suffocated. It was also very painful. I think the time he spends killing each victim is escalating, but the impaling threw us off because you kept pointing out it was a slow death." Lucas answered.

"In other words, you think a device that is going to bring death even slower than the hoop thingy," Xavier paraphrased.

"Yes." Lucas answered.

"If it were me, I'd use rats or something equally disturbing," I said.   *amused*

"Rats?" Lucas looked at me for a moment.

"A head cage sits on the shoulders. It encompasses the entire head in a box about two foot wide and about two foot tall. There is a hatch in the top and the cage wires are spaced only a few inches apart. You put the victim in the cage, open the hatch on top and dump in a handful or more of starving rats. Non-starving rats work, but starving are better. They eat the victim while they are alive."

"How are they restrained?" Xavier asked.

"Usually strapped to a chair or something," I answered, "also, he'll need to improvise this time. We have his maidens. We have his scavenger. Rats are easy to come by in a city like this. The head cage will be harder, but chicken wire would work."

"Chicken wire and rats." Xavier made a noise.

"Chicken wire, wood and rats." I corrected. "Chicken wire won't stand on its own; it would need a skeletal structure."

"That's pretty gruesome." Xavier answered.

"Yep, but effective." I remarked.   *committed*

"Most of these would take planning and set-up time. You don't just walk into the woods and chop down ten perfect sized impaling trees. You would need access to woods and trees. You don't just find four horses and get them to tear a person apart. You have to learn how to drive four horses in different directions. You can't go out and buy an Iron Maiden or a Scavenger's Daughter at your local shopping mall. As improvised as all these sound, they aren't. They have to be thought out and well planned." Lucas commented, giving me a sly smile. "There's a psychology to all of it as well. Drawing and quartering doesn't look painful until it happens. There isn't much psychological torture there, unless he were to

tell you about it in great detail before. Impaling has the
same problem. The psychological aspect comes after you
see the stakes. By then, you've been held for three days
and realized that you are going to die. Seeing the stakes
would be terrifying, but it isn't a psychological torture
method. The Iron Maiden on the other hand; that would
have a psychological effect the moment you saw it. As
Ace said, the ones we have are scary looking. Yet, not as
much as the Scavenger's Daughter. With the Scavenger's
Daughter, it is long, drawn out and there is always a hope
that you will live. Whatever comes next probably has the
same aspect, there is the possibility that you could live."

"What if he already has all the devices he intends
to use?" Gabriel entered the room. *hyperbole*

"Then we are beating our heads against a wall.
Hanging Coffins, skull crushers, maces, yokes, they all
become very real possibilities." I approved of Lucas's
analysis of the torture situation.

"Let's hope it's going to be improvised. That way
we just need to track down the guy catching the city's rat
population."

"If only it were that easy." I shrugged.

Twenty-Three

By the time dawn broke, another woman was
missing. It wasn't me. Some part was relieved. Some
part was angry. I could have stopped him. *how does she know?*

The one they had found murdered the night before
had been a fighter. He had tried to burn her body. He
had failed, luckily. DNA had been discovered in her
teeth. She had bitten him. *fought back*

Alejandro was fuming. Michael looked a little
depressed. The maiden maker had given us the
organization that had ordered the maidens. It didn't
exist. It had been paid for with a money order.

How anyone legitimately paid for five Iron
Maidens with a money order was beyond me. The only
good thing was that the blacksmith had recognized the
mark on the Scavenger's Daughter. Like the Iron Maiden
maker, he had made it for an organization that didn't
exist and paid for it with a money order.

I was dumbfounded by how blacksmiths of
exceptional skill got paid. Lucas pulled me aside. I
frowned at him. *rapper*

"What?" I snapped testily.

"You don't get it; blacksmiths don't just make
these items for show. You said it yourself; there is an
underground for just about anything. I'm sure they take
money orders from fake companies all the time and no
one gets hurt without permission as a result. I'm sure the
maker of the maiden was shocked when he learned his
work had killed." *urgent*

"I know, I know. It just irritates me that we aren't
any closer. These women have very limited time."

143

"We're guessing about three days. That seems to be how long they are kept alive. On the fourth day, they are tortured and killed. We usually find them a few days after."

"Thanks for the timeline update, but I'm guessing he isn't going to wait that long."

"Probably not. He missed some part of his ritual and he needs to get it back."

"Ritual?" The word evoked something in me. "What?"

"Ritual, the torture, not the method, is part of a ritual."

"Stay with me Ace."

"You're the psychologist," I pointed out. "It doesn't matter how he tortures them, as long as he does torture them."

"So why the medieval contraptions?"

"To lure me in. Now that I'm in, he could do anything, as long as he gets to torture the victims."

"You think that's what it was really about?"

"That verse from Revelations tells me what it was really about. When you add it up, it is all about me. I'm sure most of his contraptions are medieval in nature. He wouldn't have known how long it would take to get me involved. The languages are proving that he is smarter than me. He knows I don't know all of them."

"This is all about you?" Lucas asked.

"I think so. Why else leave my fingerprints?"

"To make you a suspect."

"But you said yourself, that I was never really a suspect. It was just another layer of mystery. What if somewhere over the last four years, I have touched that knife, but the touch was so insignificant, I've forgotten? Could he keep my fingerprints preserved for that long?"

"Longer if he wanted," Lucas told me.

"Baker just seems too easy though. And I've been to hundreds of exhibits on torture. This was just the biggest one. I've probably touched hundreds of items in the last several years relating to torture."

"Wouldn't you use gloves most of the time?"

"Cloth gloves and yes, most of the time, I would have, but with a private collection…" I shrugged. Private collectors didn't always require gloves.

"How many private collections have you seen?"

"At least three or four dozen, not to mention pieces loaned to museums for exhibits."

"How many had daggers?"

"All of them, most had multiple daggers. You don't collect torture paraphernalia without collecting other stuff, usually weapons."

"That doesn't help though."

"I know, sorry," I sighed and went out onto the balcony.

"How many in Chicago?"

"Beats me." I didn't know. "But the killings didn't start here, they just ended up here. Like the exhibit that travels, once in a while, there's a hiccup and the exhibit stays an extra day or two."

"What?" Lucas asked.

"Exhibits, occasionally they get stuck in a place and can't leave because of shipping issues or paperwork issues. It is the biggest pain in the ass for traveling exhibits."

"Damn, have you ever been to Baltimore?" He asked.

"Yes, I did a presentation there once."

"Miami, Florida?"

"Yes."

"And Birmingham, Alabama?"

"Yes." I looked at him. "Is that where all the killings took place?"

"Yes."

"Damn, in what order?"

"Miami, Baltimore, Birmingham, now Chicago." I thought for a few moments. "Nine months ago, I was in Florida, at a conference with my advisor on the Crusades. Six months ago, I was in Baltimore giving a presentation on the use of torture by the Catholic Church during the time period before the Inquisition. Three months ago, I was in Birmingham, Alabama helping out with an exhibit that on Witchcraft and the tortures used to determine if one was a witch. When I left Washington, I was supposed to move to Chicago and take a job at the Field. I backed out at the last minute. Decided I couldn't do it. I was supposed to have moved here this week."

"He's following you."

I lit a cigarette and watched the smoke curl from the tip of it. It was about me. I was back to being in sixth grade, where I was a freak for being eight years old.

"You're not a freak." Lucas said as he took my cigarette from me and inhaled deeply.

"You don't smoke," I told him.

"Not normally, I indulge in a good cigar every now and then."

"How did you know that as my thought?"

"The look on your face. I remember photos of you from Xavier's father's files. I also remember that you told him you thought you were a freak."

"Why do serial killers keep stalking me?"

"Pheromones." He giggled.

"Seriously."

"I don't know." He shrugged and giggled again. It sounded strange coming from the mountain.

"What do you know?"

"That you are going to take a year or two to break in, but once you're there, you are going to fit in nicely with this group. You'll also find that while we don't always have the answers, most of it is about the quest anyway."

"Very deep and complete bullshit. I'm not entirely sure I'm cut out for this. Once we move away from the torture stuff and the serial killer trying to get my attention, I will be flying blind." *hyperbole*

"Yes, but you will be in good company and we won't let you crash into any mountains. I know it doesn't feel like it now, Ace, but it will. Soon, it will." *flirty*

"Thanks Lucas," I touched his arm gently. "What is your deal? I've figured out Xavier. I haven't you."

"You will. When we get home, there will be a dinner party at my house. You are invited. You'll figure it out then." *mood - mysterious*

"Mysterious all of the sudden?"

"Not mysterious," Lucas shook his head. "You'll just have to wait." *suspense*

"Great and if I don't survive this?"

"You will, you always have." Lucas left me alone on the balcony again. I stubbed out the cigarette and took in another breath. When I exhaled, it exited in a plume in the cold dark air. I went back inside.

Twenty-Four

"Well we were right. She was in town for all the murders." Lucas said to everyone as I reentered my hotel room.

"Somehow, she is involved." Alejandro frowned at me, but then I got the impression he didn't smile much, so I didn't get offended. *why won't she tell?*

"Somehow she knows who it is," Lucas sat down.

"Thesis advisor?" Xavier asked.

"Female, Dr. Janice DeLong. She accepted my dissertation because it was too good to reject, but she wasn't real happy when it started evolving. She is one of those historians that would gloss over the dirty sides of history."

"Grad students?"

"Several. None that stick out."

"Undergrads?" Xavier continued.

"I tutored in English during my undergrad days. As a grad student, I worked for the history department as an assistant. Most of the students hated me, I was the one they hoped didn't grade their papers."

"How many total?"

"Estimation? Several thousand. I helped with basic European history as well as several of the advanced European history classes. Even did a semester as an assistant in an undergrad thesis class. They really hated me. Hence why it only happened one semester."

"How many enemies do you think you have?" Lucas asked.

"True enemies, very few. Students that hated me for grading their homework, thousands. Maybe tens of thousands. I was an unpopular teacher's assistant."

"Why'd they keep you?"

"Because while the students hated me, the professors loved having me as their assistant."

"That seems weird and counterproductive," Xavier said.

"Not really. I was the assistant that would take home 40 or 50 papers and grade them all in a weekend. Most of them would set amounts I could take off for grammar and spelling, knowing those were my pet peeves."

"Anyone else?"

"I don't know. I'm not a people person. I notice them when they seem out of place. I notice stalkers. Everyone else is just a flash in the pan for me. I barely knew the grad students I shared an office with." I shrugged again.

"Yeah, I get it," Lucas let out a long sigh again, "Your brain catalogues faces and names, but unless they come at you with a knife, the information is unnecessary, so it is hard to access."

"Exactly. Now if any of them had really hated me, I might remember them, but none stand out."

"None of this is useful," Alejandro said.

"Sure it is," Xavier countered. "We know who it isn't."

"Yes, but we are talking about a serial killer and we are talking about one that is incredibly smart. He could have met her in line for coffee and became fascinated." Alejandro pointed out.

"There was a guy like that, sort of. I was grading papers one weekend and it was close to summer. I had gotten in the habit of forcing myself to go to the Chinese place down the street once a week. I was walking in the door, he was walking out. Ended up covered in Orange Glazed Chicken and fried rice."

"How did you end up covered in Orange Glazed Chicken and Fried Rice?" Lucas prodded.

"He dumped both cartons on me. I ran into him, smashing the boxes. He opened up the bag and dumped them on my head. The cartons kind of hurt. The food was really hot."

"That sounds like someone with very low impulse control. Did you ever see him again?"

"No. I stopped going to the Chinese place too. I do not like Orange Glazed Chicken or fried rice."

"Anyone who cannot control their emotions that much, doesn't sound like our guy," Lucas gave another sigh.

"Look it has to be someone who either is a professional historian or archaeologist or an amateur expert in the field. Maybe an anthropologist, but it's unlikely."

"Why?" Alejandro asked.

"Because you don't wake up one morning and decide to order Iron Maidens to get my attention."

"Why?" Alejandro repeated.

"Because as fascinating as they are, think about the effort involved. It took Lucas to move them and even he struggled with the effort. They are heavy. They are cumbersome. They are expensive."

"They are expensive," Alejandro agreed.

"Using medieval means, how would you torture someone?" I asked everyone in the group.

"Burn at the stake." Alejandro chimed.

"That's what I was going to say," Michael chided.

"Ducking stool." Xavier piped in.

"Press," Lucas answered.

"Thumb screws," Gabriel added.

"See what I mean? You all picked methods of torture you learned about during the Salem Witch Trials portion of your high school history class. The only one actually meant to be lethal is burning at the stake. The others were used to get confessions out of suspected witches or to test if they were a witch. The average person doesn't know about Iron Maidens and Scavenger's Daughters. You say 'impaling' they say 'Dracula'. You say 'drawing and quartering,' they stare at you open mouthed. You say 'Iron Maiden or Scavenger's Daughter' and most just scratch their heads. They may know what an Iron Maiden is, but most think it looks like the five we have. And the Scavenger's Daughter... They are going to be like Xavier, after they have seen it; they'll call it the 'hoop thingy'. The average person doesn't know about torture. They only know recent history and whatever they retained from high school."

"My high school never taught us about Iron Maidens," Xavier answered.

"That's the point. It has to be someone who knows the time period. It could be a torture enthusiast, but..." I stopped. It could be a torture enthusiast. It was like any other fetish on the planet. Maybe not the drawing and quartering, but the others fit.

"The drawing and quartering was done first?" I asked.

"Yes." Alejandro gave me a look.

"And they were the only ones that were sexually assaulted?" I frowned.

"Before death." Xavier confirmed, "but they were definitely the only ones."

"Why?" I frowned harder.

"We don't know." Lucas admitted.

"Have we considered the possibility that it is a woman?" I looked at each of them.

"No," Alejandro said. "Women do not sexually assault other women."

"Normally they don't," Lucas corrected.

"Ok, so they don't normally sexually assault other women, but impaling is sexual assault. Penetration is penetration. The Iron Maiden and Scavenger's Daughter isn't sexual though." I said all of it slowly.

"You think it was a woman who realized she didn't have the stomach for the sexual assault?" Lucas asked.

"I think it's a theory we should explore." I shrugged. "The first set was sexually assaulted while alive with implements. The second with the stakes. For whatever reason, it isn't working for them. So, if it is a male, why no sexual assaults on the maiden or Scavenger's Daughter? If it is female, that explains it."

"Why?" Xavier asked.

"I don't know," I looked at him.

"Because when it first started, she thought the sexual assaults would fulfill some need. When they didn't, she abandoned it." Lucas stated.

"And moved to more sophisticated methods of torture." I finished.

"The progression is important to you," Lucas said.

"It isn't to you?" I looked at him.

"For me, it shows escalation. What does it say to you?"

"Sophistication of torture doesn't say escalation of torture; it says they know what they are doing. Hangmen don't put people on racks, they hang people. Torturers don't hang people, they torture. And there are different types of torturers. Some tortured for information. Some for punishment. Those that tortured for information used different methods than those for killing. Our killer crossed those lines by using the Scavenger's Daughters, it can kill, but that wasn't the intention of their creation. But our killer used it as such. That requires skill and knowledge of all sorts of torture. To me, it doesn't say escalation, it says variation. And both the maiden and scavenger were built ahead of time."

"You're going somewhere with this, I'm just not sure I follow." Lucas leaned against the dresser and frowned at me. I left the room, back to the balcony. I smoked another cigarette while I thought.

stress reliever

Twenty-Five

I finished the cigarette and walked back inside.
Two cigarettes in thirty minutes was not a good sign. I
planted myself against a nightstand, letting it hold most
of my weight. I was now across from Lucas. The other
men in the room were turning to look at me. However, it
was Lucas that needed to really understand what I was
saying.

"Why do people torture?" I asked.

"Sexual Sadism, need to control, there are dozens
of reasons for someone to torture..."

"Stop," I interrupted, holding up a hand. "Those
are all modern reasons to torture. You keep asking what
motivates our killer to use torture. It's a good question,
but is it complete?"

I took a deep breath to give him a second to catch
up with me.

"I ask why torture, it's no longer vogue." I said
after a few seconds had passed.

"Vogue?" Lucas raised an eyebrow. "Lots of killers
torture. Torture leads to gratification of some sort,
usually sexual, but it doesn't..."

"Stop again. That's the hitch. The difference
between you and me. We aren't dealing with a sexual
gratification torturer. We are dealing with a craftsman.
Our torturer probably has whatever psychological
mumbo-jumbo you want to plant on them, but that isn't
the motivation behind the torture. It's a show. Back in
the day, torturers and executioners had different
standings than the rest of society. They were reviled,
feared and yet, admired. It wasn't an office job, by any

means; you couldn't go into the office if you didn't enjoy the work, so torturers enjoyed what they did, but…" I stopped again, letting the thought form completely.

"But what?" Xavier asked.

"But it also wasn't frowned upon. Torturers were either sanctified or justified in their work, depending on who they worked for. Sanctified torturers worked for the Church. They tortured in the name of God. Justified torturers worked for the crown. They tortured in the name of the law. So, yes, they got something out of it, they couldn't have done it if they didn't, but it wasn't the driving factor behind it. They had either the power of the Church or the Crown behind them. As such, they were masters of their trade. It wasn't just a position that could be paid to whoever took the job. It required skill, knowledge, and understanding. If the torturer failed to have the necessary skills and knowledge, then their work was pointless. They either killed when they weren't supposed to or they frucked it up and didn't get the job done. Remember the horror stories of executioners who required two or three or more swings to behead a human? They weren't the most sought after executioners; they were the ones that would do in a pinch. The ones that made the most money were the ones that did it with one strike. The same is true of torturers. Looking at more modern history and more common knowledge history, we'll use the Salem Witch Trials as an example. Very few of the suspected witches were put to death. Most of the discovered witches sentences were commuted or completely negated when the tribunal frucked up. The tribunal accidentally pressed a man to death which ended the hysteria. It wasn't intentional, but they didn't know what they were doing and over did the weights. The man's ribs broke and his chest collapsed. That single event seriously changed the Salem Witch Trials. Now, take that knowledge and go back three or four hundred years. If the Spanish Inquisition had made the same mistakes, it would have changed the course of the Inquisition. The torturers were skilled monks. They were trained in the art of torture. If they hadn't been trained, if people had died by accident during the process of getting them to confess, the public would have been outraged, just as they had been in Salem. The Inquisition would have died out. It didn't. It didn't because the torturers were not just sanctified and righteous, but because they knew what they were doing."

"You think the motives are more medieval?" Alejandro asked.

"Yes, I do. This isn't just some guy butchering people because he can. It has control. It has skill. It has knowledge. It has understanding of medieval devices. Whoever this killer is, they would have been a perfect torturer for the Middle Ages. I think that is a key. The mechanisms, even when they are wrong, they are grotesquely wrong. The maidens with their long spikes are a grotesque exaggeration of a real torture method. The Scavenger's Daughter being used to kill instead of just punish, is a grotesque exaggeration of its purpose. Yet neither are unheard of. The maiden was used to kill, just slowly. The scavenger was used to humiliate, but in extreme cases, could be used to kill, slowly. That is the one thing all of these have in common, they are meant to kill slowly. With the exception of the first one." I frowned again.

"What do you mean?" Lucas had crossed his arms over his chest.

"Drawing and quartering is quick in comparison to impaling and a maiden, but incredibly painful. I think they used it first because of the sexual assaults they had committed. I think it churned their stomach, so to speak. I think that's why they made them die quickly. Impaling is much much much slower. Drawing and quartering may take ten minutes, but impaling takes days. Maidens with short spikes take days. The Scavenger's Daughter would take," I looked at Xavier.

"If they didn't die of shock, it would be an hour or more process. Probably the most painful hour they ever experienced." He confirmed.

"There you go, an hour or more. Slow death. The maidens would have been fast, but not nearly that fast. I reexamined the spikes while I was standing in there. I'm short, five foot, three inches tall. One of the spikes would have gone through my head. But a woman of taller stature, even my cousin Nyleena, wouldn't have. She's only three inches taller than me. Three inches is a lot in this situation."

"All our maiden victims were five foot six inches or taller." Xavier said.

"Meaning the only spikes to the head were through the face."

"Yes and none were lethal. I estimate it took about twenty minutes for most of the maiden victims to die. They all died of blood loss. Lots of internal organs were nicked, but the spikes had a tendency to hit bone first."

"Bad spike positioning or deliberate?" I frowned. "Twenty minutes is a lot faster than the others."

"But not as fast as the drawing and quartering," Lucas reminded me.

"Very true and the pain from the maidens would have been excruciating. I rethought the spikes and while they are long, they aren't very big. If one went through a hand or a leg, it would hurt like hell, but it probably wouldn't have hit anything vital. The spikes to the body were the important ones."

"You think it could have taken longer?" Xavier asked.

"No clue, maybe, maybe not, it would depend a lot on the women. Women who are fast clotters would have lasted longer than ones with anemia." I looked at him finally, "that is your job. Mine is to evaluate and reconsider some of your theories. My conclusion is that modern day psychology applies, but only so much, because our killer is not using modern day thought processes to do their killing. For whatever reason, they believe they are either justified or sanctified by the torture. Hence the implements."

"Then maybe we need to re-evaluate," Xavier suggested.

"Actually, I think we need to visit the museum first," Lucas corrected.

Twenty-Six

The Field Museum sits on a large campus. There are pedestrian avenues and statues and it all overlooks Lake Michigan. Despite its size, the Field Museum is not the most imposing structure on the campus. Directly behind the massive museum stands Soldier Field, home of the Chicago Bears. There are two other buildings on the campus as well; one is Shedd's Aquarium, the other is the Adler Planetarium.

As a child, I had loved visiting the museum and the aquarium. As an adult, I had visited all four buildings. Plus, I had spent countless hours sitting on the benches that lined the avenues. I had spent time wandering the park and staring off into the distance, watching the waves lap at the breakwaters.

I did this now. I stood on the shore of Lake Michigan and stared out across the span. Of course, I was facing the wrong direction, so I could see the shore on the other side of the inlet. It was still beautiful. It was still amazing to watch the sun's brilliant reflection off the gently moving water. I stood until Lucas shook me from my water-enthralled trance.

Turning away from the lake with a feeling of doom and gloom falling over me, I followed Lucas up the stone steps. We again announced ourselves at the entrance gates. A different docent called for Dr. Samuels.

Dr. Sam Samuels again greeted us. He weaved through the corridors, back into the offices. The offices and research spaces are created in a tomb like maze. Even Perseus would have had trouble navigating it.

There were so many right and left turns, that I almost lost my direction.

Finally, we stopped outside a door marked "Dr. Baker – Military Historian for the 20th Century". Dr. Samuels rapped his knuckles against the door just once. It was opened by Dr. Baker.

"Hello again, Dr. Cain." He frowned at me.

"Dr. Baker, this is Dr. Lucas McMichaels, he's a psychologist with our unit."

"Um, I'm not sure how I can help." Dr. Baker began to sweat visibly.

"I'm just interested in hearing some other expert opinions on torture and being a military historian for the 20th century, you should have some very valuable information." Lucas smiled at him.

"How do you mean?" He hadn't invited us in or even opened the door all the way.

"Well, the 20th century was full of violent wars where torture was pretty common." I answered.

"Oh, well," Dr. Baker stepped into the hall, closing the door behind him.

"Dr. Baker?" Lucas asked him, "this is probably a conversation best held behind closed doors."

"It's just that I have…" He began to stammer.

For a second, I didn't realize he had done it. He slammed his shoulder into Dr. Samuels and rushed past me. He ducked around a corner and disappeared.

"Dr. Samuels?" I asked checking on him.

"Fine," Dr. Samuels waved me away as he stood back up.

Lucas was already chasing after him. I went after them, unsure where they had gone. The labyrinth seemed to be worse, as I dashed down hallways and passed doors with people attempting to file out them.

A door marked "exit" appeared near me. I hit it at a full run and slipped as I entered the lobby. I fell on my

160

butt as my feet went out from under me. However, Lucas was only a few feet ahead of me. Dr. Baker was only a few feet ahead of him.

As I got up, Dr. Baker ran out the front exit. Lucas sprinted after him. I pulled out my badge and began shouting as I entered a bottleneck at the exits.

I shoved and pushed my way through the now panicking crowd. A security guard was trying to calm them. He was fighting a losing battle.

The crowd surged forward as I squeezed out. They began shouting and screaming. Someone was crying. I considered stopping, but Lucas was alone and possibly chasing a serial killer. That was my priority.

En masse the crowd forced their way out the door and began to skid and slide down the steps. I avoided all of it and kept on my feet. I was too short to see Lucas; my only hope was to get out of the hysterical mob.

At the bottom of the steps, the crowd dashed for Lake Shore Drive. I caught sight of Lucas running down the avenue that led to the planetarium. It was bordered on both sides by water and dead ended. The crowd was avoiding dead ends.

I turned on my heels and hit the pavement as fast as my legs would carry me. My lungs were starting to feel like they were on fire from the cold air moving in and out of them. My breathing was quickly becoming ragged. I wasn't sure how long I could keep up the pace.

Lucas stopped. I pulled one of my guns and pushed myself to the limits of my energy. Lucas was shouting orders at Dr. Baker. Dr. Baker was standing on the edge of the breakwater.

As I came up next to Lucas, Dr. Baker jumped. My body went cold, the calm washing over me. I put my gun away as I sprinted to the breakwater and plunged in behind him.

My body hit the water as if slamming into concrete. The cold enveloped me, forcing the air out of my lungs. I surfaced, my face hitting air that was even colder and gulped in a breath. Lucas was now shouting at me, but I couldn't make out what he was shouting. My body told me I had only a minute or two before my situation became critical.

My eyes searched the surface and found Dr. Baker. He was semi-floating, attempting to swim, his body in shock from the freezing lake. He was only ten feet from me. I swam as fast as I could, feeling the water drag at my clothes. I grabbed hold of him; he struggled for only a second, then gave in. His dead weight moved easily in the water. Lucas grabbed hold of the collar on my coat and jerked me from the water. He repeated the gesture with Dr. Baker.

The air seemed to instantly freeze the water on my skin. My limbs began to ache from the cold that was setting into them. It felt as if the freezing beads were entering my bones.

Someone threw a coat around me. My teeth began to chatter. I tried to grip the edges, pull it tighter, but my fingers wouldn't work.

"Let's get inside," Dr. Samuels's soothing voice assured me.

I was led down the avenue, back up the steps and into the lobby. Dr. Samuels was moving people away from us. We entered a door marked "Authorized Personnel Only". It was different than any of the other doors we had entered.

The corridor had lots of doors off of it. Again I was reminded of the labyrinth hidden from the public at the Field. He pushed open a door and as I entered, he switched on an infrared bulb. Heat instantly began to flood the room.

"We've never used this room for this, but it should do nicely," Dr. Samuels was talking to Lucas as he hauled Dr. Baker into the room with me.

"The ambulance should be here soon." Lucas said to me.

I couldn't find the words to speak. I didn't bother. Instead, I moved to stand directly under the infrared bulb.

"Why did you run?" Lucas asked.

I was pretty sure he wasn't talking to me. So I didn't try to stop my teeth from chattering. After a few moments, I realized Dr. Baker wasn't answering either. My chattering teeth had an echo.

"I'll go search his office if your security can watch him," Lucas said.

"Of course," Dr. Samuels picked up a phone.

As Lucas turned to leave, Dr. Baker suddenly began moving. He darted towards the open door. I grabbed hold of him, catching his shirt, we both collapsed into a heap.

"What the hell?" Lucas asked.

I had Dr. Baker pinned to the floor. Lucas helped flip him over and put handcuffs on him. His clothes were wetter than mine and the cold began to creep back into my body.

Lucas helped me to my feet. I put my foot in the center of Dr. Baker's back and drew my gun. Lucas demanded him to stop moving.

Xavier and Alejandro showed up. They found their way, with the help of museum staff, into the room. Alejandro surveyed the situation and shook his head. Xavier was tutting and looking concerned.

"How long has she been in these clothes?" Xavier asked.

"Ten minutes."

"Get out of them, now," Xavier demanded.

"I'm not taking off my clothes in a room full of people." I finally found my voice. The truth was I wasn't taking my clothes off in front of Alejandro. He already made me uncomfortable, being nude in front of him might be perceived as giving him some sort of power.

"Your lips are turning blue and your fingernails are as well. You have hypothermia, the blue tint is caused by a lack of oxygen and you are going to have necrotic digits if you don't listen to me. You should have shed them the moment you came out of the water. They are wet and keep the cold insulated next to your skin. Even in a warm room, you aren't going to warm up as long as you have wet clothing on. So take it all off. Someone get blankets." Xavier took charge of the situation.

Alejandro helped Dr. Baker stand. Lucas had begun to tear off my clothing. I stared at him in shocked helplessness.

He moved directly in front of me, blocking off everyone's view of me. His hands worked quickly, removing the cloth. When it snagged, he tore the fabric. Someone handed him a blanket, he wrapped it around me once I was nude and helped cinch the front of it.

"Thank you," I said, feeling the warmth start to spread under the blanket.

"Can't have you freezing to death your first time out," Lucas answered.

Twenty-Seven

Paramedics showed up. They took my blood pressure, my pulse and my body temperature and declared that I needed to go to the hospital. I ignored their requests and Xavier's protests. Instead, I followed, wrapped in a blanket, Alejandro and Lucas to Dr. Baker's office.

The room wasn't very big, maybe 6 foot by 7 foot. Bookshelves dominated the furniture, but there was a desk covered in papers and books and a couple of chairs. The chairs were obviously not used very often as they were piled with books.

Lucas and Alejandro began to systematically search through the room. I stood in the door and watched them. Alejandro was working on the desk. Lucas was working through a bookshelf, taking out books and shaking them to see if anything fell out. I decided to be somewhat useful and did the same thing to the stacks of books in the chairs.

"Cain," Alejandro snapped at me.

"What?" I turned and looked at him.

"Any of these papers important?" He pointed to the top of the desk.

"Beats me," I moved over to them.

Most were just pieces of research. The few that remained were personal correspondence and a few were grant proposals. All of it was unimportant in my opinion. I stacked them all up.

"You really need to go to the hospital," Xavier came in.

"I will, but I want to know why he ran and jumped into the lake." I told him, moving another stack of papers. I stopped and stared at the top of the desk. There was a baggy on it.

"What is this?" I pointed.

"Best guess, meth," Xavier said coming over to me.

"He ran because he was afraid we'd search his office?" I frowned.

"Meth addicts tend to be paranoid," Lucas informed me. He pulled out a cell phone and made a phone call. Whoever he was talking to was instructed to perform a drug test. He hung up.

"Might be why he had the energy to bolt a second time," Xavier offered, "if he was getting high when you came in, he wouldn't have been affected much by the cold water."

"Must be nice," my hair was still crunchy to the touch, despite being inside.

"Ok, you figured out why he ran, off to the hospital." Xavier grabbed my arm.

I followed Xavier out. We ran into the paramedics in the hall. They insisted on putting me on a gurney and strapping me down.

The ride to the hospital included inserting an IV and packing me with heat packs. They also wrapped another blanket around me and tucked it in under me. I felt snug as a bug in a rug and completely unable to move anything but my head and my lungs.

At the hospital, they took me straight into a room and began performing more tests. A doctor moved in and out, muttering under his breath. I was used to this; I often made doctors mutter at me.

Xavier came into the room. He undid the straps that held me and handed me a set of flannel pajamas. Since I hadn't packed them, I gave him a look.

"They aren't mine," he assured me, "I bought them on the way here. I also have socks and house-shoes for you. Despite not feeling like you were hypothermic, you are. They are going to want to keep you overnight."

"Uh, no. I can get warm at the hotel."

"Hypothermia isn't just about being very cold. Cell death happens, organ damage happens, brain damage happens."

"I've never had hypothermia." I admitted.

"This is only a mild case, putting you under a heating lamp probably helped a great deal."

"And here I thought those were just for lizards. Are you going to leave the room so I can change?" I asked him.

"No," he stood and turned his back on me. I shrugged, slipped from the bed and got dressed. Everything fit.

"Ok, done." I told him climbing back into the bed.

"Good, if you refuse to stay, which is your choice, you'll have to follow my orders when we get back to the hotel. Hot foods for dinner and I'll need to check on you every couple of hours."

"Check on me how?" I narrowed my eyes at him.

"Blood pressure, pulse rate, body temperature, glucose levels, the whole nine yards."

I considered my options. I could stay here and be bothered by doctors and nurses all night and if I was really lucky, I'd be out by noon the next day. Or I could go back to the hotel and deal with Xavier bugging me all night. They seemed equally disastrous.

"Ok, get me a doctor and I'll sign for my release." I told Xavier.

Xavier got up and left the room. I took stock of the stuff around me. Xavier had left a bag on the chair. I got up and snooped through it. I found my guns and shoulder holster as well as a coat and real shoes. I took all of it out

167

of the bag and put it on. The coat caught on my IV. I frowned and unhooked it. I also yanked off the rest of the wires. The monitor for my heart rate flat-lined.

Nurses rushed into the room. A doctor ran in behind them. They all stared at me, mouths hard set, eyes narrowed.

"I'd like to go now," I informed one of them as I pulled off the sticky pads still attached to my chest.

"I highly recommend..."

"I have a doctor in my unit and I'm not in any real danger at this point. So, instead of taking up valuable bed space, I'll just go back to my hotel room and sit under some heated blankets and drink plenty of hot liquids." I interrupted the doctor.

In the doorway, I could see Xavier giggling. He put a hand over his mouth to keep sound from escaping. If I had a phobia, it was of hospitals.

There was another commotion. Xavier jetted from the doorway into the hall. Several people followed. I joined them.

Dr. Baker was going into a full rage. I had never seen a meth-head explode before. He was gibbering and throwing things.

A cop in a uniform Tasered him. It didn't seem to have much effect. Another cop tackled him, they fell to the floor. Dr. Baker was all flailing limbs. Some connected weakly with the cop who had tackled him. Xavier got into the fray. He had a hypodermic needle in his hand.

He jabbed the hypodermic into Dr. Baker. It wasn't immediately effective. Dr. Baker caught hold of Xavier and jerked him over. Xavier fell onto the ground, his face slamming into the floor.

I moved in. Baker was still fighting with the other cop. Xavier wasn't moving, but his chest was rising and falling, so I ignored him. I grabbed hold of Baker and brought my knee into his head. His nose exploded, his eyes rolled back into his head and he fell to the floor with a solid thud.

"Matching wounds," Xavier said as he rolled over. Blood gushed from his nose.

A nurse tended to Xavier. Orderlies, security officers and police officers got Baker up and back into bed. They strapped him down.

"I got strapped down and he didn't?" I asked a nurse walking past me. She ignored me. I considered bitching about the injustice and stupidity of that and decided it was a battle I didn't need to win.

"Ok, let's go." Xavier looked at me. The nurse had shoved cotton up his nose. I followed him out the door.

Lucas was in the parking lot waiting for us. We got into the SUV. Lucas looked at Xavier for a moment.

"Do you have a tampon up your nose?" Lucas asked after another moment.

"No, cotton, Baker broke my nose. Just drive." Xavier huffed at him.

Twenty-Eight

Gabriel decorated my hotel room when we returned. His shoes were on the floor by the fridge, his coat had been slung across the bed and his body was reclined in a chair with his socked feet on the table. I glared at him, but he didn't seem to notice or care. They had been unwilling to let me smoke in the SUV. It had been a few hours since I'd had one. I could go a few more, but I didn't want to. I headed towards the balcony.

"Uh, no," Xavier grabbed my arm and stuck a patch on it.

"This is not the same as a cigarette."

"You are not going out on the balcony and smoking. It's cold and you are recovering from hypothermia. You'll have to do with a patch," Xavier told me.

"That sucks," I sank into a chair and looked out the glass door.

We had exhausted a good portion of the last 24 hours dealing with Baker, his shenanigans and hospitals, ensuring that we were no closer to finding our victims or our killer. My mood sank a little. We had lost a day, a day our victims didn't have.

"Come on," Lucas hit my leg.

"What?" I asked him.

"It's time to re-evaluate our torturer." He informed me.

"Re-evaluate our torturer?" I looked at him, my head tilted to the side.

"If you are right, then my profile would be wrong," he told me.

170

"Ah, I see," I moved to the small table and sat down. My attention was still drawn to the balcony door.

It took a while to notice that it wasn't as dark as it had been when we came in. Dark was slowly removing itself from the world, being replaced by the daylight. Not that Chicago is ever really dark. There were still street lights and lights from the El-Trains. Car headlights cast shadows around corners and onto buildings, warping the shadows, creating illusions in the light and dark. It did not improve the oppressive semi-darkness, but seemed to somehow make it worse, more dreadful. The people of this afflicted city would awake to their morning papers to find headlines like "Ten Women Still Missing in the Greater Chicago Area. Police Still Have No Clues About Murdered Woman Found Under Bridge."

"Ace?" Lucas brought me back to him.

"Sorry, what?"

"Do I remove likes torture from the list?"

"Not in the least," I shrugged. "There are many things about medieval torturers that aren't known, but to remove likes it, probably doesn't fit. We have every indication that they did enjoy their jobs, at least to some extent. If they didn't, they wouldn't have been able to sleep. They would have closed their eyes and heard screaming in their ears. Just because something is legal or is sanctified, doesn't mean it is still easy to do. The average person, even in the Middle Ages, would not have been able to stomach the hands on part. That's why there are hangman's bags and executioner suits. You have to dehumanize the person you are killing. The same holds true for torturers, but unlike an executioner, the event or sequence of events are going to last a lot longer. Modern humans are used to going to a job they hate. They think anyone can do it. But this, this isn't a job you can hate and do."

"Ok, what about the rest of it?" Lucas handed me a piece of paper.

"Not sure about the gender. Male, female, still a tossup unless you can show me real evidence that a man did it. Was there semen found in the sexual assaults?"

"No, just spermacide and traces of latex, an excessive amount of yeast, and..." Xavier trailed off.

"And a condom was used." I finished for Xavier. "So, you still can't say for sure it is male or female."

"What about the way they were tortured?" Alejandro asked.

"Drawing and quartering requires horses or oxen, not a lot of human strength. Impaling is a special breed of torture, but again, horses or oxen would work."

"Yes, but they would have to be tall..."Alejandro started.

"No, you begin the impaling while they are on the ground," I turned to look at him. "You lay the stake on the ground, then using whatever you want; you begin driving the stake in. You right the stake by tying it to a horse just below where it has been inserted in the victim. The horse moves forward, pulling the stake into a hole that has a reinforced back wall. The stake hits the wall and the bottom sinks creating a lever effect that uprights the stake. All you have to do is make sure the stake doesn't flip or something."

"That's sick." Michael spoke for the first time in ages.

"Yes it is, but effective. I always keep impaling in a special category. There are a few tortures that make all others look like holidays. Impaling is one of them."

"What are the others?" Alejandro asked.

"The Brazen Bull, Rats in a Head cage, The Pear of Anguish, The Breast Ripper and Impaling. These were tortures that required a lot of dehumanization. The Greeks were best with the Brazen Bull. The Church with the Pear of Anguish and the Breast Ripper. Tepes with impaling. And the French with Rats in a Head cage."

"You say the Church, why?" Lucas asked.

"Because these tortures were used by the Holy Roman Empire as well as during most of the inquisitions. The Brazen Bull, Impaling, Rats, the Scavenger's Daughter, they were mostly secular."

"Mostly?" Lucas asked.

"Impaling, much like crucifixion, was used by the Romans, so the Church sort of ignored it. They did it to their enemies, encouraged it during a couple of Crusades even, but for the most part, they considered it barbarian. The Scavenger's Daughter was made in England, after Henry VIII broke with Rome. The Bull was of ancient times. These were used more often for punishment by secular governments."

"The Maidens?" Alejandro asked.

"That is a good question. We know they were used by the Church and we know they were used by governments, but how often is a mystery. Considering the first one ever found was discovered in Germany, gives credit to the Church using it more. They were part of the Holy Roman Empire, but that doesn't seal the deal, especially since Germany didn't exist at the time of its use. After the Holy Roman Empire fell, it became Prussia. Prussian rulers were known for being methodical, but unfortunately, like Russian Czars, madness was always just under the surface and they were extremely religious."

"Meaning it could be either." Lucas said.

"Yes and probably was." I told him, frowning. My comment about Russia had struck a chord in my brain.

"What?" Xavier asked.

"Well, I just realized that The *Book of Torture* doesn't include anything Russian. I don't know why I hadn't thought of it before. None of our torture methods listed have been Russian either."

"And that's important?"

"No, yes, maybe." I shrugged. "The Russians were devout and Orthodoxy doesn't forbid torture. I know it was used often by different Czars. As a matter of fact, some of them really enjoyed it. One a woman."

"What do you mean?" Lucas mimicked my frown.

"Catherine the Great was known for her enjoyment of torture as entertainment. If it is a woman, who better to emulate? Of course, there are a few others, Catherine de Medici was pretty fond of it. She was pretty fond of murder as well. So, I thought there might be something there, but maybe not."

"Marie Antoinette?" Xavier asked.

"No, despite her plethora of sins, enjoyment of torture, murder and/or death was not among them. For the record, she never said 'Let them eat cake;' it had been in print for at least 40 years before she was born."

"Historical error number one exploded." Xavier smiled.

"Something like that," I continued to frown.

"What is it?" Lucas asked.

"Their drugged to get out of their apartments. How the hell are they controlled after that? Are there any ligature marks? Any drugs or alcohol in their systems? Torturing is noisy and fear inspiring. Nine women have to be controlled while one is being tortured. How?"

"We haven't found anything in that department." Alejandro admitted.

"Damn," light was blooming on the skyscrapers but still failing to light the roads and sidewalks enough to turn off the street lights.

Twenty-Nine

My hotel was just two blocks from the theatre district in Chicago. There was an El-stop on this block. Commuters were beginning to run to and fro. As I watched them, something occurred to me.

"All the victims are roughly the same size and shape, yes?" I asked Xavier.

"Between 5'7" and 5'9" and within ten or fifteen pounds of each other." Xavier confirmed.

"And their fingers? Feet?" I asked.

"Some bruises, broken fingernails and toenails, the odd broken bone, nothing that can't be explained during their initial struggle or struggling to not be tortured."

"True," I turned back outside. The thought still forming in my head. Two inches wasn't a lot of height difference. Ten or fifteen pounds could be, depending on the body shape, but perhaps not enough.

"Why?" Lucas held suspicion in his voice.

"Because I think I can explain how they are being held." I got out my book and flipped until I found the page.

"This is called a Hanging Coffin. They are supposed to fit like a glove, so that the captive can't move too much. In the old days, they were made to order. They had hanging cages, but those left a lot of room for movement. These were different. The victim was put inside, the door was closed and for several days, people passing by could hurl rocks or food or sticks at them. Eventually, the victim was either let out or left to starve to death. There weren't injuries involved except what was done by the people passing by or the futile attempts

175

to escape their fate. Because the Hanging Coffins fit so tightly though, it is hard to move much more than your fingers and toes. Considering the victims were the same size, same body shape, you could just order ten Hanging Coffins with those specs. It might raise eyebrows if you ordered them all from one person, but then again, it might not."

"It would raise my eyebrow," Alejandro commented.

Michael cleared his throat. I smiled at him. I had been right.

"They are popular with a couple of subcultures," I started. "I have seen them at Goth clubs, but I also know if you go for something a little darker, you can find them in the vampire underground and some of the fetish groups."

"I've seen them in a few death metal clubs and at raves," he admitted. "I didn't know what they were called though."

"No and they have been popularized by vampire and medieval based movies. There is even one in Monty Python and the Holy Grail." I added.

"So these things while being difficult to make are not exactly unique, rare or uncommon." Xavier sighed.

"No, but again, they require a master smith. You couldn't just look at a picture and get one made. They are hinged, the entire front opens, then locks. The metal that makes the latitudinal slats are made slightly different than the ones that make up the longitudinal slats. They have been fitted properly. Like anything else made of iron or steel, it takes true craftsmanship to create it."

"Why do you keep saying things like craftsmanship and skilled?" Alejandro asked.

"Have you ever been to an artisanal community?" I asked him.

"No." He answered.

"Ok then, communities of the Middle Ages were artisanal in design. You didn't have importers or exporters and if you did, the populace couldn't afford it. So, everything was made there, in the community. You got bread from a baker, meat from a butcher, metalwork from a smithy; even your torturers and executioners were parts of these communities. The executioner was paid by the state, he had to then pay for everything he bought in the community, but he also helped with law and order to some degree. Some people knew he was the executioner, some didn't. Those that did kept clear of his bad side. In the modern age, where master smiths are as uncommon as artisanal communities, it requires a bit of luck and a lot of work to find a master smith, especially one that works with iron. Everything about this case reeks of the Middle Ages, meaning that everything to do with this case is not modern in nature except our techniques to catch them. I can't help but ask myself if we shouldn't be time traveling with them. What are these women's offenses? Are they flirts? Atheists? Shoplifters? Something about these women, other than their size, has to connect them and I imagine the connection is as medieval as the methods used to kill them. My first thoughts are heresy or adultery or something similar, but it could be secular instead of ecclesiastical. It doesn't have to make sense to us, just the person doing it. Which means there is a lot of theories and ground to cover."

"Not necessarily," Lucas looked at me. "If it is ecclesiastical, it is most likely a woman, very devout. If it is secular, then male and this is feeding his need for some sense of justice."

"Great, we just need to find out what imaginary offense has been committed. Why and how the killer relates to Cain and how it relates to that book, if it does at all." Alejandro stood up. He pulled a pack of cigarettes from his pocket and lit up in the room.

"Balcony," Lucas pointed.

"Fine," Alejandro walked out, blowing smoke at Lucas as he did.

"Why is it more likely to be female if it is religion related?" I asked once Alejandro had departed the room.

"Because women are more likely to act on religious fervor than men."

"Then explain monks." I asked.

"Monks are not acting on religious fervor, they are acting on faith. Cult leaders tend to be male, but most cult followers are female."

"I thought that was just because the leader didn't like to compete for sexual favors."

"There is a bit of that, but in reality, women are twice as likely to join a cult because women already have more inclination towards religious fervor."

"Explain zealots then."

"Zealots are a special breed, as you put it. They are acting upon their own desires and calling it providence. Huge difference." Lucas assured me.

"You use the word providence and questioned me on the use of vogue?" I gave a quick flash of a grin.

"Well, I figure if you are going to use outdated references, I would as well," he winked at me. For the first time, I suspected I knew Lucas's secret.

"Religious fervor doesn't normally include murder," I went back to our original conversation.

"No, no it doesn't, but normally isn't always. One thing we found in common is that they were all out-going. Several were described as flirty." Michael spoke again. "As a matter of fact, several were flirty even on their Facebook pages and blogs."

"It's amazing what you can find out about people now-days with the internet," I commented.

"A Google search is a great thing for finding information about people." Michael retorted.

Thirty

With the rush of traffic now steadily flowing through the city streets, I yawned. Lucas and Xavier took the cue. Lucas smiled at me.

"I'll go back to the museum today and see what else I can discover through my powers of perception," he said.

"Go get 'em Holmes," I joked with him.

"I'll go to make them feel comfortable. They met me two days ago," Xavier said.

"I will go find out who makes Hanging Coffins," Michael got up.

"Tired?" Alejandro asked.

"Yes," I told him as the others shuffled out of the room.

Alejandro stayed behind. He studied me for a few moments, without saying a word. He lit another cigarette.

"What is it that you don't like about me exactly?" I finally asked, ignoring the fact that he was smoking in my non-smoking room.

"I haven't put my finger on it yet, there is something that bothers me about you."

"I have that effect on people from time to time." I didn't add they were normally alpha males and serial killers.

"If I was my father or grandfather, I'd say it was because death seems to follow you around. Luckily for you, I'm not them."

"Meaning you don't think a spiritual cleansing would help much because you don't believe in them."

179

"Are you implying you do?"

"I have done many things in my pursuit of knowledge and understanding. I've been to see priests about exorcisms and shamans about cleansing my spirit, I even saw a voodoo priestess to lift my death curse."

"And what did all of them tell you?"

"The priest told me I wasn't possessed. The shamans told me that my soul was clean. The only helpful one was the voodoo priestess. She did some prayers and some rituals and told me death would stop following me. Two days later, someone slaughtered a pig on my front steps. So it seems that she was wrong, but at least she tried."

"Why did someone slaughter a pig on your front doorstep?"

"That is a question for the ages. I don't know why I attract the violent types, but I do, always have. The poor pig was slaughtered to get revenge for breaking someone's heart. Odd, considering they probably wouldn't have lived if they had continued to date me. It was only a couple of months before I met Gerard Hawkins. Had I still been with the pig butcher, Gerard Hawkins would have followed us both; probably killed him or I would have been killed because I would have been distracted by the addition of another being in my lair."

"You choose to live in solitude instead?"

"No, I have Nyleena and Malachi when I get lonely. My mother is always just a phone call away. I choose to live this life because it is safer. There are things that aren't in the files. Things that probably should be, but never made it that far. Things like the pig. Things like the last time I visited this city, I came here for an opening at The Field. Nyleena met up with me. We went to a play. We stayed in this very hotel even. The play was at the Schubert Theatre, 'Spamalot' to be precise. The play was amazing. The hotel was nice. The exhibit at the museum as grisly and gruesome as expected. What we didn't expect though, we went shopping, some way from here. We took a car instead of the El because of the neighborhood. There is a leather shop there that does amazing work. It was late in the day and as we were leaving the shop, someone approached us, demanded Nyleena's keys. I stared him down. He pulled a knife. I stayed still until Nyleena went to hand him her keys. When she did, I stopped her, told her it wasn't going to happen, not today. I turned back to the man and told him the same thing. I don't know what he saw there or didn't see, whichever the case maybe, but he didn't take the car. As a matter of fact, he dropped the knife and ran from us. From me. Something about me convinced him that his life wasn't worth Nyleena's car. We considered reporting it, but since I don't exactly have a spotless track record, we didn't. Instead, we continued on with our day. We went to dinner at a pizza joint where they served deep dish pizza upside down. Nyleena had a glass of wine. I had a soda. We talked, laughed and for some reason, it was like it never happened. That night, as we were going to sleep, Nyleena told me she was never afraid when she was with me. That there was something about me that made her feel safe and secure even in the worst neighborhoods. I told her that night that I was a sociopath. She gave a small laugh, said that explained so much, rolled over and went to sleep.

"So, yes, Alejandro, I can believe that you can't name whatever it is that you don't like about me. It could be the cold demeanor I always seem to have or the lack of emotion or the lack of fear. I don't know any of it better than you do. You aren't the first and you won't be the last to tell me that. As a matter of fact, I hear it a lot from men. With very few exceptions, that is what has ended most of my dates. There is just something about me that makes them uncomfortable. They don't know why, they think I'm a wonderful person, with intelligence and a good personality, if a little hard to get to know, but for some reason, I don't make them feel comfortable.

"The only males that do feel comfortable around me are as screwed up as I am. Men like Malachi Blake, a true psychopath who may or may not always be on the side of the law. Lucas McMichaels is comfortable in his own skin or mind. Xavier Reece is only happy when death is around. You and Michael will either come around or you won't. It depends on what is wrong with you. Lucas and Xavier took to me quickly because we are kindred spirits of a sort. I don't know what fractures your mind has, so I don't know if you will be more like Lucas and Xavier or more like the serial killers who are fascinated by me. Only you can make that decision."

"Your perception of the situation is admirable and astonishing. When Lucas came to me with the idea of hiring a historian, I thought he was kidding; now I can see why he thinks you would be an asset."

"History was written by the person with the best publisher. It requires perception and attention to detail. However, I admit, that those skills are probably why I became a historian and not the other way around. Perception and attention to detail are what have kept me alive, coupled with a strong survival instinct. I don't imagine our relationship will get better with time. You're an alpha male with a chip on his shoulder. I'm a girl with survival skills that would rival any predator. I think that will cause constant conflict. Can you work with that?"

"I agree with your analysis of the situation. I can work with that, if you can, Cain, but that is a question for you to answer. Can you have a superior alpha male with a chip on his shoulder and a diagnosis similar to your friend Malachi's with just a few more problems?"

"I don't know. Either we will get along and learn or we will kill each other."

"At least we both admit it. Get some rest, you look like shit." Alejandro walked from my room. Cigarette still burning between his fingers.

Thirty-One

The curtains were still closed when Xavier and Lucas let themselves back into my room. I was on the bed, eyes closed, blanket tossed over me. I had rested my eyes and my body, but I hadn't slept. My mind had been churning over details.

"Should we wake her?" Xavier whispered.

"I was never asleep," I answered, not moving. I heard them both come further into the room.

"The museum employees are strange, but that isn't a crime." Lucas told me.

"There's an anecdote that I want to share with you," I sighed and rolled over to face the other bed in the room. Lucas and Xavier were both sitting on it.

"Ok," Xavier said expectantly.

"How do you tell the difference between a historian, an anthropologist and an archeologist? By how they begin their conversations, because by the time the night is through, we all have the same three things to talk about." I told him.

"What's that?" He asked.

"Sex, death and religion," I thought for a moment. "It should apply to sociologists as well."

"Is that helpful?" Xavier looked puzzled.

"Yes. We have a clue; so to speak, we think we know how the killer is getting victims, how the victims are being held and why they are being picked. The question now becomes, how long does it take to find ten women who have violated that code and fit the body profiles? Days? Weeks? Months? I've been considering the care and planning that goes into the torture devices, without realizing the care that goes into the victims. And obviously, they don't just pick ten women. They have back-ups in place. Our killer proved that by finding an eleventh that fit so perfectly into the Hanging Coffins after the unexpected death of one of the chosen. It just suddenly hit me. This is not an easy thing. Especially in these days. I should have thought of it this morning, when I watched all the people scurrying about. All the different shapes and sizes of people, most of them cookie-cutters of each other in personality. Yet, they are finding perfect women at the drop of a pin. That doesn't happen. They are putting just as much care and time into picking the victims as they are picking the torture. In my mind..."

Lucas interrupted, "it means that each victim is picked for a precise torture as well."

"That's exactly what I was thinking. So, I got to considering offenses. Drawing and quartering was a thief's punishment most of the time. So did those ten women have sticky fingers? Tepes impaled debtors, were those ten drowning in debt? Or if they were being impaled for another reason, was it for their religion? The Crusaders impaled 'heathens'. The Romans impaled Christians and other 'heathens'. The Ottoman Empire impaled non-Christians and then went even further when they broke from Rome and began impaling Catholics for not being Orthodox. The maidens were used on female heretics and adulteresses. It was scarier than a scarlet A on their chest. The Scavenger's Daughter was used as punishment for a plethora of crimes, but again, it wasn't meant to kill, just maim and embarrass. There's a break from the pattern there. However, in England, the scavenger was an alternative to the stockade. Considering it is being used on females, I'd guess women who nag or women who have cuckolded their husbands.

And yes, being a nag was a punishable offense in medieval England and other places in Europe."

"You think each committed a different offense?" Xavier frowned at me.

"Haven't you ever heard the saying 'let the punishment fit the crime'?"

"Who hasn't?"

"Well, if they were all the same offense, why not just use one punishment? Why go through all the trouble of multiple punishments? Especially the very elaborate punishments? Did you find out how long it took to make the maidens?"

"Michael said about 18 months."

"See, 18 months of planning and preparation to kill ten women. It would be..." I shrugged unable to think of a word I wanted.

"What?" Lucas asked.

"I don't know. I can't imagine planning a murder for 18 months and then grabbing ten random women in one night. If I'm right about restraining them using Hanging Coffins, that's another 12 months just waiting for the opportunity to grab the women. Even if each coffin is ordered through a different master smith, that's still got to be a month or more worth of work. They are so precise."

"Michael checked. The smithy that made maidens also completed an order for three Hanging Coffins by the same company. It took him roughly five weeks for each Hanging Coffin." Lucas sighed.

"So I was right about the coffins and the time. Before any of this began, our killer had to have those coffins. The guy that made the maidens was probably very quick with the coffins. They require skill and precision, but they aren't as consuming as the maidens. A different smith might have taken longer on his order of coffins."

Alejandro burst into my room. His face was set in a scowl, hard lines appearing on his forehead. It looked like he was grinding his teeth.

"Locking my door is pointless around here." I noted that he had broken it from the hinges.

"This was delivered to you." He handed me an envelope.

It was a brown, legal size envelope. It was padded on the inside. I could see the bubble circles. What I couldn't see was what was inside the envelope. Carefully, I undid the clasp and the tape that held it.

"Ew," I said as I looked inside.

"Severed finger?" Xavier asked, trying to look inside.

"Nope, teeth," I got out of the bed and poured them onto a napkin on the table.

"All of them are canines and there are twenty of them." Xavier poked one with an ink pen.

"I'm not sure why I was given teeth." I looked at Alejandro.

"Really? I thought you knew everything."

"These are not recent removals either and none of our victims were missing their teeth." Xavier was now bent over them, looking at them through a magnifying glass. I wasn't sure where it had come from. I suppressed a giggle I felt rise up, he reminded me of Sherlock Holmes.

"You mean there are ten more victims?" I asked.

"At least ten women who don't have canines," Xavier corrected, "I'll know more when I can look at them under controlled conditions. If they were pulled out while alive, could mean that's all they did. If the tissue was dead when they were removed..."

"What do you know about teeth?" Alejandro asked.

"Very little. They were often scavenged from battle fields to make dentures. Um, some cultures remove a few teeth as a sign of this or that. A few removed all of them when they got married. People have long been pulling teeth that bothered them. Even the Egyptians did it. Some of the more violent cultures wore them on necklaces to show how many they had killed. That's about it."

"In other words, these mean nothing to you." Alejandro slammed the dresser into the wall with enough force to put a hole in it.

"That would be correct. Considering they are canines, I'd go with vampire myth, but an anthropologist would be the person to ask about teeth, not a historian."

"Why send them to you?" Alejandro asked.

"Because I have bad teeth." I retorted before I could stop myself.

Thirty-Two

Everyone turned to look at me. I opened my mouth and took out the bottom row of teeth. I set the dentures on the table and frowned at them.

"You have false teeth?" Lucas asked.

I put them back in.

"Only on the bottom. No enamel to begin with, some of my permanent teeth grew in with holes. Add to it the soda and starches, plus the violent lifestyle and I had dental implants at 15. When two of them were knocked out a year later, along with three other bottom teeth, I got the bottoms pulled and had dentures put in their place. I have six implants on the top and will have a seventh before long. I give it another two years before I replace all the top teeth with dentures."

"How many people know you have bad teeth?" Alejandro asked.

"Not many. A couple of dentists, Nyleena, Malachi, my pseudo-serial killing stalker, my brother, and a handful of others that I have known over the years."

"This is critically important. The handful of others and your pseudo-serial killing stalker, who are they?" Alejandro moved towards me like a looming storm.

"That's the thing; I don't know who the handful of others are. I rarely take them out. I've had them for ten years and I spent a fortune on them, I only really remove them to clean them. I've had college roommates who have seen them; I don't know who they told. I don't know if Nyleena or Malachi has ever gotten drunk and told anyone. I don't know if my brother or mother has told. It

happened after my sister and father were killed. I'm sure
people know, it just isn't common knowledge and I'm not
sure who would care that much. Furthermore, I can't fit
twenty teeth in the bottom of my mouth. That seems like
a strange number to send me. My mouth always had
extra teeth to begin with. They were the first to be pulled
and not replaced. I had one removed from each side of my
jaw on the top and bottom. I have no wisdom teeth. But
honestly, I don't talk about it and I don't know why
anyone would know I have bad teeth." I shrugged at him.

"Damn it, Cain, someone knows."

"I'm aware. I don't know how my pseudo-serial
killing stalker found out, but he did. That means I'm sure
others know, I just don't know who or why. Hell, it could
be from a newspaper." I had a sudden memory.

"When I graduated high school at 16, I had just
been fitted with them. They didn't fit right, but I won an
award and full scholarship to several colleges. For some
reason, my local college paper did an article about me.
They took my picture. I didn't keep it because I'm not the
scrapbook type, but my mom did. Now that I think about
it, my mouth looks funny in the picture, like my bottom
jaw and top jaw don't align right. Anyone with any
knowledge of what a person with false teeth looks like
when they first get them would know that I have
dentures."

"There are over 100,000 people in your hometown
and you're telling me that any of them could know,"
Alejandro said.

"That's correct. Luckily, it is just over 100,000 and
a portion of that is migratory because they are college
students. I don't know the enrollment figures for the
University of Missouri, Columbia College or Stephens
College, but I'm sure that some of them get figured into
the population. Having said that, even fewer people read

The Missourian that is put out by MU. It doesn't have the circulation that the Columbia Tribune has."

"That is supposed to help?" Alejandro glared at me.

"No, it is supposed to make something poignantly clear." I glared back.

"What is that?" He asked, backing down a bit and giving me some space.

"It means that anyone who saw that picture might know, but there is no way to check the circulation records from ten years ago and that you, specifically, cannot hold me responsible for anyone knowing that I have bad teeth or that I even had bad teeth to begin with. If you had lived the life I have lived, you'd be missing a few as well."

Alejandro seemed to think about that for a while. He moved away from me completely. Once back by the dresser, with fifteen feet or so between us, he calmed down.

"Now, back to the problem of the teeth. We don't have any victims missing teeth and Xavier says it is unlikely these came from the newest victims. That means we've missed a set of victims. If I had to guess, I'd say they were beheaded, had their hearts removed and silver coins put over their eyes and filling their mouths. Unfortunately, that isn't a form of torture; it's how you kill a vampire. It doesn't fit the pattern, at all.'"

"You got that from teeth?" Lucas asked.

"No, I got it from the kind of teeth. If there is something significant about teeth, I don't know it. The only thing I know is that suspected vampires would occasionally have their canines removed so that their fangs couldn't come out. It was rare though, very rare. I can't imagine why it would be done. Most cultures just killed suspected vampires; a few removed the teeth thinking that would 'cure' the vampire because they wouldn't be able to drink blood."

"I am not a vampire-enthusiast, you'll have to explain." Alejandro was still glaring at me, but at least he was across the room doing it.

"You know what a vampire is right?" I asked him.

"Get on with it." He rolled his eyes.

"Ok, in some instances, when a person was sick and vampirism was suspected, they would remove the canines so that the vampire couldn't go out and feed at night. If the vampire died as a result, the human would heal. This was of course complete bullocks since vampires don't exist and most of the people thought to be vampires were actually infected with TB. Removing the teeth didn't help much, so it was a rare thing to do."

"Thoughts on the matter?" Lucas asked me.

"It is weird to send me teeth. It is weird to send anyone teeth. It doesn't fit with our pattern of torture and either it was done in an act of madness or to throw us a curve ball," I concluded.

Thirty-Three

Xavier took the teeth and went wherever Xavier went to examine things. I was told to stay in my room by Alejandro. Lucas kept me company while Alejandro and Michael went to find all the Hanging Coffin makers.

"Now that it's just the two of us, what do you honestly think of the teeth?" Lucas asked after several minutes of silence.

"I don't think they have anything to do with the case. Our torturer isn't going around removing teeth. It isn't part of the deal. I think it's The Butcher and I think he is kicked back now having a hearty laugh at me."

"Explain your relationship there."

"I already have."

"No, you told us about it, you didn't explain anything."

"There's a difference?"

"Yes, I want to know your thoughts and opinions on him."

"I think he's for real. I don't think he's just some crackpot writing me letters and things. I think he is actually a serial killer. I think he is actually killing people and doing a damn good job of covering it up. When it first started, I thought it was Malachi. Some years later, I don't think that anymore. Malachi might be a serial killer, but he wouldn't taunt me with it. I searched through the victims' database and found nothing that corresponded to the stuff in his letters. He is too exact, too precise to be faking it. If he isn't killing people, he has the imaginative abilities of Edgar Allan Poe or HP Lovecraft. Since I think there is a better outlet for that sort of creative ability, I think he's real. I know nothing about him except that he always seems to know where I am. I've had my stuff swept for bugs, changed my phone numbers and it never helps. Within a few days, I have notification from him that he still knows where I am. I think the teeth are a reminder. A taunt, 'I know where you are and what you are doing, here's the proof of it.'"

"And you're alright with that?"

"Yes. He doesn't want to kill me. I'd like to capture him, don't get me wrong, just to find out who he is. But I know that there are two psychos in the world watching out for me. When I get in over my head, they let me know it."

"Two?"

"Malachi and The Butcher. You know, when I was fighting with the guy in Seattle, I was pretty sure I saw someone watching. He was outside my window, on the fire escape. The window there was nailed shut, but should I have started losing, really losing, I think The Butcher would have come through that window. I think he is responsible for the hit and run that killed my date as well. I haven't exactly figured out what he wants from me, but something tells me it isn't my death."

"That should scare the shit of out you."

"It should, it did in the beginning, but now, he's just another person. Another serial killer that is in my life. I can accept that as long as we can co-exist without him attacking me. Eventually, I know that he'll screw up and I'll nail his ass, find all his bodies and watch him go to the Fortress. Until then, I just wait for him to screw up."

"And the others in your life?"

"Nyleena is terrified. Malachi is fascinated. My mother doesn't know or she'd be chaining me up in my bedroom and never letting me leave again."

"Explain those relationships."

"Nyleena stays because it doesn't bother her. It might be why she picked the profession she picked. She doesn't like Malachi, but then very few people do. Malachi likes her well enough, but she is essentially just a blip on his screen. She exists, he knows it, they live in peace because they have to. Both love my mother dearly and my mother loves both of them. When I went to school, it was their suggestion that my mom move to Kansas City. She could be closer to both of them and my brother. Wouldn't take no for an answer. Malachi hired the movers, Nyleena took her house shopping. I couldn't survive the way I do without either of them. You think I don't know that Nyleena has been carefully feeding my trust fund for ages? Malachi does it as well. Nyleena out of some sense of guilt and need. Nyleena can't protect me from the horrors of my life, she feels guilty for it. So, she secretly gives me money. Malachi doesn't think I need protecting from myself, but does realize that I will never function like he does. So, he also feeds my trust fund."

"How do you feel living off the generosity of others?"

"I hate it, but I have never been quite sure what to do about it. I've told them to stop, but that hasn't worked. If this job works out, maybe they will stop then." I shrugged. "Isn't there something else we could be doing?"

"Not at the moment. The Chicago Police are interviewing family and friends. You are persona non-grata at the crime scenes and just about anywhere else. Alejandro wants an analysis of you, so we are doing that."

"And what have you discovered?"

"That you and he are going to have a very stormy relationship that will probably end badly."

"Why?"

"Because Alejandro is all about control and you are not someone or something he can control. Your life outside of your work is always going to be an issue. Things like this are always going to happen and as a result, he will eventually lose his temper with you. You are going to respond in kind."

"I don't always respond to anger with anger."

"No, that would be too simplistic for you. You are too logical for something like that. In this instance, you are too you to let him lose his temper and not be punished."

"Good to know. What will you tell him?"

"The truth. You are a valuable asset to the team. Right now, you're our resident expert on torture, but you have already started to work as a sounding board for both Xavier and myself. You are smart enough to be our sounding boards. I can't talk out psychological theories with Xavier, Alejandro or Michael, they don't really get it. Xavier can't talk about wound tracts and anatomy with us, it makes Michael green. Alejandro doesn't give a shit and my anatomy classes are so far in the past they are unhelpful. You don't have that issue. You understand psychology, sociology, anatomy, forensics and a multitude of other disciplines. Did you know that every adviser I spoke to said you would have excelled in whatever area you had wished to pursue? Did you also know that most were surprised by your choice to become a historian? Did you know that I have seen your transcripts and agree with them? You aren't just smart Ace, you're a genius. More so than any of us, which says a lot, because none of us are exactly intellectual slouches. Not only are you smarter than us, you are less emotional, more logical than us. You see teeth and say you are being taunted; they don't have anything to do with the case. I'm inclined to agree with you because there is no reason for them to be there."

Thirty-Four

"Well, they were alive when they were extracted." Xavier said, walking into my room with all the teeth in an evidence bag.

"That tells us what, exactly?" I asked.

"It tells us that they aren't from any of our previous victims. Also, the teeth are old, older than our current victims. Older than anyone born this century. I'm taking them to the museum to have them carbon dated. Wherever they came from, they aren't new victims from another serial killer. One of them had a filling in it that tested positive for mercury and lead. There isn't a snowballs chance in hell that the filling was created this century. It probably wasn't even created during the last century."

"Mercury in a filling?" I frowned.

"It isn't unheard of, just rare." Xavier informed me.

"Yes, I know. Fillings themselves are rare in old teeth. Are we sure it was a filling?"

"Well, it was a hunk of metal shoved in a tooth," Xavier shrugged.

"You know the stories about radium right?"

"What are you going on about?" Xavier frowned.

"Ok when radium was first discovered..."

"Yes, girls who worked with it would paint their teeth to make them glow in the dark. It was used to cure everything from tooth aches to cancer, which is ironic in its own right. So?"

"So, it is unlikely to be a professional filling. I'm not an expert on the subject, but if your tooth broke and you couldn't pull it, but you had access to mercury..." I shrugged back.

"You think it was a do it yourself job?" Xavier frowned harder.

"Wouldn't be the first time I've heard of something that weird. Several professions worked with both mercury and lead, hatters being the prime example."

"Why would someone do their own fillings?" Lucas asked.

"I don't see why not, most so called dentists before the 1900's pulled teeth, they didn't save them. Hence the scavenging of battlegrounds for teeth."

"I don't understand what you mean when you say that." Lucas informed me.

"After any major battle, the governments would pay people to clean it up. Mostly it was a matter of burying or burning the dead. But there were others there too and cleaning up a battlefield doesn't exactly pay well. Let's take Waterloo for example; roughly 40,000 soldiers died during the battle. That's a lot of dead to bury. It's also a lot of teeth to harvest. They would extract the teeth of the dead or dying and put them into barrels to be shipped somewhere. Barrels, not small boxes or containers, but actual barrels. The teeth would arrive at their destination. Dentists would then have patients come in that were either missing some or all of their teeth. If teeth could be found to fit the holes left by the missing teeth, they'd do that. What was left would be used to make dentures for patients."

"That was common practice?" Lucas raised an eyebrow.

"Yes. You had dentures made of wood, ivory, some even of metal, but quite a few were made from human teeth."

"You mean we have old teeth that have nothing to do with our actual serial killer?" Xavier shook his head.

"Most likely, yes. Battlefield dentures wouldn't hold in today's world. Twenty canines tell me they were taken from TB patients or for some other unknown reason. While they are old, they don't fit with our pattern. Taking out teeth is painful and torturous in its own way, but it isn't the same as torturing someone and none of our victims are missing teeth. Not to mention the age of the teeth."

"Another dead end." Xavier said.

"Seems so," I answered.

"What now?" Lucas asked.

"Hopefully, Alejandro and Michael will have more luck with the coffins," Xavier sat the teeth down on the dresser. We all stared at them.

"Just because they aren't from our serial killer, doesn't mean they aren't from a serial killer," I suddenly said. "If my serial killer sent them, it is probably because they mean something. He would know I was here and working on this case. I imagine the teeth have some meaning."

"You said that about the maidens," Xavier reminded me.

"And they do have meaning, finding the context is a whole different story." I told him.

"The *Book of Torture*, the Iron Maidens, the sexual assaults, now the teeth, does everything in your world have symbolism connected to it?" Lucas asked.

"No, but in this case, I think they are all somehow related, I just can't grasp the relationship. It is worse when I have to include myself in the equation. It is much easier to be objective when you aren't personally involved. That dagger makes me personally involved."

"Maybe we need to look at it like a puzzle. We have the extreme planning that went into the capturing and torture of the victims as well as the selection of the victims. We have an obscure book that some of it has been recreated from. We have a dagger with your finger prints on it, but no memory of where you touched it. And now a bag full of teeth." Lucas offered.

"That didn't help me much," I said after a very long silence between the three of us.

"Maybe the pieces are still too big." Lucas offered.

"Then we have a serial killer with knowledge of the medieval era. We have Hanging Coffins, Iron Maidens, Scavenger's Daughters, impaling spikes and horses. We have a bag of canines that may or may not have anything to do with the case, but were definitely not sent by our killer. A replica military dagger..." I stopped.

"What?" Xavier asked.

"The dagger you recovered with my fingerprints. It's carbon steel, indicating that it was a military grade replica. I don't know the significance because I don't know what knife it represents. The circle at the top is meaningless without the insignia that should have been on it. We can rule it out as something common, like a K-Bar, they weren't that decorative."

"No, the US military doesn't use a lot of decoration on any of their daggers or knives," Lucas told me.

"Sort of figured that, but I don't have the military expertise to figure it out. Besides, it is way outside my timeframe. It would be a 20th century dagger. I don't know the significance or the origin or anything about it other than it's a 20th century dagger. If we consider the options for it..."

"That would be staggering," Xavier answered. "The Swiss Guard, KGB, The British Royal Guard, The Scots Guard, Beefeaters, they all have their own special marks and insignias and symbols. That's just touching a few of the highlights from the 20th century."

"Exactly and I imagine we missed quite a few. Officers and servicemen with distinction get ceremonial daggers that are practical as well as symbolic of their

station. It's been that way for years. The Knights
Templar had their own sword smiths who specialized in
making the broadswords that we associate with the sect.
Even secret societies have them; there are records from
the late Middle Ages of daggers specifically designed for
Masons with their own unique symbols. It could belong
to any country of the last century or so." I shrugged at
him.

Thirty-Five

"Well, that was pointless," Michael came barging into my room without even a knock. Although, since Alejandro had broken it earlier, I figured it didn't matter. I was pretty sure that someone would be up to fix it, eventually, and until then, I'd just play revolving door.

"What was?" I asked him as he sat down some containers of food. It smelled like Chinese. I searched for and found a box containing Cashew Chicken.

"The Hanging Coffins. We found out our company did order ten, but again, the company doesn't exist."

"How long did it take to get all of them?"

"About seven months. One smith took an extremely long time making one." Michael pulled out Sweet & Sour Pork.

"Back logged." I commented without surprise.

"Exactly. Hence why they only built one of them. Do you realize the amount of work these smiths get?"

"I imagine it is a lot and it is all unique." I answered.

"You have no idea. We talked to a guy that said last year alone, he made seven Hanging Coffins, six Pears of Anguish, a Brazen Bull, three show piece Iron Maidens, and that wasn't counting all the other stuff he normally makes or the special orders from museums."

"It's a specialized business," I commented dryly again.

"Why don't you seem surprised by any of it?" He asked.

"Because I once had to order a replica for a class that I was helping teach. For some reason, someone had

stolen the leg irons that belonged with a stockade.
Anyway, it took nine weeks to get them. Leg irons aren't
complicated by any means. Besides, I've put together
exhibits and done consulting with museums before and I
know the sort of stuff they order."

"And?" Lucas prodded.

"And I've been to Goth clubs, death metal clubs,
fetish clubs; they all have this sort of stuff around. I was
once in a Goth club that had a maiden and a Hanging
Coffin. Both replicas of course, but still... These things
draw a crowd. Society likes to carefully interact with its
darker side. When a museum offers an exhibit on torture
or surgical tools or death or taboos or superstition, they
always have big turn outs. They can have huge fund
raisers based around them. The small museum that was
connected with the University of Washington did it one
year as a fundraiser at Halloween. They raised more
money at that fundraiser than they had in the three
months previous from donations. The reason I was in
Baltimore was to give a short speech on The Spanish
Inquisition and its use of torture as a means to extract
information. The entire fundraiser was based on torture
methods used by the Inquisition. They raised a ton of
money. It's where I got the job offer for the Field as well
as three other museums."

"So for historians, the dark side is big business."
Xavier said.

"Yes, go to any large university campus and take a
class on the Middle Ages and some portion of the
curriculum will be dedicated to torture, crime and
punishment, executions and other dark stuff. Students
need credits in different departments, so when they offer
those sorts of classes, the enrollment fills up very quickly.
Money gets shipped into the department based on the
student head count. Campuses offer them. History,
Anthropology and Sociology departments all do it. Rarely

does someone major in it, like I did, but I'm the exception, not the rule. It is part of the reason I am considered a resource in the academic world and why museums want to hire me. I can bring the darker side to life for them. Most Medievalists specialize in specific kingdoms or governments or time periods, I specialized in torture."

"Sounds like you did more than specialize in it." Michael gave me a grin.

"I'm human; I can appreciate the darker side of humanity. To be honest, every historian can. Show me a professor of cultural history and I'll show you a professor that knows all about the dark side of whatever civilization they specialized in. That is the reason I am unique. I didn't pick England or The Franks and get my degree there. I took the dark side of all the Middle Ages and got my degree."

"That's very gloomy," Michael frowned.

"Yes and no. It is gloomy when you think about all the time I put into studying it, but in reality, humanity has been dominated by sex, death and religion from the beginning. All I did was get my degree in one of the things that has dominated humanity. It would have been gloomier if I had gotten my PhD in 20th Century American History."

"Why?" Michael asked.

"Because it was dominated by two world wars, the Korean War, the Vietnam War, assassinations, the rise of the mass murderer and the rise of the serial killer. In comparison, the Middle Ages seems like a trip to Disney Land. There was far less death during it."

"Hard to imagine that the Middle Ages had less death than the 20th century," Xavier said.

"Yes, yes it is, but in the long run, it isn't that much of a mystery. Death has become an industry in the 20th century. War reached technological highs. Mass murderers became a dime a dozen. Serial killers became prolific and normal. Of course, that's not counting diseases and other causes of death."

"They had diseases back then," Xavier countered.

"They did and they were bad, but there was less population to kill off, so if a third of Europe dies from plague in the Middle Ages, that's a few hundred thousand people. If it happens now because of a particularly virulent strain of flu and that's millions. Population increase makes a significant difference in the amount of death. 40,000 people died at Waterloo, that many and more died in the Battle of the Bulge, but we don't realize it because of the population increase."

"You are trying to point out that everything is relative." Lucas said.

"Everything is relative," I agreed, "relative to your current position in the world. Forty years ago when serial killers began to rise in numbers, it was the topic of every newspaper headline. Now days, it's an editorial found near the back. Our torturer will start making headlines when they hit 100 people or when they do something so horrifying that it can't help but shock everyone in the nation."

"That should have happened with the drawing and quartering." Michael said glumly.

"But it didn't because we've had six Jack the Ripper copycats in the last 15 years alone. We've had countless mass murderers since then, including my brother, who only made headlines because he was popping off prisoners behind a fence. Numbers and shock-factor attracts attention, a small drawing and quartering doesn't count. Impaling doesn't count. If our torturer sticks ten women inside Brazen Bulls, it might get noticed, but even that is questionable."

"You're obsessed with maidens and Brazen Bulls." Xavier gave me a weak grin.

"I can't think of a worse way to die than a Brazen Bull. Impaling comes close, but I have a fear of burning to death and actually burning to death, not dying of smoke inhalation."

"That's twisted," Alejandro came into the room. "Someone is on the way up to move you to a different room. It is closer to Xavier and Lucas, you'll be protected. You've got another letter."

Thirty-Six

I opened the envelope. I had seen the script many times in the past. Small neat block letters, handwritten but looking so much like they should belong to a typewriter.

"I hope you got my gift and have figured out their significance. I hate to see you struggle with something like this, someone like this. If you didn't get the significance, you should think a little harder. I'm sure it will come to you."

There was no signature. It wasn't necessary. I folded it and put it back into the envelope.

"Well, the teeth are from The Butcher. He says they are significant. Beats the hell out of me why they are significant though." I handed the letter to Lucas.

"Fingerprints?" Lucas asked.

"You can check, but I find it unlikely you'll find any. Never have in the past." I shrugged.

"Never hurts to double check." Lucas looked over the envelope. He turned it over twice, examining it. He even sniffed the envelope.

"Find anything?" I asked.

"It smells like formaldehyde." He answered.

"They always do," I shrugged again.

"They always smell like formaldehyde?"

"Yep."

"Do the teeth?"

"I didn't smell the teeth." I commented.

"They smell like formaldehyde." Xavier stated.

"Ok, that tells us they were stored. I'm thinking that your letters are treated with formaldehyde for a reason."

"What reason? Other than to slowly poison me."

"I think that's a question for your serial killer," Lucas left me hanging.

"Well, that didn't help much." I sighed.

"Yes, actually, it does. Formaldehyde would prohibit oils from sticking to the paper." Xavier stated. "It's a preservative, but it preserves flesh, not oil. Hence, no fingerprints. The teeth were probably stored in it ages ago."

"I didn't know that about formaldehyde," I admitted.

"You know about a lot of other things," Xavier teased.

"Does this help at all?" Alejandro frowned at all of us.

"Probably not," I admitted. "Mainly because I don't know the importance of the teeth."

"How old do you think the teeth are?" Lucas asked.

"I don't know. I don't know for how long DIY dentists were using mercury or lead or both in their teeth. It wasn't covered in any of the books I read. Honestly, I don't know much about dentistry in general. I know some unusual facts here and there, like the radium thing. That's it."

"If you don't know anything about dentistry, then the clue must pertain to something else." Lucas stated.

"Teeth. During some time periods, the removal of teeth was vogue, others not so much. It was occasionally used as a torture method, but that was actually earlier in history or in other parts of the world. The Europeans did it, but it wasn't really their thing. They were more likely to remove fingers and toes than teeth as a form of torture.

The removal of teeth didn't mark you, brand you or stigmatize you in Europe. The Europeans were all about the symbolism behind their tortures."

"Could that be it, the lack of European symbolism?" Xavier asked.

"How so?" I countered.

"Teeth mean nothing to Europeans, unlike the other tortures you've named. Could that be part of it?"

"I don't see how. Most cultures have their removable bits. This was the European removable bit. They didn't perform many lobotomies or castrations or splenectomies."

"Maybe we need to narrow it. What year did you have your bottom teeth removed?"

"February of 2006."

"What happened that year?"

"I got my driver's license. I graduated high school. I moved to Michigan. I'd had a stalker for a year."

"What prompted you to remove your teeth?"

"I was in a gas station and someone tried to rob it. When I didn't submit to their orders to empty my wallet and get down on the ground, they hit me in the mouth with the butt of their gun. It broke out two more bottom teeth. By that time, I'd had implants and I just decided to do something different. A few days later, I went to the dentist, he pulled the rest of the teeth and I got fitted for temp dentures."

"Is there a police report?" Michael asked.

"Yes," I frowned at him. "There is a report. He busted out my teeth, I broke his nose and the store keeper knocked him out. The police arrived, rushed me to the hospital and arrested the guy."

"Is that important?" Alejandro asked.

"Maybe. Did it appear in the papers?" Michael continued.

"No, there was far more interesting stuff going on at the time. There was a Jack the Ripper in New York that had killed several and left their mutilated corpses around the city. That was taking up most of the front page news that month. The middle pages were filled with other, important things. I don't remember what, I just remember being grateful that I wasn't in the papers for it."

"If you had your stalker then, maybe he remembers something you don't." Lucas offered. "Did you meet anyone new that month?"

"Uh, if I did, they didn't register, meaning they didn't stick around for another meeting. Aside from the robbery it was a quiet month."

"Did you have a lot of months that year that weren't quiet?" Lucas asked.

"Not really. March was rough. August was rough because of the move. I got my driver's license in September. I drove home and had a car accident in December. That about covers 2006."

"What about prom?" Xavier asked.

"I didn't go to prom," I gave him a stupid look. Like anyone would ask me to prom.

"Now the year before that was interesting. The Butcher appeared, my brother went on a shooting spree and was convicted, the press hounded my mother about it for months, three of my classmates were murdered in the school parking lot by a random drive by shooting, someone tried to blow up the other high school in my town, and Malachi graduated from high school that year, the one they tried to blow up. He actually found the bomb and moved it to a safer location before it detonated. Nyleena finished college and was instantly offered a job in KC and moved. Her first case was a serial killer case that she won. The NYC Jack the Ripper appeared and killed eight or nine in the first five days."

"You can stop," Alejandro held up a hand and shook his head.

"What happened first?" Lucas asked.

"The Butcher. I got my first letter from him in January 2005. I thought it was a prank, but turned it over to the FBI anyway. They also thought it was a prank."

"After that?" Lucas continued.

"School shooting. Classes had ended for the day. There were about forty or fifty students in the parking lot. Someone drove by and opened fire. Over twenty were injured, including the guy that was supposed to give me a ride home that day, three were killed."

"When was that?" Michael asked.

"Oh, that I'll never forget. April 1, 2005, it was a Friday. That's why this guy was giving me a ride home. It was Malachi's birthday. He normally picked me up from school, but didn't because he was going out to party that night."

"Did they catch the shooter?" Xavier narrowed his eyes at me.

"No. I was the only one that could give a description of the car." I frowned at him.

"Could it be the same person?" Lucas asked.

"Who?" I asked back.

"The person in the car and our killer now?"

"Sure, in a world where coincidences are a dime a dozen, I suppose so. I can't imagine the drive by shooter and this methodical killer are one in the same."

Thirty-Seven

"Did you have enemies back then?" Lucas asked.

"I have never exactly been popular, but aside from a few serial killers and other violent criminals, I'd have to go with 'no'. I've never really had enemies. Nyleena and Malachi are both popular people, I was always sort of the odd person that hung around with them. So while I was never really well liked, people didn't detest me. Usually, people were too afraid to talk to me; they believed I was damaged goods. My town wasn't very big before I was kidnapped and killed my kidnapper, after that, it got even smaller."

"Why did you get an admirer?" Lucas continued to prod at me.

"I don't know exactly. I think I know. I think it was because of an incident in November 2004."

"What incident?"

"Police reported that on the night of 21 November 2004, a group of thieves broke into an occupied home. The homeowners, plus four minor children were inside at the time. Police went on to say that because of the bravery of the homeowners and one of the minors, the group was subdued and arrested. They have been linked to twenty other home invasions, including one that left a child in a coma and one where two people were shot." Michael answered.

"That would be the incident," I confirmed.

"Explain." Alejandro looked at me, his eyes darkening.

"I was at my friend's house, when three men broke in. They waved guns around and corralled Malachi,

212

myself, his two younger brothers and his parents in the living room. While two went and ransacked the house, one stayed to watch us. Malachi got loose first, dislocating his thumb to pull his hand free of the ropes. Once Malachi was free, the ropes that had bound both of us were loose enough to slide off my wrists with a little help from the corner of the coffee table. Malachi attacked the gunman. The gunman fired a shot and the other two came running. By then I had managed to use a pocket knife to cut his parents loose. Malachi was tall, even back then. He was already 6'10", wiry and psychotic as can be. Malachi subdued the gunman that had been watching us and then got hold of one of the others. I helped his dad with the last man while his mom called the police. Since I had been in the spotlight before, Malachi and his parents told them that I had been tied up with his younger brothers during the struggle. There was a cop or two that didn't believe them and it went into the report with a question mark. Malachi got a letter that January too, but not the same kind. Just definitely from the same person. Malachi became less interesting as he graduated high school, went to college and then went into law enforcement. My letters probably would have stopped too, but things kept happening to me."

"They didn't to Malachi?" Lucas raised an eyebrow.

"Oh no, they did, just not the same types of things. Serial killers seem to want to take me on. They seem to want to run away from Malachi. He's actually scarier than I am."

"I find that hard to believe," Xavier muttered.

"Trust me on this. If you ever run into Malachi on a dark street in the middle of the night, I wouldn't even wave. Just walk on past and hope for the best. I'd suggest turning around, but he'd probably take that as a sign of guilt or weakness and pounce on you."

"You've seen that side of Malachi?" Lucas asked.

"Malachi lives in the darkness. He always has. I may be his only true friend in the world. Everyone else is just a passing shadow. Ask him who his girlfriend all three years of high school was, he can't even remember her name."

"That is a bad sign." Lucas agreed.

"I once saw Malachi pick up a baseball bat and beat the hell out of a guy for slapping a girl that Malachi didn't know at a bar. His temper is a thing of nightmares. Even worse, it isn't really a temper because he doesn't experience anger. Only rage. He has three emotions, rage, euphoria and nothingness. About ninety percent of his life is spent feeling the nothingness. The other ten percent is scary. Even euphoria is strange on him. Malachi even..." I stopped and thought for a moment. Malachi. "In 2006, Malachi tracked down a guy."

"What?" Lucas asked me.

"In 2006, Malachi had a run in with a guy that he had purposely tracked down. Left him in a coma. However, it was self-defense, to some degree. Nyleena and I were out one night. We had gone to see a rock concert at the Blue Note. Great band, good show. Anyway, this guy there kept harassing us. When we went to leave, he followed us to Nyleena's car. Grabbed hold of her arm and jerked her around. Nyleena kneed him in the groin, but dropped the keys to her car in the process. I went and picked up the keys. When I did, this guy attacked Nyleena's car. He slashed her tire, took a knife to the door and scratched it up, broke out the driver's side window. He just lost it. Nyleena filed a report. The police took our statements and found the guy. He plead to something stupid, he got six months unsupervised probation. The next time we went to the Blue Note, Malachi insisted on joining us. Different concert, but the same jackass was there. He started harassing Nyleena again. Malachi told him to back off. He didn't. As we left, Malachi hung behind some. This frucking moron followed us to her car again. He began hurling obscenities at Nyleena, calling her a whore and a slut and all kinds of stupid shit. Then he punched her car. Malachi grabbed him, pulled him away. In his defense, he just tossed the guy away and told him to leave. By this time, we were gathering a crowd of onlookers. For some reason, that seemed to embolden this guy. He charged Malachi. Malachi punched him in the face. We all heard the guy's jaw shatter. He was too drunk or high to notice though. He charged Malachi again, this time with his knife drawn. Malachi put him in the hospital, in a coma. Malachi ended up getting a misdemeanor assault charge, but the prosecutor on the case didn't really want to press or file charges to begin with. The only reason he did was because Malachi got stitches and this asshole ended up in a coma. There were plenty of witnesses that said Malachi was being defensive, not aggressive. It went away a month later when Malachi turned 18."

"Why is that significant?" Alejandro asked.

"Because when Malachi shattered the guy's jaw with the first punch, he broke out all the teeth in the guy's mouth. I remember the guy spitting them out onto the ground. One had to be surgically removed from Malachi's hand as well."

"This guy still in a coma?"

"Yes." I said.

"Then how does that help us?" Alejandro frowned.

"Because the guy wasn't alone either night. He had a girl with him. Turned out to be his younger sister."

"Why would she hold what Malachi did against you?" Michael asked. I went out onto the balcony to smoke a cigarette.

215

Thirty-Eight

I finished my cigarette, dropping it into a mostly empty Coca-Cola can to keep from flicking it off the 7th floor balcony onto the passing crowds below. For another minute or so I stood there. I was debating with myself. How much could I tell them about Malachi?

"Remember I said that I might be Malachi's only friend?" I asked, coming back into the room.

"Yeah," Michael said.

"I think that's because he can only afford one friend. Malachi has his own unique code that he lives by. It doesn't make sense to anyone but him. One of those things is fierce loyalty. And he is, loyal, I mean, at least to me." I sat back down and looked at them.

"I met Malachi when I was in the first grade. I had just started at that particular school. It had been in session maybe two months. I know it was starting to get colder, but it wasn't the holiday season yet. It was recess. Our school had a big tree that we could play under. I sat under it every day and read a book at recess. That particular day, I was reading The Count of Monte Cristo. Only time I ever read it, didn't really enjoy it. Too much revenge for me. Anyway, some of the sixth graders came over and started picking on me. One of them grabbed the book and started tearing pages out. Malachi came over to see what the commotion was about.

"When he saw it, he stopped it. He got my book back and picked a fight with the sixth grader. Malachi was in fifth grade at the time. They both ended up suspended. As his parents were escorting him home, I happened to be in the hallway. I ran up and thanked him for not letting them destroy my book entirely. I have always been a bibliophile. It was the first time I saw Malachi smile. Anyway, I thought long and hard about how I could repay Malachi for helping me. When he returned to school the following week, I had a gift for him. It was a signed baseball. Nothing extraordinary, my brother had taken me out and helped me get it from some sports store in town. It cost me fifty dollars. I forgot to take the price tag off of it. I wrapped it up and gave it to him at recess his first day back from suspension.

"After that day, Malachi and I were thick as thieves. We went everywhere together. Malachi was popular, I wasn't. It didn't matter to him though that I preferred books to people. What did matter was that I had been so thankful for his help, that I had bought him something and let's face it, fifty bucks to a first grader is a ton of money. Shortly before Christmas that year, he and I were talking about how I could afford the baseball and I admitted that I had been saving up to buy a leather bound edition of Poe's complete works. I had been ten dollars short when I spent it all on his thank you present.

"Malachi has been my friend since then. As a result, he is fiercely protective of Nyleena and my mom. Not because he has any significant attachment to them, but because I do. A few years ago, when Nyleena had a contract taken out on her by some cartel she was prosecuting, Malachi asked to be put in charge of her security. He took a bullet for her. He also killed the would-be hit-man who had taken the contract. He doesn't do this for her. He does it because he can't bear to watch me lose her. When the press was hounding my mother after my brother did his thing, Malachi camped out at our house and escorted us to and from the car, made sure they couldn't get to her or me."

"Just like the jackass at the concert," Lucas said.

"Just like the jackass at the concert." I parroted and pursed my lips together. I rubbed both eyes.

"Ok, so why would this girl hold a grudge against you?" Michael repeated.

"Because Malachi could and would have killed the jackass, but I stopped it." I shook my head.

"And that matters?" Michael asked.

"It does considering the circumstances. Malachi reached a point where he couldn't stop himself. I saw it. I walked over and put my hand on his waist. He instantly stopped. It was like it brought him out of the calm. He dropped the guy, who was unconscious and leaned back against a car. He just stood there, waiting. The police were only a couple of blocks from us. They showed up and arrested Malachi. We all had to give statements at the scene. The guy's sister said..."

"Jessica Thompson, sister of the victim, age 19," Michael interrupted me. "She said the following in her statement. 'The girl with the assailant could have stopped the fight earlier. All she did was touch him and he stopped beating on my brother. Had she stepped in a few minutes earlier, my brother might not have lost his teeth, let alone all the other damage the maniac did to him. She should be arrested with him for not doing anything about it. She should have known my brother was not in his right mind and not let her goon beat him to a pulp."

"That would be correct. At the courthouse, during Malachi's sentencing, she threw a brick at me. She missed thankfully, but she still tried."

"The police report also notes that Malachi was sober and not on drugs, while Eric Thompson tested positive for PCP, LSD and alcohol. That's some combination. Tests conducted on his hair proved him to be a frequent user of PCP and LSD as well as cocaine." Everyone turned to look at me.

"Malachi took on this guy, bare handed and won?" Xavier said.

"Yes." I let out a breath I had been holding.

"That's sort of amazing and absolutely terrifying." Lucas commented.

"And the sister held Nyleena and me responsible for the beating her brother took."

Thirty-Nine

"Well, at least we know the importance of the teeth." Xavier gave the bag a look of disgust.

"I guess so. We also know that means The Butcher knows about the incident." I gave Lucas a look. "Malachi and I have always thought he might be law enforcement. Someone that knew my dad. Mainly because even when things didn't make it into the crime blotter, he seemed to know the details."

"We'll deal with your pseudo-serial killer later," Alejandro was glaring at Michael.

"I'm on it already," Michael waved him away. "Searching for Jessica Thompson, hometown, Columbia, Missouri."

"Well?" Alejandro asked after several minutes.

"Well, so far, I haven't found much after the incident. It appears that she dropped off the grid about six years ago. No credit cards, no background checks, nothing is popping on her social security number. Even if she changed her name, like our Dr. Cain here, her social would remain the same."

"People don't just disappear off the face of the planet," Alejandro snapped at him.

"They can, it just takes a lot of effort," Michael snapped back.

"Can you find her?" Alejandro turned all his attention to Michael. The weight of that gaze would have shriveled lesser men. Michael just shook his head at him and made a huffing noise.

"Why don't you go shoot something?" Michael dismissed him with the wave of a hand.

"We have to figure out why she would be doing this." Lucas interrupted them.

"Well, the women would all have Nyleena's body type." I pointed out. "She's not quite that tall, but she is taller than me by several inches."

"But they don't have her hair color or anything else that she has, so why these ten?" Lucas continued to press.

"At the time of the incident, Nyleena had poison green hair. She wore it well, surprisingly. Most women couldn't get away with poison green hair, but Nyleena has the pale skin for it. I would look like I had jaundice."

"That's your contribution?" Alejandro scoffed.

"What do you want me to say? I barely remember the girl. If you showed me her picture from back then, I probably wouldn't recognize it. I'm not as bad as Malachi, but there are some people gaps in my memory. This girl barely registered. She was there. Things have happened since."

"Malachi nearly kills her brother and you can't remember her face?" Alejandro made a noise deep in his throat.

"I remember her brother pretty vividly." I defended myself. "She was just there. She bitched that I didn't do anything to stop it, but she didn't either. If she hadn't told the police she was his sister, I would have thought she was just another bystander watching the action. Do you remember the face of every jacked up junkie you encounter?"

"I don't deal with many jacked up junkies," Alejandro told me.

"Fine, but don't crucify me just because of a memory gap. That was over ten years ago. There's been at least two serial killers and a serial rapist in my life during that time. For some reason, they made more of an impression."

"Found her. Sort of." Michael interrupted.

"What do you mean sort of?" Alejandro glared at me while talking to Michael.

"First, I couldn't get away from your attention and now I can't get it." Michael prodded our team leader. I didn't know Alejandro well enough to know how he would react.

His face changed. The scowl left. He turned to face Michael, all the malice gone from his posture.

"Here's the deal, she has two blips in her file. Both classes, both of them at the University of Washington. Both of them had Ace as the professor's assistant. She had changed her name. She is now using Jessica Welbourne. It appears she was married for a couple of years, then she just disappears again. Then she pops up at the University of Washington, she audits two classes, both of them under Ace and then she disappears again."

"Welbourne," I thought about it.

"Name ring a bell?" Lucas asked.

"Yes, but you don't want to know why." I told him.

"Why?" Alejandro asked.

"Nyleena is dating a guy whose last name is Welbourne. He's a doctor in Kansas City. I don't know if they are related or not."

"Smart money says there's a chance. How long have they been dating?" Alejandro asked.

"Dating may be too strong a word. They've been sleeping together for at least the last six years. I don't know much about him. I've met him a couple of times. I try not to get involved in that section of her life."

"Why?" Lucas asked.

"Uh, I attract serial criminals like honey attracts ants. She doesn't need me complicating her sex life." I said it as if it deserved a "duh" at the end. Lucas picked up on the unspoken ending and smiled at me.

"They could be related or it could be a massive coincidence." Xavier stated.

"We'll go with the assumption that they aren't coincidences," Alejandro was digging out his cell phone.

"Who is he calling?" I asked Lucas.

"My guess, the Federal Guard Apartments where Nyleena lives."

"You think Nyleena is in danger?" I frowned and pulled out my own cell phone.

"What are you doing?" Xavier asked.

"Calling the one person I know will keep her alive." I stepped out onto the balcony.

Forty

"Blake," Malachi answered on the second ring.

"Hey Malachi." I said quietly.

"How's the new gig?" He was grinning, I could tell over the phone.

"Unbelievable. I need you to do me a huge favor. Kidnap Nyleena and keep her in my apartment or your house until further notice."

"You say the most interesting things."

"Seriously, Malachi, our past or rather, your past is coming back to haunt us. Remember that guy, Thompson, from the KMFDM concert?"

"Yes."

"We are pretty sure his sister is our serial killer and she's torturing women who look like Nyleena. So, if you wouldn't mind, I'd like you to be the one to protect her. I'm sure the federal officers are good at their job, but this might be a special breed of crazy and I don't want to take any chances."

"And?"

"And the girl has the same last name as Nyleena's doctor friend. I'm sure it's just a coincidence, but..."

"Better safe than sorry." Malachi finished for me.

"Pretty much. I'm going to text Nyleena and tell her you are going to be her personal body guard. She'll be expecting you. How long?"

"If you can get Mr. Evil to pull some strings, I can be officially assigned to her in thirty minutes. If you can't, it might take as long as two hours."

"Mr. Evil?"

"Your boss, Alejandro from Hell."

"Not a fan?"

"Alejandro doesn't have fans. If you weren't as crazy as you are, I would suggest getting the hell out of there. However, since you aren't normal, I'm sure you'll be fine. Just make sure you sleep with a gun under your pillow and a dagger strapped to your leg when he's around. I'm not sure he'll kill you being a member of his team, but I've been wrong before."

"Encouraging."

"Alejandro doesn't like women. He really doesn't like women who are strong willed, quick witted and easy to fire off their mouths. You, my dear, are all three. Think of him as a Puritan, women should be seen and not heard, they certainly shouldn't have opinions and god forbid they know how to defend themselves."

"I've talked to him."

"And?"

"We agree that we aren't going to get along."

"Good to know, I'd prefer you survive the encounter. I like having you around. Now go talk to your boss and see what we can get done. Should I go to her office or the courthouse?"

"It's Sunday, she'll be in her office by now."

"Got it," Malachi hung up. I finished my cigarette.

"Can you arrange for Malachi to be on her security detail?" I asked Alejandro, who was already hanging up the phone.

"I did already," Alejandro informed me, a scowl set deep on his face.

"Good."

"SK knows us, might be related to Thompson disaster. Malachi headed your way." I texted to Nyleena. It took less than sixty seconds for her to respond.

"Thompson? Now? Why?"

"I don't know. Trust Malachi and don't kill him." I responded.

"Done," I said, looking up. "Had to warn Nyleena about...

"Ew, oh my God, that's just wrong and twisted and sick and now I know why she's a serial killer." Michael interrupted me with his exclamations.

"What?" Several of us said in unison.

"Poor Jessica had a tough run of it. She didn't get divorced, the marriage was annulled."

"Ok," I looked at him sideways.

"Jessica met Marcus Welbourne the summer Malachi jack hammered her brother. They dated for a year and then married. The Thompsons carry a rare genetic disorder that affects infants and causes high infant mortality rates. After the two married, well had been married for a year, they both went for DNA testing to see if he also carried the disorder and get an understanding of the chances of their child having it. The DNA test showed they were related, half-brother and sister to be exact. An investigation was done and it turns out that before her parents married, her father got a woman pregnant. They split up; she put the baby boy up for adoption. The baby was Marcus Welbourne."

"How long ago was that?" I asked.

"After the annulment, she completely disappears."

"That would be hard to live with." Lucas stated.

"True, but it isn't the first time it has happened. There are a few publicly known couples who are actually siblings or half-siblings and for whatever reason were unaware of it when they married. The most famous is in Germany." Xavier noted.

"Does that help?" Alejandro asked.

"No, just a bit of information," Xavier answered.

"If it isn't relevant, don't offer it up," Alejandro shook his head and muttered something under his breath.

"She appears on the roster of two of my classes?" I frowned.

"Yes, but no one seems to have seen or heard from her during that time. Her parents listed her as missing."

I sat and scanned my memory. If she just audited the class, she wouldn't have had to turn in homework or anything. I wouldn't have graded her papers; she wouldn't have made much of an impression. Lots of people had audited classes I had been involved with.

Then a really scary thought entered my mind. I frowned.

"You realize the Butcher knows who our serial killer is?" I asked everyone.

"Yes." Most agreed.

"That means he could be killing by proxy. Maybe that's what the letters are. Maybe he stalks serial killers and tells me about what they have done. Serial killing by proxy. That means he could save these women and he's not going to do it. Worse, he expects me to save them."

"I had already thought of that." Lucas sat down at the table next to me.

"Can we use that somehow?" I almost pleaded.

"Probably not, we would need more information about him. Information that we don't have."

"Shit. Ok then, let's work with what we know."

Forty-One

"What do we know?" Alejandro prodded.

"We know that Jessica has had a rough time of it since her brother's encounter with Malachi."

"Which seems to be a pattern with Malachi," Alejandro offered.

"I won't argue that. Anyway, she marries, finds out she has married her half-brother, goes off the deep end because now she has a brother she didn't know existed and one in a coma at a hospital. We know that our killer is torturing women based on a book that I own. However, Jessica has never been in my presence at a social function and I never took the book into my office at the university. This would suggest that she somehow managed to get into my apartment, look through the book without my noticing. Since I'm pretty keen at noticing when anything is out of place, that seems unlikely. I don't remember her from my classes and even though I'm bad with faces, you'd think I'd remember that. And now, she has disappeared which seems even more interesting and unlikely. We know Nyleena is 'dating' a guy named Al Welbourne, which is an odd coincidence. And our killer currently has 10 women in their possession that will all die very painful deaths. Oh and they use a hallucinogen to kidnap his victims. Anything else?" I asked

"Yes, it seems unlikely to be a woman." Lucas offered.

"Why?" I asked.

"How do you get a drugged woman into a Hanging Coffin without a lot of physical strength?" He cocked an eyebrow at me.

"Good point, but psychopaths are known to have more strength than the average person because their body..."

"I know that, but true psychopathic women are rare and I'm not going to place all my eggs into that basket."

"You think it could be a man?" I frowned.

"What about Marcus Welbourne. He marries, finds out he married his sister, then learns he has a brother that is in a coma and all because of the three of you. That would be a lot for a man to take in as well."

"Ok, I'll give you that." I sat back down.

"I can't find much on Marcus either. He has an adopted brother, no name listed though. Some petty crime before he turned 18. Looks like after 18 he became a model citizen, after the annulment, he dropped off the planet." Michael chirped.

"What if they are working together?" I offered.

"Killer couple?"

"Why not? They have disturbing history together."

"What makes one person break, doesn't necessarily make another," Lucas reminded me.

"True, but some people are just born broken, look at Malachi." I countered.

"You think Malachi was born that way?"

"I think Malachi and I were both born this way. I was crazy before I had a run in with Callow. Malachi was crazy when I met him in first grade. So, yeah, I think some of us are just born this way and considering the persistent increasing trend of dysfunction, I think there's a very good chance that we are now breeding psychotics who grow up to be serial killers."

"There isn't a genetic link."

"Yet, Lucas. You should add that to the end of your sentence. Remember about nine years ago the scientist that put forth the theory that serial killers were an evolutionary step in mankind's history?"

"The one that was then killed by said study group?"

"Yes, that one. I met her once; we debated if it was a new thing or a sign of devolution. She believed that it was devolution at work and that most hunter/gatherer tribes were either sociopathic or psychopathic. She also believed it was genetic because it did seem to run in families and nature explained situations like Malachi better than nurture especially since his brothers are fine."

"This isn't helpful," Alejandro interrupted us.

"Actually, it is," Lucas took a moment to stare off into space.

"How?" Alejandro asked.

"Because we've been missing the elephant in the room," Lucas suddenly focused all his attention on me, "while we can't prove it is genetic, we already know that violent people attract other violent people. If you knew your brother was a PCP addict, would you go out with him? No, because his behavior would be violent and unpredictable with no real way to estimate when that violence would turn on you. However, looking at Ace and Malachi, she goes out with Malachi and Malachi with her, why? Because they know when things get hairy, they are just crazy enough to deal with each other's madness. If Jessica knew she was just as dangerous and violent as her junkie brother, he wouldn't scare her. She then takes up with Marcus Welbourne, petty criminal until he becomes an adult. Probably damaged goods and probably some history of violence. He scares her about as much as a serial killer scares Ace, meaning none. She can act and react to his violence accordingly. Most psychologists believe that for whatever reason, violence doesn't beget violence, it attracts it. Especially in our day and age. Serial killers follow Ace home because they sense there is something off about her, but they don't know what, they just know they find it attractive. Ace understands what they sense and lures them in. You get clash of the Titans at that point. Most people look at it like Ace is bruised and beaten at the end, but the truth is, she isn't defeated. At least, not yet."

"I hadn't considered that," I admitted. "I wouldn't go out with my junkie brother."

"Yes you would, but only to corral him. Jessica did nothing to break up the fight. Most would think it was because she was scared to intervene. Two men, one of them high, going at it like enraged bears. But what if she didn't intervene for the same reason Ace didn't intervene? What if she stood on the sidelines and watched the blood flow because she enjoyed it?"

"I didn't let it happen because I enjoyed it." I defended myself, "I just knew better. There is a point of balance in Malachi and stopping it before the balance tips, is dangerous. He is still emotional or as emotional as Malachi gets until the balance tips. I had to wait for him to enter his calm state. Once he did, I broke it up."

"Fine," Lucas frowned at me, "that isn't the point. The point is, most women would not stand idly by and watch their brother get their ass kicked unless they were terrified or wanted to watch it happen. Since there is no mention of Jessica being hysterical when the police arrived, I find the terrified theory, hard to believe."

Forty-Two

"Now our theory is psychotic girl meets psychotic boy, they marry and when the dust settles and they find out they are actually half-siblings and they go together over the deep end. They begin planning a series of crimes that are bound to get my attention. Once they have it, they also have to get Malachi and Nyleena's attention, because they are as responsible as I am. There is just one problem. They don't have Malachi or Nyleena's attention yet. Instead, they get The Butcher's attention. Since he doesn't like competition, he sends me a couple of clues and now we have a protective detail on Nyleena with Malachi at the helm."

"Hm," Lucas frowned.

"Which is exactly how to get the attention of Malachi and Nyleena," I rolled my eyes.

"Yes, I think they wanted the protective detail on the two of them, I don't think this is how they planned to get it though. I think this next round of bodies was supposed to be the catalyst for it. Actually, I think the last round of bodies was supposed to be the catalyst, but it was interrupted. They deviated from the original killings with the Scavenger's Daughter because it wasn't a plate in the book. I've been thinking about that. I can't see any reason to copy plates from a book when there are hundreds of books on torture. Meaning they copied it because it was in your library and looked well used," Lucas said.

"Speaking of the plates in that book," I shook my head. "There are far worse tortures described in that book, some in great detail. Why pick the plates and not something far worse?"

"Because they don't read German," Xavier answered almost before I had finished the question.

"Then why deviate?" I asked.

"You don't read German, but you know the book is on torture. You also know that one of your targets has used it several times as reference material. You pick out a few plates and copy them. You get one target's attention. You deviate. You grab for something else. In this case, the Scavenger's Daughter. Something was supposed to grab one of the other target's attention. But it backfires, for whatever reason; you can't leave your clue. You grab ten more women to leave the message."

"Shit," I looked at the floor. "The Scavenger's Daughter was meant to get my attention focused on Malachi."

"Why?"

"The first serial killer case that he worked, the bodies were put into a trash compactor. Same technique, just more modern equipment. That's why the teeth were old. It was a way to show me that a different mechanism can be used with the same results. Old teeth v. new teeth. Trash compactor v. Scavenger's Daughter."

"Is this Butcher going to be a problem on all our cases?" Alejandro scowled.

"Unlikely. He got involved with this one because it is directly aimed at two of his favorite things, Malachi and Ace. It also let him show off, 'I know the killers. I know where you are.' He was taunting us while helping us." Lucas commented.

"Just crushing a few women wouldn't bring Malachi into a case, no matter how much it reminded you of his first one. Just like the symbols were missing, there was something else they were supposed to do and didn't get the chance. Something that would specifically shout

'Malachi Blake needs to be involved.'" Xavier crossed his arms over his chest.

"Something that will probably turn up if we don't find the victims before they are killed," Lucas added.

"Doing anything that gets Malachi's attention is dangerous at best." I pointed out.

"You know that, we know that, but do they know that? They probably think it's two against one, they could take him." Michael added.

"No, Jessica would know that she couldn't. Like me, she would have seen the point where emotion turned to calm and life meant nothing to him."

"How can you be so sure?" Alejandro asked. I frowned at him.

"Because Ace does it from time to time, even the interviewee at the prison commented on it being scary," Lucas answered for me. "Anyone who has spent more than a second staring into the depths of that darkness would know better and Malachi's would be much worse."

"Imagine the Portal to Hell reflected on someone's face." I looked at Alejandro. "He smiles when he reaches that point, it isn't a happy smile."

"We don't have time to debate how scary Malachi is," Michael interrupted us.

"Very true, we'll just go with he's very scary," I finished and looked back at Lucas.

"I can only think of a few ways to guarantee Malachi would get involved. Me, his brothers, Nyleena, his mother, my mother. I'm not sure it would faze him if it was his father."

"What about ex-girlfriends?" Xavier asked.

"Unlikely he would remember them, once they are gone; they are well and truly gone. Malachi doesn't form emotional attachments, so everyone, even the women he sleeps with are background noise."

"You both live in lonely worlds." Lucas looked at Xavier. "Why did you mention ex-girlfriends?"

"Because the Chicago police just found a picture of Malachi in one of the new victims' in her apartment."

"Name?" I asked.

"Trisha North." Xavier answered, looking at his phone.

"Trish, wow, I haven't seen her in ages. They dated..." I sighed heavily.

"What, Ace?" Lucas asked.

"They were dating when Malachi went postal on Jessica Thompson's brother."

"You remember Malachi's ex-girlfriends?" Xavier tilted his head sideways.

"Most of them are very nice to me. They want me to like them. Trish was special though. I think Malachi did her wrong. We kept in touch for a year or two after they broke up. Then she got married, had a kid, got divorced, the child died..."

"Give her a list of all the victims," Lucas interrupted me.

"Why?"

"Find any more of Malachi's girlfriends on it?" Lucas said as he handed me a print-out.

I scanned through the names. One jumped out. She had been placed in the Scavenger's Daughter, Anna Rochelle. I sighed and pointed to it.

"Who is she?" Xavier asked.

"She was nice enough, never took a shine to me, but I understand that. She cheated on Malachi, not that I hold that against her, he isn't exactly a model of fidelity and he's emotionally distant even at the best of times. When he dies, women will come from miles around to dance on his grave. However, she didn't live in Chicago."

"No, she lived in Bloomington Indiana." Lucas frowned.

"She was a professor at the university there." I filled in more information.

"How did her and Malachi meet?" Alejandro asked.

"Not a clue, but at the time they met, she was living in St. Louis Missouri." I told him. "With Malachi, it could have been a trip to Six Flags or in a car accident or a talk he gave at SLU. Malachi isn't a dummy either. Universities beg him to give guest lectures on social matters."

"I forgot about his degree in Sociology," Lucas said.

"Not just that, he only got his bachelor's, but he got an honorary doctorate from SLU in Sociology after he wrote a paper that made it not only into the FBI's profiling report, but into a major scientific journal. I forget which one. Anyway, I believe Anna was his last girlfriend. It has been a few years since he has attempted to date."

Forty-Three

"What would get Nyleena's attention?" Alejandro looked at me.

"A nuclear bomb?" I suggested.

"This isn't time for fun and games," Alejandro scolded.

"That's the problem, I don't know. She doesn't have the issues that Malachi and I have. Nyleena is a mostly normal, well-adjusted human being. She's taken on the Cartels, gun runners, serial killers, mass murderers and human trafficking. Killing anyone she knew could wake her up to a brutal reality or she might just shake it off because it comes with the territory. She chooses to keep a best friend whom death follows around like plague. She decided a long time ago that she could tolerate Malachi and The Butcher to be friends with me. So, I just don't know what would and wouldn't bring her running."

"If I wanted to ensure I had Nyleena and Malachi's attention, I'd kidnap you." Lucas made this sound very matter of fact.

"I'm not going to fit into the Hanging Coffins, unless they designed one for me and I'm not a good victim. Getting a hold of me is a battle in itself. I'm not above being kidnapped, but I don't think two psychopaths could do it and while they may not know it, I do have that very bizarre pseudo-serial killer watching me. I don't think he wants me dead. They'd have to contend with him as well."

"We could use you as bait then." Alejandro suggested.

"I don't think that works," I frowned. "Kidnapping me gets them Nyleena and Malachi's attention. Kidnapping Nyleena does the same thing and she would fit in the Hanging Coffins and doesn't have a serial killing stalker. Getting past Malachi might be an issue though. What do they do for the three days?"

"Huh?" Xavier asked.

"They keep them alive for three days. Why? Doesn't that strike anyone else as odd? Especially since they aren't physically torturing them or raping them? Are they psychologically torturing them for three days? If so, why? To what purpose? That would make the deaths, even the most painful of them, seem like a release, not a punishment. So what the hell are they doing with them for three days?"

"This is like the Maidens." Lucas shot me a warning glare.

"A bit, yes, but we found stuff out about the maidens. Might find out more stuff from the maidens." I quipped.

"What we discovered from the maidens was pretty unhelpful," Michael added.

"True, to some degree, it was pointless. However, it helped me realize that these things were planned long before they happened. It made Lucas re-evaluate some of his theories."

"That's true. We think the victims are planned, not random. Two people would be better than one, especially at grabbing ten women in a single night. We know they have back-up women just in case something happens to their first ones. We know they plan far ahead."

"The next torture device is going to be the same; they are going to use the Scavenger's Daughter on these ten." I closed my eyes.

"But we have their hoop thingy," Xavier commented.

"No we have a hoop thingy. Surely they had more than one made. If they can afford five Iron Maidens, they can afford more than one Scavenger's Daughter. How are they getting the money for these things if they are off the grid? How many ways can you make non-traceable money?"

"Not many; drugs, prostitution, robbery, burglary, illegal gambling," Lucas started listing.

"I think we can ignore prostitution and illegal gambling." I told them.

"Why?" Alejandro asked.

"Because it is too chincy. There's too much that is left to chance. What if Jessica were arrested for prostitution? What if they lost all their money gambling? What if they were accused of cheating in some backroom of a Russian club? These are not risks the two of them are going to take. It would negate all the planning," Lucas said.

"That leaves drugs, robbery, burglary and..." I started listing things.

"The internet," Michael suddenly perked up. "Far easier to run a porn site on the internet and if you are routing it through multiple servers, it becomes harder to trace and porn is legal. However, we are talking about sums that would require hundreds of thousands of dollars."

"And you can't make that off internet porn?" I frowned at him.

"You could, but the IRS would be all over it, regardless of how many servers in different countries it was routed. Besides, with all the new child porn regulations in place, it is becoming harder and harder."

"Poor word choice," Lucas chided him.

"Sorry, it is becoming more difficult to run internet porn sites anonymously," Michael said.

"So we are back to burglary and robbery," I said.

"Yep," Lucas seemed to be thinking.

"What?" I asked him.

"They are kidnapping ten women at a time; surely some of those ten have money and things at their houses. The rest could be supplemented with other burglaries and robberies," Lucas said.

"And muggings," I suggested, finding the idea ridiculous, "you can't make a couple hundred thousand a year off burglary."

"No, no you can't," he deflated like a balloon, looking smaller. His entire frame seemed to shrink.

"Other ways to make that kind of money?" I asked.

"Drugs." Xavier suggested.

"Again, that seems rather chincy. Too many variables that you can't control. Same with weapons dealing. But maidens aren't cheap," I cocked my head to the side.

"Trust funds?" Lucas asked.

"Not that I can see." Michael answered, "of course, if they did have trust funds they emptied at 21, they might have disappeared. I'll do more digging into their backgrounds."

"Jessica didn't seem like the trust fund type," I sighed again.

"What is it?" Lucas asked me.

"I feel like I can't see the trees for the forest." I told him.

"Normally it is the big picture that gets missed, not the details," he counseled.

"That's just it. I can't seem to find the details. I have the big picture; Jessica and Marcus take revenge for their brother. They used the *Book of Torture* to lure me in. They are killing off Malachi's ex-girlfriends, but that's a never-ending list and won't have much impact on Malachi. It will bother me more than him. They may or may not go after myself or Nyleena; either would strike me as poorly thought out, which is the exact opposite of what they have been doing. They are buying incredibly expensive replicas of torture devices but they don't seem to have any money coming in. Hell, they don't seem to exist. I guess they could be day-laborers, working with illegals, but that wouldn't make them enough money. We're still missing something, something important. Something that I can't grasp."

"Maybe it's lack of sleep," Michael chimed in, his fingers working frantically over his keyboard.

"I've gone days without sleep. It starts to bother me after about 48 hours. I've slept in the past 48. That rules out sleep deprivation."

"Well, we need to figure something out because while we sit here spinning our wheels, those women get closer to dying," Alejandro suddenly became livid. His face went red with rage. Sweat beaded on his brow. I frowned at him, he reminded me of something.

"Get out," I told him quietly. "And so help me god, if you ever break down another door that I'm on the other side of, I'll put a bullet into your brain."

The calm washed over me. I felt myself slide into that special place where no emotion filtered through. Alejandro moved closer to me.

"Out Alejandro," I said it calmly, felt myself begin to reach for a knife I had strapped to my wrist.

"You will not order..."

"You will not stand here, hulking out on me and expect me to back down. I said to get out. I meant it."

Alejandro looked at me for a couple more heartbeats. He snarled, turned and left.

Forty-Four

"What was that?" Michael asked after the room had settled down.

"Call the front desk and make sure Alejandro arranged to have me moved to a new room." I told him.

"Everything all right?" Michael had stopped typing.

"Our fearless leader has an issue, one that is going to be a problem giving his opinion on women." I looked at Lucas. Lucas nodded once.

"Just call them, Michael," Xavier agreed.

"Not until someone tells me what is going on."

"Alejandro isn't naturally that big, he's using steroids. I've encountered 'Roid Rage' once or twice before; it isn't normally a problem for me. Plus, he doesn't like women, especially women like me, women who think and talk and have opinions. So when we are together and he flies into a rage, I'm going to be the target of his abuse. I refuse to be his victim. He can battle that demon all on his own. He also has a drinking problem." I told Michael.

"Oh, yeah, I'll call the front desk," Michael picked up the phone in my room.

"On second thought, don't bother," Lucas grabbed my bag and started shoving my clothes into it. "Michael, you and Xavier are going to bunk up. I'll share with Ace."

"Great, kicking me out of my own room," Xavier pretended to sulk.

"At least for now." Lucas looked at him.

"I know he juiced not long ago, probably to keep himself awake while we investigated." Xavier shook his head. "One day, he's really going to lose it and someone is going to have to kill him."

"If we are taking bets, I put money on Malachi," I picked up the soda I was drinking and followed them all down the hall.

We entered Lucas's room. He tossed my bag down on the bed and took a seat at the table. I sat down on the bed. Watching Lucas and Xavier move around proved that sitting on the bed wasn't practical. The bed was springy and seemed to bounce each time I moved my head to follow them.

"Back to what you were saying." Xavier said, picking up his own duffle bag.

"Wow, this room looks a lot different than mine," I commented. The two double beds were arranged on one wall, with the TV and dresser across from it. There the similarity stopped. Their table was bigger. They had a mini-fridge and a microwave. Even their bathroom looked bigger and there was a small recliner. I moved from the bed, taking a seat in the chair. It fit like I was Goldilocks.

"Done?" Xavier asked, Michael unpacking his computer next to him.

"Yep, I'm good now." I relaxed a little. The room seemed safer suddenly.

"Now, what were you saying about the three days? Does it mean anything to you?" Lucas continued unabated.

"I don't know, it just seems like an odd length of time to keep anyone. Three days. Why keep someone three days if you aren't going to torture them? And our victims do not seem to have been physically tortured in the three days. Psychologically torturing them would work, but that makes death a release, not another form of torture."

"You don't think they are psychologically torturing them during those three days?" Xavier asked.

"Would you? Honestly? You want the full weight and horror of their death to weigh upon them. You show them the device or describe it and then wait three days. Ok, I can grasp that. But these are people. What do they do for the three days? Do they listen to their captives plead, beg and scream for three days? That seems more like torturing the torturer. A couple of hours of it, maybe, but three full days? Doesn't that seem extreme? By the end of the third day, the captives are just grateful that the wait is over and they can finally die. Also, that's a long time to leave someone in a Hanging Coffin. They aren't fool-proof, nothing is after three days. I can gross you out with some stories about what the human body can do to metal."

"You're talking about acid in urine and bacteria in feces," Xavier said.

"Not to mention bile," I agreed.

"The Hanging Coffins have to be cleaned after each event," Xavier countered.

"That's true, but how much acid can metal take? Iron begins to corrode fast. Start pouring stomach acid on it and it goes that much faster. Each of these coffins has now housed at least three women. I know I pee a lot in three days. If I was terrified for three days, it would be much worse. The reality of the situation, even in the Middle Ages, was that Hanging Coffins were meant to be displayed and the victim was left to be turned into something subhuman, but you certainly didn't walk under them."

"Stomach acid is a mild sulfuric acid," Xavier looked thoughtful.

"My point exactly. Sulfuric acid is hard on organic material and metals. Look at common household products that use it. Like..." I thought for a moment, "drain cleaner. It can strip the finish off of porcelain, ceramics and it corrodes metal. Add to it that sulfuric acid is one of the harder acids to neutralize. It takes a lot of other materials mixed with it to bring down the acidity. Still drain cleaner is more concentrated than stomach acid, but on raw iron..."

"And we know that they are raw iron," Michael hastily jumped into the conversation.

"Raw iron is porous." I reminded them.

"Easier to succumb to bacteria and acids," Xavier agreed.

"That becomes a risk factor for them. They have to know this or if not, they should have researched it better. There are stories of people getting stuck in Hanging Coffins and asphyxiating from the floor falling out of them."

"We've used iron for centuries," Michael countered.

"Yes, but in things. We moved out of the Iron Age for a reason. The tensile strength of iron is great, but it's corrode rate is terrible. It's porous, which means anything from weather to dirty air to human touch breaks it down just that much faster. Ten Hanging Coffins, made of raw iron is not only expensive but terribly impractical."

"You just run from detail to detail." Lucas smiled at me. "Why?"

"Because every time I think of one thing, another pops into my head."

"Trees for the forest," he mimicked.

"Pretty much," I stepped out to the balcony.

Forty-Five

The day was ending. Commuters were filling the streets again. I watched them scurry to and fro. Their coats were turned up against the cold winds that blew off Lake Michigan. Snow flurries were beginning. People with hats and gloves were pulling them tighter. Winter was about to descend upon Chicago with a vengeance and fury, encouraged by arctic winds coming from Canada and sweeping across the Great Lakes.

Tomorrow or the next day, there would be real snow. Today flurries and sleet. You could feel it in the air. The threat of snow was oppressive.

The pieces almost fit together, but not exactly. It wasn't just that we were missing a few key pieces; it was that the pieces we had seemed to have slightly different size connectors. I clung to the thought and tried to smooth it out, figure out what was wrong with them.

Below me, an El-Train screamed to a halt. Indistinct talking filtered up to me. The muffled sounds of thousands of footsteps drifted with the voices.

"You'll freeze on this balcony without a coat. It isn't as sheltered as yours," Xavier wrapped a jacket around me.

"Look at them. All those people. All of them oblivious to us. We stand up here, trying to figure out where to look for serial killers and missing women and they go about their lives like it isn't happening."

"That's because for them, it isn't. It isn't their family or friends that are missing. They don't know anything about the serial killer except what they see in the news or read about in the paper and that isn't very much. They continue forward. Tomorrow they will wake up and start the routine over, the same as they have every day for the last year and the same as they will start everyday for the next year. In their world, we exist, but only as background noise."

"We're still missing something, something big and important. Something that keeps everything from coming into full focus." I turned to face him as I finished the cigarette.

"I know. The answers don't seem to be on the bodies or in the devices or in your past either."

"Where do we look for it then?"

"That's too philosophical for me." He shook his head and took the butt from me. He dropped it in a soda bottle. "I didn't think sociopaths got depressed."

"I'm not depressed, I'm irritated."

"I can't imagine what you're like when you are mad then," Xavier smiled and dragged me back into the room.

"Ace is still hung up on what we're missing." Xavier said as I closed the balcony door.

"Why?" Lucas asked.

"Because I think that is where the answer lies. You don't become an expert on torture in a few days. Where are they getting their information? There isn't exactly a 'how to' manual or a 'torture for dummies' guide."

"Yes there is," Michael looked at me. "You wrote one."

"No, I wrote a scholarly thesis on it. It's not a 'how to' manual."

"But you were turning it into a book for the layman, yes?" Michael pressed.

"Yes."

"In it, you had to go into details about some of the lesser known methods."

"How do you know?" I frowned at him.

"Because I hacked your computer and have it." He smiled back.

"That's just scary."

"True, but you have good security. It's very unlikely you've been hacked before. Anyway, I'm looking at your book and every torture device, including the Scavenger's Daughter, has a lot of detail," Michael said.

"Who knows you are writing the book?" Lucas asked.

"My publisher, my thesis advisor, Nyleena and Malachi. I'm sure The Butcher knows, but he hasn't said anything about it."

"Seriously, could it be your serial killing stalker?" Michael asked.

"Unlikely," Lucas dismissed Michael's question. "Her serial killing stalker is about terrorizing her, which he doesn't get, so he continues to press her buttons to see what she reacts to. This isn't his thing. If he was going to start killing to do more than terrorize her, he'd have a much different method. He'd probably be a Jack the Ripper copy-cat. Back to her book though."

"It does go into some pretty gruesome detail," I admitted. "Everyone loves a horror story, but it's still in draft version. Nyleena has a copy. Malachi has a copy. My publisher doesn't. My thesis advisor doesn't."

"Both live in secure areas," Xavier frowned.

"Yes they do," I frowned with him.

"But Nyleena has a boyfriend." Lucas chirped.

"She has an insignificant other, not the same thing. She wouldn't show him a copy of it."

"What if he stole a copy of it. You admit that you don't know his first name. Why?" Lucas prodded.

"I do know his first name, it's Al." I reminded him.

"Oh, well. Michael, see if Al and Marcus are related or if it is just a coincidence," Lucas shrugged.

"On it," Michael's fingers began to move swiftly over the keyboard again.

"Why didn't we do that earlier?" I asked.

"Because Alejandro had a moment." Lucas answered.

"Why is he the boss?"

"No one really wants the job. He isn't the first we've had in three years. Hell, even your buddy was approached about it and declined it. Our supervisors have short life expectancies." Xavier informed me.

"Alejandro's doing good at five months," Lucas agreed. "He's outlived the last one by a month and a half."

"You telling me the position is cursed?" I gave him a sideways smile.

"Something like that," Xavier muttered. "When we do capture a serial killer, the supervisor does all the interviews and things. Since we have a high capture rate, this makes the supervisor a target. So no one ever wants the job. It is usually the last stop on your way down in the Marshals Service."

"One has quit," Lucas added cheerily.

"How many have you had?" I asked skeptically.

"With Alejandro, we've had seven in the three years we've been up and running." Michael said his fingers still moving over the keyboard.

Forty-Six

Michael frowned at his laptop. He looked up at me. He looked back down at the computer. For a moment, he reminded me of a bobble-head doll. He looked back up at me.

"What is it, Michael?" I snapped at him.

"Well, I couldn't find an Al, Allen, Albert, or Alfred with a medical license. I did find a Marcus Alfred Welbourne with a medical license."

The world swam for a moment. I shook my head. He was in Nyleena's apartment when I left for this trip. Would he have had the time?

"Tell me you're joking?" My throat felt dry.

"No, I'm not."

"He was in Nyleena's apartment when I left," I sat down. "She has this thing though, she hates when they spend the night, so she came downstairs and slept in my apartment until he left. She was incredibly drunk. I mean just hammered. She would have wandered off a cliff if I had told her it was the way to the bedroom."

"The thing is the marriage certificate has his middle name listed as Jeffery."

I thought for a moment. My head uplifted, my eyes staring at a spot on the wall. The wallpaper trim was done in reds and oranges. The design had no real shape; the mind searched for a pattern but failed to come up with one.

"Multiple middle names?" I asked.

"What do you mean?" Xavier asked.

"I mean that sometimes when you have multiple middle names, they will only put the first one on a document. Or clerical error. I have a friend whose passport has her middle name listed as 'Preator', but it is actually her maiden name. However, because of the error, she eventually changed her middle name to Preator instead of what it was."

"You have friends?" Lucas raised an eyebrow.

"She was actually a professor I had at the University of Michigan. I tutored several of her students."

"He doesn't have the same social security number." Michael offered.

"Hm," Lucas frowned at him, "there is a way to get your social changed."

"Witness protection?" I asked.

"That would be a really good way, but no. If you steal an identity," Michael grimaced. "He would have had to steal the identity after Welbourne married Jessica."

"If Jessica helped, it would be easy." Lucas shook his head.

"The concept makes my head hurt," I told them.

"I'll explain..."

"Please don't, it is already complicated enough. I get it, but it means we are missing a body. Where is the real Marcus Welbourne if he isn't sleeping with my cousin?"

"Good question," Lucas answered.

"Yep and I'm open to suggestions. Are all your cases this complicated?"

"You're familiar with Occam's Razor?" Xavier asked.

"Of course," I frowned at him.

"Toss it out the window."

"I like Occam's Razor." I told him.

"Yes, but in our line of work, it is usually the opposite. The weirder the theory, the more probable it is correct."

251

"That's not exactly correct," Lucas gave him a look. "We theorize until we get a better theory or another piece to work from. At the moment, it seems likely that Jessica and another are our serial killers. The coincidence of Marcus Alfred Welbourne being Marcus Jeffrey Welbourne is a pretty big coincidence. So we work with the theory that they are one in the same. That begs the question: is Al Welbourne real or is he someone else? Since he is a doctor who is also half-siblings with Jessica, it seems likely that he is real. But that doesn't mean we can't discount the theory that Jessica replaced the real Marcus with a different psychopath. Someone she could control. Being a doctor would explain where they are getting the money from. It would be even better if he were a judge or an FBI agent, but a doctor gets paid pretty well too."

"And the different socials?" I dreaded asking.

"That lends credence to the theory it is a stolen identity." Lucas stopped to look at Michael who had started making guttural noises from his spot at his computer.

"What?" He finally snapped at the younger man.

"Uh, it's the same social. He inverted it on his employment forms."

"Oh god," I moaned. "My cousin is fucking a serial killer."

"In her defense, she doesn't know he's a serial killer." Xavier grinned.

"Not helpful," I scowled at him.

"And he's in Chicago." Michael added.

"Well, that's something, I suppose." I grabbed my cell phone.

"Aislinn?" Nyleena's voice came over the receiver on the third ring.

"Tell me you are still in Missouri and that you are with Malachi." I sighed.

"I am in Missouri, but not by choice. Al asked me to go to Chicago with him, but then Malachi showed up and busted it up, told me I was being held in protective custody, but no one will tell me why." She sounded pissed.

"You're sleeping with a serial killer," I told her, "actually, a suspected serial killer who is currently operating in Chicago. You cannot call him about it. Let's just say, you are probably the target and it would be best if you didn't contact him anytime soon or take his calls."

"What?" The anger drained from her voice, replaced by something else.

"Al Welbourne is really Marcus Alfred Welbourne, half-brother of Jessica Thompson. We think they are killing women who look an awful lot like you and we think they have gotten access to information through you. Have you shown Al my thesis?"

"Yes, of course, I was so surprised when you gave me the draft of the manuscript that I showed it to him ages ago."

"Define ages?"

"When you first sent it to me."

"So, years actually. Was he ever in your house when you had a copy of my book on torture?"

"Of course."

"Ok, found the pieces. Thanks, listen to Malachi, I'll be back when I can."

I hung up on her before she could pump me for more information. Malachi was about to catch hell, but that was Malachi's problem. Mine was catching our serial killers.

"Found what pieces?" Lucas asked.

"Nyleena is the link. When I first wrote my dissertation, it turned itself into a book. I gave it to her to edit down. It read even more like a how to manual on torture in the Middle Ages. She also speaks German; it is our code language and she has borrowed my book on torture a few times when putting together cases against modern day torturers. Al Welbourne had access to all that information, plus whatever info he wanted on me, Nyleena and Malachi."

"Found the trees?" Lucas asked.

"Sadly and Nyleena is terrified of rats. Al asked her to come to Chicago with him. Malachi showed up in time to stop it. I'm terrified of being burned alive."

"And he knows this?"

"I imagine he does."

Forty-Seven

Ignoring the rest of the inhabitants in the room, I tossed myself onto what was obviously Lucas's bed. I had considered the one Xavier was about to vacate, but I wasn't entirely sure how often he showered yet. I closed my eyes.

Instantly, my mind started to whirl. The thoughts danced as the neurons fired. Nyleena was the link. How could we have missed that? That brought the dagger to the forefront of my thoughts.

Suddenly, it hit me. Some years ago, there had been a replica set of eight. Three had been stone blades, one silver, one gold-plated, one bronze, one carbon steel and one with a hook. Each was a ceremonial dagger from some point in history. I had wanted the one with a hook and the one made of bronze. The hooked end dagger had been a Thugee Cult replica. The bronze had been an accompaniment to the Brazen Bull ceremony.

I sighed. The other six. Nyleena had taken one of the stone daggers and one that was gold plated. Malachi had taken the other two stone daggers. The last two, I had left at my mother's house. The carbon steel had been a modern piece, based on a German SS dagger from World War II. I hadn't seen or even thought of it in years. That was the one they had found. The lightning bolt SS design had been chipped off, hence the complete lack of recognition.

If I opened my eyes now, I would have to explain it to them. I kept them closed. When was the last time I had slept? How many hours had it been? How had they gotten into my mother's house and what was I going to do about that?

"I know about the dagger," I said.

"Really? Memory flash?" Lucas asked.

"Pretty much. I bought a set of eight long before I went to college. Nyleena has two. Malachi has two. My mom had two. I had two."

"You said had, not has on the last two." Lucas picked up on the past tense.

"One was a bronze dagger; it sits in an evidence box in Michigan. I had it once, I have it no more. I'm guessing the same is true of one of my mother's. There was an SS replica in the set. I didn't want it. Neither did the others, so we just put it away at my mother's house. Shortly after, she put both on display in her living room. Just to be different I think. One was the SS dagger. I didn't recognize it because the stylized SS wasn't on it, but it is definitely the same design of dagger. Since it has my fingerprints, I can only guess that they have been in my mother's house. Which is a serious problem."

"Yes, it is. Would Nyleena have taken him over there?" Lucas probed.

"No, Nyleena keeps her personal life personal. She doesn't even tell her parents about Dr. Welbourne. She wouldn't have taken him to my mother's. That means they know who my mother is and where she lives."

"I'll scramble someone over there," Xavier was already digging out his cell phone.

"Tell them to get Malachi and Nyleena to meet her somewhere and they can all go back to Malachi's house."

"That's a lot of work for Malachi." Lucas commented as Xavier spoke into the phone.

"Maybe, but it would be a labor of love. If Malachi is capable of such emotion, he has it for my mother."

"Romantic?" Lucas questioned.

"Definitely not. She doesn't question his personality disorder; she accepts it, like she accepts mine and thinks nothing of it. For that, Malachi may love her like he would his own mother, if he had that sort of attachment with his own mother."

"He doesn't?" Lucas prodded.

"No, no he doesn't. For either of his parents. He respects them to some degree, but familial love isn't part of their relationship. He feels they lost that..." I stopped myself. "That is his story to tell, not mine."

"I understand," Lucas made a noise. I finally opened my eyes to look at him.

His face was set hard. His eyes barely open. His lips partially parted.

"When was the last time you slept?" I asked him.

"It's been a while," Lucas admitted.

"Come on, crawl in, we'll nap together. I could use one."

"We still have Michael and Xavier." Lucas said.

"True, but I'm sure Michael has computer things to do and Xavier looks like hell, he probably hasn't had much sleep either. He can take the other bed. When he gets up, I'll have housekeeping come replace the sheets so I can sleep in it later."

"I heard that," Xavier said quietly, covering the mouthpiece on the phone.

"You'd share with me over Xavier?" Lucas opened his eyes fully.

"Of course, you're much safer than Xavier and cleaner." I closed my eyes again and yawned. Sleep was rushing at me.

In my dream, the Iron Maidens stood in a line. They were in a field of thistle. Their doors open, blood dripping down the spikes, pooling around the bases. It was dark with a full moon casting the only light on the field. There were no trees, just thistle as far as the eye could see and those maidens.

I walked towards them, fearing what I might find when I arrived. I expected to see Malachi and Nyleena in front of them. There were no bodies. Just the maidens and the moonlight.

Somewhere behind me, I heard feet scamper. I turned to see the thistle rustling. Several small things were running through the thistle. I didn't have to see them to know they were rats. I looked around some more, expecting to see a Brazen Bull, both our fears coming through in the dream. There wasn't one though. Just the rats and the maidens and the moonlight.

I awoke gasping for air. My heart was beating a million miles an hour. My lungs felt like they had an iron band around them. A panic attack. I reached for my rescue med and found Lucas's arm instead. His breathing was regular and deep. The panic began to recede. I was in our hotel. And I knew what had interrupted our killers and their work with the Scavenger's Daughter.

Lucas whispered to me. His breath tickling the hair on my forehead. I couldn't make out the words, just the understanding that he was awake and there for me. As I calmed down and my own breathing began to match his, the mountain fell back asleep, his hand protectively on my side.

Forty-Eight

"Lucas," I shook the large man that slept beside me.

"What?" His voice was thick with sleep still.

"I know why they didn't finish the job with the Scavenger's Daughter."

"Can this wait another hour?"

"No, I don't think so."

"Ok, I'm waking up," Lucas sat up in the bed. He stretched and yawned.

"Awake?" I asked after a few moments.

"Yes."

"I interrupted their use of the Scavenger's Daughter. I moved. Nyleena called Al before we left Washington. She called to say she would be back early and that I was coming with her."

"You think that's what it was?"

"It fits. Look at the time frame. Xavier estimated they had been dead about three days. That's how long it took me to move, get into my apartment and then come to Chicago."

"You're right," Lucas stood and moved to the other bed. He began to shake Xavier.

"I spent one night in my apartment. Just one, before we were called here. For whatever reason, my move to KC, made them rush through the use of the Scavenger's Daughter."

"It was probably the fact that you weren't moving to Chicago." Xavier rubbed his eyes. He looked worse than before he had slept.

"That could be." I commented, realizing no one knew my intentions to move back to KC, back to my family and friends.

"It fits," Xavier yawned. "Can I go back to sleep? Michael and the Chicago Police are scouring the area for any trace of either suspect. There is nothing for us to do at the moment."

"Yes, you can go back to sleep," I told him, cracking a hint of a smile.

Lucas sat, looking at me. Xavier rolled over and instantly began snoring again. He took a second to glance at the smaller man.

"I've always envied his ability to do that." He sighed.

"Sleep like a narcoleptic?" I asked.

"Yes," Lucas continued to frown. "This is not a good start for you."

"I had that exact same thought. Maybe this job isn't for me. I'm a death magnet."

"Actually, I'd say it is perfect for you. After all, you are a death magnet."

"Stop analyzing me. I keep spewing information about myself and Nyleena and Malachi, things I never talk about."

"I don't think that's the shrink in me." Lucas said with meaning.

"No, it probably isn't. I can deduce and avoid all the shrinks I've ever met. With you, I just keep spilling my guts."

"Might be that you have to expand your list of friends."

"Might be, if we survive this." I did my own frowning.

"You seem upset about having friends."

"I am. I keep a wall around myself for a reason. It keeps people from dying."

"We are more like Malachi than your average, everyday person. We will take care of ourselves and you. Likewise, you will take care of us and yourself. Like you have with Nyleena and Malachi."

"Doesn't it bother you?"

"Not in the least. An intelligent, attractive woman to hang off my arm when I need one for a function who doubles as a friend and confidant. I like the idea."

"I'll keep that in mind. I'm not good at sitting on my hands."

"You're not good at sleeping either."

"No, I'm not."

"Go back to sleep, Ace. You're safe and sound in here."

"I know. I just wish I could do more to find these women."

"Like what? Go door to door with Welbourne's photo and ask all the residents of Chicago if they've seen him?"

"Unrealistic, I know."

"Very, let Michael do his magic. He'll have something for us soon."

"The sun is setting," I told him.

"I know."

"That means we are almost through day two. They have one left, maybe."

"I know."

"Soon may not be soon enough," I put my head back on the pillow and felt myself begin to slip back to sleep.

The maidens were back. So was the field of thistle. My subconscious was cobbling the previous dream back together. Something told me I would wake up the same way as before.

The rats were also back. This time, the Brazen Bull had the full attention of the moon. A small fire was burning under it. It wasn't moving, the only thing keeping this dream from being a nightmare. The fire was just small enough to look unimportant, but I knew from the accounts that the bronzed beast was already heating up on the inside.

I tried to force myself to wake up. I knew I was dreaming. But my eyes wouldn't open onto the hotel room. My brain kept them transfixed on the Brazen Bull.

Lucas appeared. His voice floating to me through the thistle. It seemed to carry on a wind.

"Get up, Ace." His voice finally broke the dream, it faded away. My eyes flew open and I was safe and sound in the hotel room.

"Thank you," I told him.

"You were mumbling in your sleep."

"I believe it."

"Do you have a lot of nightmares?"

"No, I don't sleep enough to have a lot of them and I always know when I'm dreaming that I'm dreaming."

"Why were you chanting 'don't let it start rocking'?"

"There was a Brazen Bull in the dream. If it had moved, the dream would have officially become a nightmare."

"Why?"

"Because it would have meant there was a person in it and I am terrified of burning to death. There were also rats. I'm sure if Malachi had a phobia, it would have been in the dream as well."

"No phobias for the psychopath?"

"No fears at all." I told him.

"Mount up," Alejandro's voice came through the door. It was bold, confident.

"Looks like you won't have to sit on your hands anymore," Xavier was jumping out of the bed.

"That'll teach you to be careful what you ask for," Lucas smiled at me as he tossed my shoes onto the bed.

"Ah well, could be worse."

"Don't say that." Xavier shook his head as he grabbed my coat.

Forty-Nine

"Where we going chief?" Xavier asked as we entered the hall.

"Somewhere you won't need that," Alejandro gestured to my coat. I watched it sail back into the hotel room as Xavier tossed it.

"Where?" Lucas made a face.

"Michael got a hit on Welbourne; he's three floors above us in a suite."

"Well, that's probably not a coincidence." I pulled on my holster and checked that the guns were loaded.

"Probably not." Alejandro pointed to the stairs.

Lucas grabbed the door and we slipped into the stairwell. The hotel designers had tried to keep it from looking drab. There was very thin pinstripes on the walls following the angles of the stairs. They were set low to the ground, barely noticeable. The paint was beige, the pinstripes were hunter green.

Lucas took point. Despite his massive size, he moved silently. His footfalls making almost no noise in the enclosed stairwell. I was not as stealthy. My footfalls sounded like thunder. Even my breathing seemed loud.

We reached the tenth floor. Lucas peeked out the door before opening it. We hadn't been given a room number. There was no need. Alejandro, Michael and Xavier had already piled out of the elevator and stood outside the door, guns drawn.

Alejandro made hand motions to Lucas. Lucas moved, I shadowed him, unsure what else to do. I didn't understand hand signals.

I stood slightly behind Lucas. Alejandro moved in front of the door. I had seen enough movies to know to expect him to kick it in and watch it explode. Or have it be rigged up to fire a shotgun directly into the chest of our "fearless" leader. Alejandro drew back and kicked the knob at the handle.

I held my breath. Nothing happened. I exhaled loudly.

"Were you expecting something?" Lucas grinned.

"I was expecting more than nothing," I admitted.

"Life is rarely like the movies. It is usually far worse."

"Are you two done?" Alejandro had his gun trained in the room. Everyone else was staring at us. I blushed.

"Good," Alejandro started into the room. He let out an audible gasp.

Lucas pushed me in behind Alejandro. I couldn't help but let out a gasp either. The room smelled of death. Not the romanticized version they talk about in movies, but real death. All the sphincters in the body relax; this includes the valve at the top of the stomach, all of them in the intestinal tract and the couple between the bladder and the outside. Decomposition also begins immediately. Creating more gasses to release.

I gagged. I tried to breathe through my mouth, but the smell was already in my nose. Then my eyes found the bodies.

Ten women, hog tied. Their legs were to us, pulled up; I couldn't see how they had died yet. Xavier came up next to me. He handed me a breath mint and some peppermint balm. I spread the peppermint balm under my nose and inserted the breath mint into my mouth. It helped, but I could still smell the death in the room and the skin on my upper lip tingled from the peppermint oil.

"Oh my fucking god, RATS!" Lucas let out a squeal and ran to the bathroom.

He slammed the door behind him with enough force that it rebounded against the frame, failing to latch. His massive frame leaped up onto the toilet. For a moment, he stood perched on the center of the toilet lid, his eyes darting around the room like a terrified prairie dog. There was a loud cracking sound. The porcelain lid on the toilet gave out. Lucas let out another squeal as his feet plunged through the lid and into the toilet.

"Ew, toilet water!" His voice was high pitched, almost shrill. I stifled a giggle as he pulled his feet from the toilet and tried to precariously perch on just the rim. His hands had a death grip on the towel rack overhead. One of his wet feet slipped from the toilet edge, slamming into the floor with a deafening thud. The towel rack broke free and crashed into his head.

I held one hand over my mouth. My side was starting to hurt from not laughing out loud. Some part of me was worried that he might have cut himself on the lid, but it was overshadowed by the insanity of the situation. Xavier grinned at him. Michael was beside me, trying to hold in his own laughter. Alejandro frowned.

"Are you done? We have dead bodies and a serial killer."

"We also have rats." Lucas told him, scurrying onto the rim of the bathtub.

"Rats won't kill you," Alejandro scolded him.

"What about Plague? Rats carry Plague. That can kill you." Lucas retorted.

"Fleas carry Plague, not rats," I said between giggles.

"Get down from there and get to work," Alejandro gave him another blood-chilling look.

Lucas seemed unaffected by it. He continued to look around for the rats.

"Lucas, go outside, we'll clear the rats," Xavier told him.

"Ace, how dangerous are rats?" Lucas asked.

"Not very, not if you are a healthy, strapping human being like yourself. You could step on them and kill them and they haven't carried fleas with Plague in a very long time," I reassured the bigger man.

Lucas began to climb down from the tub. I walked over to him and put a reassuring hand on his shoulder. He looked at me with the same terrified look.

"I'll Taser any rats that come near you," I told him.

"I'd feel better if you shot them," he told me.

"Ok, I'll shoot any rats that come near you. You have to help me, I don't know what I am doing," I whispered the last.

This seemed to do something for him. He had a task; he could stop thinking about the rats as much. Besides, I really would Taser any rats that came near me. They could still carry diseases other than Plague. We exited the destroyed bathroom together.

"What the hell?" Xavier asked, looking at one of the bodies.

"What?" Alejandro asked.

"Head cages," I tried to keep the disgust out of my voice.

"They look like that thing one of the ghosts wear in *Thirteen Ghosts*." Xavier pointed out.

"The Jackal." I told him.

"Yeah, that one," Xavier slipped into gloves.

"How many rats?"

"Not nearly enough," Xavier looked around the room. "I'm sure there are some that got free, they are pretty wily."

"How many are you thinking?"

"Well, I'm seeing dead ones, but they wouldn't account for this damage unless they had been at it for days, possibly weeks. That means there are more rats."

"Ouch," Alejandro shouted.

"What?" I asked, beginning to kneel down next to Xavier.

"Fucker bit me," Alejandro said back.

"Bag all the rats," Xavier told him, he was moving closer to the first head.

"They probably won't have tongues." I told him.

"Start the rats feeding if the victim is bleeding."

"Exactly Dr. Seuss. Plus, they can't scream if they don't have tongues."

"How do we get these open? I need to see how the rats died."

"Probably killed each other, fighting for food." I stared at the cage, trying not to see anything other than the metal.

"Unlikely, how do we open the cages?"

"There should be a spring latch," I said examining it without touching it. "The latch will open the cage around the neck; you just pull the head out at that point."

"Where's the latch?"

"Here," I found the small button. Xavier pushed it. The cage separated at the victim's neck.

"What the hell?" Xavier began looking at the rats more closely.

"What?" I frowned.

"These rats have been poisoned. The bloody foam at the corners of their mouth would indicate cyanide."

"Maybe they were rabid." I offered.

"Nope, definitely poisoned."

"Why poison a rat or a group of rats?"

"Maybe they were poisoned before and it took a while to act?" Lucas offered.

"No, this was quick. They pretty much died where they were and fell into the bottom of the head cage. Someone poisoned the rats intentionally."

"That seems like a waste of time and energy." I told Xavier.

"Maybe they could be linked back if they were alive when found?" Xavier offered.

"Maybe he figured out they have plague. The Hippocratic oath and all," I gave an inappropriate giggle that stopped me from thinking too much about what I was looking at.

There was a noise behind us. We turned to see Alejandro lying on the ground. His body was twisted unnaturally, it jerked and spasmed.

Xavier jumped up and rushed over. He checked Alejandro's eyes with a small flashlight.

"Ace, check the counter." Xavier ordered.

The counter looked clean except for some rat droppings. I shined a light over it. It was coated in a fine layer of dust.

"Uh, Xavier, does cyanide come in powder form?"

"Yes," Xavier was still examining Alejandro.

"I think he might have cyanide poisoning."

"We'd smell almonds."

"Can you smell anything other than death and mint?" I asked pointedly.

"Not really," he admitted.

"Xavier, I think she is right," Lucas joined me.

"Why would anyone cover a counter in cyanide?" Xavier asked.

"Beats me, but it would explain the death of the rats." Lucas answered.

Fifty

Alejandro was carted to an ambulance. Michael followed the ambulance to the hospital. Xavier went back to work on the bodies. Lucas stood, arms folded over his massive chest, watching Xavier. Xavier handed me a pair of gloves and made me put them on. Together we removed one of the head cages.

"These were done simultaneously and they don't have the markings," I told him as I held the head cage in my hand.

"Why send messages when they've pulled us in?" He asked.

"I don't know, don't serial killers have MOs and things?"

"Normally, yes, but the writing may not have been part of the MO. The writing could have just been an attempt to show how smart they were. They proved it here." Lucas shrugged at me.

"Learning anything?" Xavier asked.

"It's very high quality, nothing like the originals. Originals could be made of almost any metal. The rats had a free meal; they weren't likely to run away. The victim was bound, so it wasn't like they were going to get out of it. If they did, they were still tongue-less and usually eyeless."

"I think the heads have cyanide on them." Xavier said.

"Why would Alejandro react that fast? Did he ingest it?" I asked.

"The rat bit him," Lucas answered.

"So? I didn't see a blood smear on the counter."

"It's stupid, but the human condition says 'ouch, blood' and when it is on something like a finger, we stick the wound in our mouth automatically. He probably ingested the cyanide. My guess, the rat was coated in it, Alejandro grabbed the rat, the rat bit him, he stuck the wound in his mouth after dropping the rat. The rat scampers away. The cyanide gets ingested. Alejandro reacts to it."

"Will he live?" I asked.

"Maybe, it depends on several factors," Xavier answered.

"Is there an antidote?"

"Yes," Xavier answered. "We have always been able to treat cyanide poisoning. In the last five years, it has gotten better, but it depends on how much he ingested and the type of cyanide."

"I see." I frowned at the head cage. "This is really well made and it's steel or some sort of alloy."

"Steel is an alloy." Lucas told me.

"You know what I meant, it could be carbon steel or stainless steel or tungsten or nickel; there are other alloy options."

"I knew what you meant," Lucas gave me a thin smile.

"Sorry, head cages don't have a lot of information in them."

"Unlike Iron Maidens," Xavier chirped.

"Unlike Iron Maidens." I agreed.

"Do you have any information about this particular set of head cages?" Lucas asked.

"They were made by the guy that made the Scavenger's Daughter. His stamp is on here just like it was with the screw mechanism. This time, it's on the latch mechanism."

"Does this bother you?" Lucas asked.

"I feel useless, other than that, no." I admitted.

"You aren't useless. Tell me about the rats."
Lucas said.

"Rats were used because they were convenient.
Honestly, the entire contraption is convenient. It was
most popular in France. It wasn't hard to tie a person up
and find a way to contain some rats over their head. In a
professional setting, the rats would be kept for a day or
two without food. The head cage was placed over the
victim, the rats inserted through the top." I pointed to
another latch.

He nodded. I clicked it and it sprung open
revealing a square about three inches by three inches. I
closed the cage, hearing it latch and then mimed putting
rats in through the open trap door on top. Lucas frowned.

"It wasn't pretty; the rats can do a lot of damage in
just a few minutes. Some will crawl out of the holes, most
won't. Sensing the helplessness of the victim, the rats
would set to feeding."

"And they did," Xavier brought our attention back
to the bodies in the room.

"What do you know?" Lucas asked.

"I'll know more when I get them on the tables. I'm
pretty sure the bodies have a stray rat or two on the
inside. I thought I saw something move a few seconds
ago that wasn't consistent with post-death twitches. I'd
say the deaths were painful and slow."

"Not as slow as some deaths," I quipped quietly.

"Very true." Xavier took off the gloves.

A couple of men appeared. They took the bodies
and put them inside bags. I watched it with detached
awareness. For several minutes, I just stood. Men and
women were moving all around me. They were scraping
things, cataloging things, doing things I couldn't even
begin to fathom.

Lucas stood next to me. He watched everyone
moving about the rooms. Xavier had already left,

following the bodies. I diverted my attention to the bloodstains on the floor.

"You look lost in thought." Lucas said.

"The scavenger was the first; the rats were second, what happens if there's a third?"

"What does the third mean?"

"We'll be pulling baked bodies out of a giant bronze bull and it will horrify me to no end."

"Wait." Lucas turned on me.

"What?"

"How many people can build a giant bronze bull? Especially one that is hollow inside?"

"I doubt there are many."

"I think we've been chasing the wrong torture device. How certain are you that a bull is on the list?"

"After finding the rats and the Scavenger's Daughter, about 98%. It explains the scavenger as well. It didn't fit. But if you think about Malachi and his crushed bodies case, it explains the scavenger. The rats were Nyleena's weakness. The bull would be mine."

"So you said."

"I'm terrified of it." I admitted.

"You are truly afraid of being burned to death?"

"In something like that? Yes. You don't die in a few minutes because of smoke inhalation. The bull doesn't allow for the smoke to enter. Instead, you cook. You are literally baked alive inside it and your struggles make the bull look like it is dancing. I can't think of anything more horrible."

"Then I think we should investigate the bulls and their makers."

"To what end? Even if we find the makers, how will we know who the killer is?"

"What size are these things?"

"Depends on the make. If it fits just one, it is significantly smaller than one that fits two or three

273

people. One person, it's usually a cavity where the person is forced down on hands and knees. More than one and it varies."

"And how long does it take to work?"

"Hours, sometimes longer. It depends on who is stoking the flames."

"Come on," Lucas grabbed my arm and pulled me from the crime scene.

Fifty-One

We were back in the morgue. Xavier was looking over the bodies of the new victims. Carefully, he removed the head cages.

"Now, tell us about the Brazen Bull." Lucas got comfortable on one of the empty tables.

"The legs are filled with metal. The top opens from the outside; occasionally the ass end does as well. It works on a hinge system with a lock. The legs keep it balanced even while the person inside is fighting to get out."

"Ignore that part; tell us about the uses, the specifications." Lucas interrupted.

"Ok, well, there's a fire under it. The flames control the pace at which the victim dies. Large flames heat the metal quickly, small flames heat it gradually. The big thing though is the air inside. The speed at which it heats up has a lot to do with how long the victim lives. If the air stays cool on the inside, this means the victims that are on all four limbs, suffer from third degree burns long before they die. Most victims probably die of shock. There is usually an air hole through the nostrils. It provides air that can come and go, keeps the interior cooler than the exterior. It also allows the bull to make 'noise'. The skin will begin to peel away as it burns from touching the metal. The part that kills you though, is when the air inside gets hot. You breathe it in; it begins to cook your throat and lungs."

"How long does it take?" Xavier asked.

"Hours upon hours, depending on how long you want it to take. There is one described as taking days because they kept the flames minimal, so it'd be like being in an oven at 100 to 150 degrees. There are others though where the victim died in less than four hours because the flames were stoked."

"Four hours is still a long time, three hours is a long time, when you have ten victims. If we can get the specs, can you tell how many will fit inside of them?" Lucas asked.

"Yes," I frowned at him.

"What?" He asked.

"That's the complicated part. The more people inside, the less stable, which means a stabilization mechanism would have to be attached. Also, it means they are going to die a lot slower unless they don't have air holes or the air holes are small. The largest one ever made, would allow a human hand to come out the nostril. The seams where the metal met at the hatches were left with tiny gaps to allow more air circulation."

"They were getting their money's worth," Xavier said as he turned on a small drill. I looked to see him working on a rat.

"What are you doing?"

"I think the girls were sprinkled with the cyanide after they died. Probably to kill the rats. Rats have a different absorption ratio than humans when it comes to lethal doses. I need to know how many absorbed it and how many ate it."

"Why will that be helpful?"

"Because if I can figure that out, I might be able to more accurately pinpoint how much we missed him by." Xavier spoke as if it should be self-evident why he was doing a necropsy on the rats.

"I see."

"Since there were rats still alive, but covered in cyanide," Xavier looked up at me and shrugged.

"We didn't miss him by much." I finished his thought.

"Exactly."

"Back to the upcoming horror," Lucas brought my focus back to him, "if you were going to do this and wanted it to be as easy as possible, how many bulls?"

"Two, you would never be able to create one that would hold ten. Six is the most I've ever heard of." A light was starting to dawn.

"Where do you store two bulls large enough to hold five people apiece?"

"A storage facility, but you'd need two rooms and the likelihood of someone seeing you move in two very large metal bull sculptures would be high."

"Everyone makes mistakes." Lucas stood up and looked around the room.

"Michael is with Alejandro," I reminded him.

"Then I suggest we join him, because without his computer skills, I'm not sure I can find him."

"Good idea," we left the morgue and the stench of death behind us. The smell didn't leave us behind though. Even nurses moved out of our way as we trekked to the ER. The waiting room was crowded. Lucas showed his badge and while a petite brunette behind the desk tried not to gag, she hit the button to let us in.

We were definitely in a hospital. The back rooms smelled of bleach and ammonia. Most curtains were closed. The few open ones revealed people, trying to go about their life and curtailed by the whims of the human condition. One room had a girl of about nine years old in it; she was getting a cast put on.

"Lucas," Michael stuck his head out of a door and motioned us over.

We followed Michael through the filmy curtain. His face was dark and set.

"That bad?" Lucas asked him.

"They don't think he'll make it. The doctor is calling it a double dose. He got some in the rat bite that went straight to his blood and you were right, he ingested it. One without the other and he might be fine. Together and the antidote isn't working very well. We've called his sister. She wasn't all that keen on coming, but she'll be here within a day. Pretty sure he won't last that long though." Michael told him.

"Did they tell you the type of cyanide?"

"No, it's still a mystery. Xavier figure anything out?"

"Not yet. We did though," Lucas hooked a finger at me.

"What?"

"We want you to search storage units for the name of the company that orders the torture devices. If you find none, find double units and see if anyone noticed someone moving in two very large bull statues. We also need the dimensions for the bulls ordered. Ace thinks the skill required would put the maker of the Iron Maidens at the top of the list."

"Now that you mention it, he did say something about some odd bull sculptures. Different company, but he said they were massive and bronze."

"Sounds like the ones. What was the company name?" I asked.

"Alexandra's Dream Salon." Michael told me.

"Oh you have got to be kidding me," I sighed.

"What?" Michael asked.

"My middle name is Alexandra and my first name means 'dreams'."

"Wow, why don't they make it more obvious." Michael thought for a minute.

"I bet when we find out who ordered the head cages, it will have something to do with Nyleena. What was the name of the other company?"

"Mala's Custom Home Interiors," Michael answered.

"Mala? CHI? I should have asked earlier. Malachi."

"Huh," Michael pursed his lips. "The invoice was addressed to a Blake McCain."

"Son of a bitch, it was there all the time." Lucas bowed his head. "From now on, we need to do a better job of sharing all information."

"Alejandro wasn't an information sharer," Michael said.

"Well, even if he recovers, he won't be coming back to work, so we'll have to train our new liaison on info sharing," Lucas looked at that bed, "I always expected him to die. But, I figured someone would exact revenge with a machete."

Fifty-Two

Michael and I left Lucas with Alejandro. We walked back down to the morgue. Xavier was still examining away.

"They don't think Alejandro is going to make it," Michael told him.

"Pity, I was just getting used to him."

"Does anyone feel anything about this?" I asked, slightly appalled.

"Yes, but not what one might expect. Alejandro is and was a complete bastard. We've talked to the head guy twice about replacing him. He makes our lives hell and he's so paranoid that we have trouble sharing information, even information important to our cases. Since he started as our liaison, our capture rate has dropped. So, are we sad he's going to die, yes. It's terrible to lose a life. Does that mean others might get saved as a result? Yes, so it serves a purpose," Xavier had a mask on.

"You?" Michael asked.

"All life should be mourned." I told him coolly. I had no particular like for Alejandro, but I was of the opinion that even jackasses had families and people that cared about them. I was sure Alejandro was no different.

"Well then, back to the case at hand," Michael began his ferocious typing.

I watched Xavier. He had gotten all the head cages removed. There were rats strewn about the room. Some had been dissected. Some hadn't yet. He was moving meticulously from rat to rat.

"I hate to admit this, but I find hanging out in the morgue to be morbid." I told them.

"Go back to the hotel; god knows you need a shower. Get Gabriel to take you. He's our FBI contact here." Xavier told me.

I left. Gabriel was hanging out in a lounge area just off the cafeteria. My stomach growled.

"Don't go in there, half the people will lose their appetites, the other half will lose their lunch," Gabriel said as I took a step that way.

"I smell that bad?"

"You smell worse than that." Gabriel stood up, "what can I do for you?"

"I need food and a shower."

"So, hotel." Gabriel dug his car keys out of his pocket, "no coat?"

"Didn't need one originally."

"Here, take mine, you can have it cleaned at the hotel." Gabriel handed me his coat. He had a zippered hoodie under it. Together, we left for the hotel.

"Shower, I'll get room service ordered while you do. What do you want?"

"A Philly would be great," I told him, grabbing some clothes.

"No, don't take anything you intend to wear into the room with you. Take and put the clothes you are wearing into a trash bag and set them outside the door. I'll make sure they get picked up to be cleaned. Put my coat with them."

"Really? It's that bad?"

"You can't smell it anymore. Try to remember when you first walked into that room. That's what you smell like."

The memory surfaced. I put my clothes and Gabriel's coat into the bathroom trashcan and tied up the bag. I set it outside the door by slipping it through a small crack. Gabriel was on the phone, ignoring me.

The shower was blissful. The water was hot enough to turn my skin pink. I lathered with soap, over and over again; my nostrils began to clear of the smell of death. I could smell it again, faintly. I washed my hair for a third time. The tiny bottle of shampoo was empty. The bar of soap was nothing more than a speck by the time I exited. I wrapped a towel around myself. My clothes were in the other room.

For a couple of seconds I debated asking Gabriel to just bring them to me, but I have never been the shy type and any modesty that might have tried to form was squashed when I was eight. I exited the bathroom, watching for a moment as the steam rushed out the open door, filling the small hallway.

"Feel better?" Gabriel asked.

"Yes, much."

"Michael called. He thinks he found the storage unit and they cleaned it out earlier today."

"Fruck," I said it with very little emotion. He still didn't have any victims to put in it. That was something.

"My thoughts exactly, especially if what they tell me about them is true. There were only two of them."

"That's going to suck," I shook my head. Gabriel turned his back to me. I got dressed.

"Are they heating them up before they fill them?" Gabriel asked, turning back around.

"That would be my guess. A cold bull takes even longer than a hot one."

"That sounds dirty for some reason."

I broke a smile and shook my head. In a way, he was right, it did sound dirty. He smiled with me.

"Why are you doing this?" He asked after another second.

"Because I don't know what else to do," I told him.

"US Marshal by default then," Gabriel nodded, "I know a couple of people like that."

"Well there isn't much for a damaged, serial killer magnet with a degree in history to do in this world. It's either this or deal with classrooms full of students. Since stats would dictate that I would have a serial killer every two years in one of my classes, this seems safer."

"They are on the rise," Gabriel stood as there was a knock on the door.

Our food was here. Gabriel took both containers and brought them into the room. He kicked it shut with his foot. I got up and put the locks on.

"Concerned?" Gabriel handed me one of them.

"Habit," I admitted, opening the box. The Philly smelled delicious. The green peppers and mushrooms were cooked to perfection. The beef was thinly sliced and slightly salty. I chomped into it and had half of it devoured before Gabriel had finished putting condiments on his baked potato.

"Wow, you were hungry."

"Starved." I told him. There was another knock on the door.

Gabriel got up and looked out the peep hole. He frowned and started removing the locks.

Xavier entered the room. Lucas with him. Behind them there was a man with a gun. He fired one shot into each of them. Then turned the gun towards me.

The bullet ripped through my shoulder. I felt my knees go weak, before they collapsed and tossed me onto the floor. My body twitched. Gabriel went down. All I could do was watch as the two people in black masks entered the room.

Fifty-Three

I awoke in the dark. The floor beneath me was slightly warm. I opened my mouth and took in a deep breath.

Someone clamped a hand over my mouth. It smelled of death. I let the air out of my lungs slowly.

"There are five of us in this thing and yes, I believe it is your worst nightmare. However, if you scream, you will panic the other woman with us. I am not sure they counted on Lucas's size when they tossed him in here. I also think if you keep your calm, you can help us find a way out. Right now, the metal is only warm to the touch. We have some time." Xavier whispered to me.

"I'm bleeding," I whispered back.

"The bullets were small caliber, but they seem to have sedatives in them or on them. I'm not sure. The sedatives are wearing off slowly. You, I and Gabriel are awake. Lucas is still out, but they shot him twice. The other girl is also still out. There is room to move around, but not as much as there would be if Lucas wasn't with us."

"I will warn you, I heard screaming a little earlier. I believe they have the other bull filled." Gabriel added.

"Not helpful," I told him, placing my hand against the metal as I rolled over onto my side. It was warm. It wasn't hot. We weren't yet baking. My skin wouldn't blister and fall off anytime soon. My inner stillness took over. I looked and found the air holes. The nostrils of the bull were pretty close to my head.

The holes were large, large enough to stick my arm through. However, I had a horrible suspicion that if

I did stick my hand out of the bull's nose, someone would chop it off. I put my face close to it. It was dark outside. The air was cooler, cold even. I took a deep breath of the fresher air.

"That's why it isn't warming," I said very quietly.

"What?"

"The weather. The Brazen Bull was Mediterranean in origin. This one is bronze. Bronze doesn't heat evenly," I whispered.

"You said something about a stabilizing mechanism?" Xavier whispered back.

"Yes, a bull of this size would need a stabilizing mechanism."

"What kind?" Xavier asked.

"Cross bars most likely."

"I don't remember seeing cross bars on the surveillance video Michael found." Xavier answered.

"Ok, then perhaps it doesn't have any." I felt around.

My fingers found a seam. I traced the line with two fingers, moving around as much as possible as I did. The seam ran over my head and down, under me.

"The head moves," I told Xavier.

"What?"

"The head opens."

"Is that important?"

"Think of the shape, it would require its own latch and hinge. We might be able to force it forward. If it falls forward, the bottom hinge might give, based on the amount of weight in this thing and its own momentum."

"I only sort of understand."

"When we get out, I'll explain why the heads didn't open. Until then, how long before Lucas wakes up?"

"I don't know. I've checked him as best I could, but..."

"It's dark and cramped." I finished for him.

"Pretty much."

"Anyway we can speed the process or drag him over here?"

"Not really," Gabriel joined the whispering.

"Whatever we do, Lucas needs to be the one in the head. I and the other woman needs to be near the rear. If we knock it forward, I don't want to be on the bottom of that pile."

"Can you climb towards the back now?" Xavier asked.

"I can try." I began wriggling and wiggling inside. I pinned my body against the side and felt the bull move ever so slightly from the force of my weight moving. I found Lucas and climbed over him, my back scraping against the top.

"Well?" Xavier asked.

"I'm there." I answered.

"Is there room for the rest of us back there?" Gabriel asked.

"Only if Lucas moves," I found I could almost sit up in the belly of the beast. Back here, the metal was cold to the touch. I checked on the other woman. She was like me, breathing but bleeding. I touched my shoulder. The blood had clotted. It had been a while since I had been shot, snatched and shoved into this thing.

"Ugh," Lucas moaned. I gave him a good kick to the arm. The pain shocked him, he yelped.

"Don't yell," I told him.

"Where... This is bad." Lucas answered his own question.

"True, but we have a plan. You need to move away from me. The front of the bull has a hinged head. If we can get it to fall forward, the hinge might give. If not, they certainly aren't going to get it standing with us in it."

"What about the stabilizing mechanism?"

"They weren't intended to have hinged heads. Aside from the air holes, the heads were solid. This one isn't built that way. The head is hollow. We can get weight in it and empty the back. Put it off balance. Let our weight and its own carry us to the ground. It is going to hurt like hell, which is why I am not going to be in the head," I hissed almost wordlessly to him.

"That will work?"

"If it doesn't, we'll have to figure something else out. We need our fifth here to wake up though."

"Put your finger into her wound like you did me with your heel."

"Oh, good plan." I found the wound and stuck my finger in it.

The woman woke up. She was screaming. I covered my ears. The sound resonated and echoed in the tiny metal chamber. I heard someone swear and she stopped. Or rather, it became quieter.

"My name is Aislinn Cain. I'm a US Marshal and there are five of us in this torture device. I think I have a plan to get us out. But you'll need to stop screaming and help us." My fingers searched for her face. I found it. There was a hand clamped over her mouth.

"I'm going to let go, please don't scream," Lucas said gently.

Fifty-Four

Lucas let go of her mouth. She didn't scream. She took several deep breaths.

"Now, you are trapped with three US Marshals and one FBI agent. None of us have any intention of dying in here, especially me. If that means I have to chew through the metal with my teeth, I will." I didn't add that this was a particular horror that I would do anything to escape. I didn't figure she needed to know that.

"My name is Lucas McMichaels, there's Xavier Reece, and Gabriel Henders. You've met Ace. What's your name?"

"Cassandra Clachan."

"Oh, Cassie," I said, horror filling my voice. If I thought cooking me alive was bad, adding my family to it was much worse.

"Aunt Aislinn?" She said my name slowly, quietly.

"What happened, Cassie?"

"Mom opened the door, someone shot her. I tried to take Kyle and hide, but he found us. I thought we died when he shot us." My niece was sixteen years old. Her younger brother, Kyle was fourteen.

"I think we can safely guess two of the occupants of the other device," Gabriel said sadly.

"Yes, I think we can." I shook my head in the dark. "Cassie, you and I are going to slowly move forward after we get the men into position. The goal is to get this thing to fall forward. When it does, we are going to get bumped and bruised and tossed around. We are going to have to ignore the pain. Once we are free, you are going to run like hell. If we are in a building, find a place to hide. If we are outdoors, run towards trees, woods, roads, whatever you see. Got it?"

"Got it," she said after several seconds.

"After we get out, we are going to get the people responsible and save everyone else."

"Serial killers?" She asked.

"Yes."

"Figures." She gave a sigh.

"Think you can work with us?"

"Yes. If we live, I'm making sure mom spends more time with grandma." She said.

"Good plan," I told her confidently. My desire to get out was growing by the second, "Lucas, move forward, the rest move back. The bull rocks with movement, so expect it to move, but try to keep it to a minimum."

In the dark, I could hear the shuffling of their clothes. I grabbed Cassie as the bull began to rock with us in it. She didn't yell or let out a single noise, just grabbed my hand. Unlike Malachi, I had attachments to my family.

"There," Lucas whispered. His voice echoing in the chamber.

"Ok, move feet first into the head, fill as much of the hole as possible with your body. As he moves, the rest of us need to move. Xavier and Gabriel, scoot up to his back and move as he does. Cassie and I will move with you." I took hold of the shirt to the side of me and put it into Cassie's hand.

"We don't have guns, what do we do when we get out?" Gabriel asked.

"We kill them. Guns are a convenience, not a necessity," Lucas answered.

I did the same with the shirt in front of me. I waited until I felt them move. I pulled Cassie with me.

In unison, the five of us wiggled through the body of the bull. We scooted across the warm sections of the belly slowly. The bull rocking more and more. Not just side to side, but I felt the legs come up in the back.

"Now, Lucas, move fast, now," I suddenly ordered.

The filled legs would work to our advantage. I felt them lift again. Cassie grabbed my arm tighter. The back legs lifted higher. My feet went around whoever was in front of me. I wrapped my legs around them tightly, adjusting my weight to put more of it into the head.

It was the tipping point. The bull didn't come back down, it tipped forward. My face hit the roof. There was a little give at the hatch, but not enough to work with. We heard voices yelling.

"Son of a bitch," Xavier yelled as the front legs gave out and the entire structure tumbled forward.

We were all slammed into different parts of the bull. My face hit the side and I felt blood begin to pour from my cheek. I grabbed Cassie and pulled her head into my body. Locking her between my chest and the back of the man in front of me. I was sure the position wasn't comfortable, but at least she wouldn't bust open her head.

We crashed to the ground. The sound of bronze hitting the concrete rang like a bell inside the bull. Cassie screamed. The entire bull broke apart. The hinges giving under the stress of the weight and mangled metal.

Something sharp and most likely metal was stabbing me in the leg. Cassie was moving, trying to untangle herself from the heap of bodies. She was failing miserably. Her arm was pinned under Gabriel who seemed to be out cold.

"You know the problem with hinges is that they are always a weak spot," Xavier quipped. I turned to look at him.

"Lucas, what does your psychological training say about people who kill in groups? I count five people."

"We call them cults," Lucas groaned back, "I think my arm is broken."

"So help me god, if you shoot me or her with that fucking thing one more time, I'll make it the last thing you live to regret." I told someone who was now towering over me. He wore a mask. He held a gun.

Xavier started giggling. Everyone turned to look at him.

"He's already made that mistake. What do you think is going to happen when he gets to the Fortress and your brother finds out that he's one of the assholes that kidnapped his wife, son, daughter and sister? Normally, he is kept under lock and key, but I'm sure the guards would let him out at an inappropriate time to deal with these guys. They are sympathetic to his reason for being there."

"I hadn't thought of that," I was waiting for a sign. Something to tell me to go for the gun.

The screaming from the other bull came to us. The flames had suddenly shot up higher. I looked and found an automated bellows under it.

"Forget it, Ace," Lucas said to me.

"Forget what?" I asked innocently, getting the message. I waited another second, took a deep breath and let the stillness overwhelm me.

Fifty-Five

In the calm, the world slows down just a fraction. It's as if time has trouble getting through the calm. As it washed over me, I saw the eyes of the man standing over me. They widened slightly in reaction to my lack of emotion. I imagine it showed in my eyes as well as my face.

I reached out, grabbed hold of the man at the wrist and pulled. He crashed into the scraps of metal, losing the gun in his fall. Cassie grabbed it and finally jerking free of Gabriel, began to run.

The other men took a moment to react. By then, Lucas had hold of one. Someone shot him. He growled with rage. There was a second gunshot. It sounded muffled compared to the breaking of bones as Lucas broke his neck. Lucas let go of the dead man. I moved, pulling my leg off whatever was stabbing it. As I yanked my leg forward, off the twisted piece of metal, I shoved the man's head down onto it. I felt it go through his skull. He gurgled once and began to twitch.

Xavier had his hands full. He was wresting the gun from another. Lucas had a second man within his grasp. He grabbed him and tossed him onto the mangled remains of the bull. The man began to move, I grabbed his shirt, moving it into the flickering fire. It instantly caught.

Xavier had finally gotten the gun. He flipped the guy over him, he thudded as he hit the concrete, the air knocked out of him. Xavier shot him, twice, once in the leg, once in the crotch. The fifth man began to run.

Xavier shot him in the head. He fell. His body being forced forward, his face slamming into the ground.

"The other bull!" I shouted to Lucas.

Lucas ran at it. He hit it in the side. It tottered before smashing to the ground. Xavier found the cord for the bellows and unplugged it. I hobbled that direction.

Ignoring the heat, Lucas tore at the latches and opened it.

Five people crawled from it. They were suffering some burns. I opened my mouth in horror.

Malachi's two younger brothers, my sister in law, my nephew and Nyleena's boyfriend crawled from the belly of the bull. I looked at Al Welbourne in shock.

"Doctors," he said to me.

"On their way," Xavier fell to his knees and began examining them. Gabriel had woke up and was currently handcuffing the guy Xavier had shot in the leg. The burned one was gasping on the floor, alive and no longer on fire.

"What the hell is he doing inside the bull?" I asked Lucas.

"I guess we were wrong. Who are these other guys though?"

"I don't know, I don't think I've ever seen them before."

"We'll fingerprint them and see what that get..." Lucas finished his sentence with a growl.

A woman stood several feet from us. She had Cassie in front of her, her arm holding her in place. I recognized her face, Jessica Thompson.

"Let her go," I told Jessica.

"Or what?" She looked around. "You don't have a gun."

"I've never actually needed one." I told her.

"You would in this situation, I have a gun on your niece, without a gun of your own, it would be hard to kill me before I killed her."

"So you think," I didn't look around. I already knew what I wanted.

Behind her were a stack of pallets. If I could set those on fire, it would make her have to move. I watched Cassie as I knelt down. I found a flaming bit of wood. The heat singed the hair on my hand and arm. I stood back up, holding it.

"Fire?" She looked doubtfully at me.

"Fire," I agreed and tossed the stick.

Jessica ducked and laughed. Her hair began to smolder. I hadn't considered setting her on fire.

"Your hair's on fire," Lucas told her.

"Yeah right," Jessica said and stopped. The gun waivered just a bit, Cassie stomped on her foot and jerked out of her grasp.

Jessica began to scream. She dropped the gun as she swatted at her hair. It was now starting to grow flames.

"Stop moving," Xavier wandered over to her and tossed a jacket over her head.

As the coat fell over her, he punched her in the face. Her body went limp. She collapsed to the ground.

"Well, not bad work," Lucas looked around. "The fire was ingenious.

"I was hoping to set the pallets on fire, not her. Setting her on fire was a bonus," I told him. He smiled at me.

Cassie came running out. She ran over and hugged me. I tried not to groan as it shot pain down my leg.

"I think your mother and brother will be fine after a day or two," Xavier told her. "They are a little burnt, but it could have been a lot worse."

"Thank you," Cassie blushed at him.

Malachi and Nyleena came running through the doors. They stopped a few feet into the doorway. Malachi's eyes darted over everyone. His gaze fell on me. He nodded once. I nodded back. The unspoken words asked if I was alright and reassured him that I was. He found his brothers, they were sitting up finally. He rushed to them.

Nyleena let out a small yelp that ended in a whimper. Her eyes were following the trails of blood that seemed to be slowly flowing down my body, helped by gravity. She came to me, afraid to touch me. I knew she wanted a hug. I also knew she wouldn't touch me first. The blood and my calm were enough to keep her within arm's reach, but not closer. Tears welled up in her eyes.

"It's not as bad as it looks," I told her. "Besides, I just survived my worst nightmare. The blood is the least of my concerns. Al's off the hook though and he looks like he could use some help."

She stared at me for another couple of seconds. I took her hand, squeezed it once. She smiled and turned. She found Al and began talking very quietly to him. I collapsed onto the floor and lay still, the thought of moving made me feel ill.

Following like lost puppies was a squadron of police officers, paramedics and firemen. They dashed about, trying to do everything that needed to be done. They were examining the injured, putting handcuffs on bad guys and shouting loudly at each other.

"Let me help you," Lucas came over to me. He offered his arm. I frowned at him.

"What? It's a good arm."

"It's broken and I'm five foot, two inches tall. You are six foot something tall. I don't think that will work."

"Fine," he bent and carefully picked me up.

"Doesn't that hurt?"

"Yes, but the pain keeps me from passing out from the sedatives." He told me as he put me on a gurney.

"I think you could use one yourself, big guy." I told him. He sat down on mine. There was a second when I thought it would give way under our combined weight, but it only gave a small hiss and a groan. A paramedic attempted to attend to us, we both brushed him away, sending him to deal with the injuries worse than ours. We were good so long as we were sitting down. We watched them silently.

"Don't pass out, either of you," Gabriel walked over to us.

"That sounds suspiciously like an order," I told him.

"It should. I just heard from your director. Alejandro is going to live, but there was significant damage done. He's going to get a nice fat pension and for some reason, I am getting promoted from FBI liaison to team leader," he told us.

"Hope you're better at it than he was," Xavier said. "Do you understand the need to communicate between all five of us as individuals as well as a group?"

"Yes, if we had done it earlier, we might not be in this mess now." Gabriel answered. "Now, off to the hospital with the lot of you."

Fifty-Six

I sat in the hospital room. My jeans had been cut off and tossed into a ball near the trashcan. A doctor was stitching up my leg. Gabriel had just left. Lucas was sleeping off the sedative laced bullets plus the good drugs they had given him for his arm. Xavier was being tended to and Gabriel had a concussion. My mother was on her way up to look after Cassie while her brother and mother recovered. The doctors expected them to be out in a few days.

Malachi entered. His face was grim. He looked tired.

"How's it look with Mark and Mitch?" I asked him.

"They'll be ok. Good thing you got that stupid idea though. If they had been trapped in there another half hour or so, chances are, they wouldn't be fairing as well."

"Ah well," I shrugged. It hurt. The shoulder had already been stitched.

"Aislinn, look..."

"If you apologize to me Malachi Blake, I'll shoot you," I told him, looking at the doctor.

"How'd you know?"

"I know you, better than you think sometimes, better than you know yourself."

"I know that," Malachi sat down and sighed.

"What's up?"

"I can't believe this came back to haunt us all."

"It happens, Malachi. With the lives we lead, it happens more than we want to admit. Nothing to be done about it. I'm sorry our families were brought into it, but us..." I finally looked up at him. "With us, it's an occupational hazard."

"And a life hazard." Malachi told me.

"And a life hazard," I agreed.

"So you are definitely taking the job?"

"Oh, I thought about turning it down. I don't like waiting for the crime scene techs and the specialists and sitting on my hands, but I also know that if I hadn't been trapped in that bull, ten people would have died. Ten good people. Instead, only three bad guys died. I doubt we will ever be in that situation again, but I can think on my feet and keep my cool when I should be screaming and running for cover. Who knows, I might be good at this."

"I think you will be and I know Xavier and Lucas have taken to you."

"I think I've taken to them as well," I smiled.

"A few more friends to add to your very short list."

"It's nice," I admitted, "what was the deal with Al?"

"Oh, Jessica stole his identity and since he was trying to hide his past with her for obvious familial reasons, he wouldn't report it. Gabriel is going to talk to some contacts and see if they can really get his social security number changed."

"That would be good," I sighed at him.

"What?"

"I was just thinking that you are starting to look old."

Malachi Blake was six foot ten inches tall. He weighed roughly two hundred pounds dripping wet. All of it was solid muscle. His skin was tanned by the sun. He kept his head shaved so that no one would see the brown hair with a dusting of ginger color or the curls that start the moment it leaves his scalp. His eyes were a vibrant green, a rich color that reminded me of malachite, not emeralds.

Time, work and life were taking its toll. He had a five o'clock shadow that was quickly turning into a beard and mustache. Lines were starting to form at the corners of his eyes and the furrows of his brow were getting deeper. His mouth, once young and sensuous was starting to look thin and always seemed wearied. He didn't smile easy, but he didn't frown either. It was the only thing that kept the wrinkles from invading the corners of his mouth. A part of me was sure that if he did grow out his hair, it would be streaked with grey.

A few scars decorated his face, one jutting up from his cheek to his ear. One bisecting an eyebrow. Another on the lining of his bottom lip. I knew where all of them had come from. I knew there were actually hundreds more hidden behind long sleeves, jeans and cowboy hats. His body was bespeckled with gunshot wounds, jagged knife cuts, multiple surgical marks and anything else the human body could endure. He'd been set on fire once. The burn scar had melted away some of the previous scars that had been on his leg.

"I feel old," he finally said.

"Me too," I told him.

"Your hair is graying."

"I know and I'll have some new scars to list on my distinguished features portion."

"I'm glad Lucas and Xavier found you."

"Why?"

"They'll help keep you alive, despite attempts by others or indifference for yourself when others are involved. Your survival instinct is strong, but you still aren't willing to sacrifice those you love for it."

"Said the psychopath to the sociopath," I gave him a look and got a grin out of him.

"Aislinn Cain, you are the only person I would exchange my life for."

"I know and you'll exchange your life to keep me from being in pain or angry at you."

"True."

"It's about as close to love as you'll ever get Malachi. I know. I also know you're glad I didn't die today."

"Yes indeed." He stood up.

"Malachi," I said, stopping him from leaving.

"Yeah?"

"I'm glad you care about me. If things were just a little bit different, I'd give it a go. Since we are who we are, we'll both have to be content to live life as we do."

"I know, Aislinn."

"Thank you."

"For what?"

"For caring, for coming today, for being my friend and for being you."

"Most people aren't that enthusiastic about me being me."

"Most people aren't me." I told him. He gave me another flash of a smile and disappeared from the room.

The doctor finished stitching me up as Xavier came into the room. He looked at the doctor and took the seat vacated a few minutes earlier by Malachi.

"Well?" He asked.

"Well what?" I asked in return.

"Think you'll stick around?"

"Yeah, I can't think of anything I'd be better at. A vigilante maybe, but it doesn't pay well."

"Jessica Thompson has spent the last couple of years plotting revenge and gaining a following of psychos to follow her. They didn't seem to know anything about you or Nyleena or Malachi."

"Pity they didn't get a chance to meet Malachi."

"If they thought we were brutal, they would have been in for a serious wake-up call." Xavier smiled.

"Indeed."

"I'm here to extend a formal invitation. We'll be leaving Chicago in a couple of days. We have to wait on Lucas and you to heal. There's a dinner being prepared for our return. It will be at Lucas's. All you have to bring is yourself. We've invited Nyleena as well."

Fifty-Seven

The following morning, Nyleena and Malachi were in my hospital room. Malachi looked grim, but then he usually does.

"Well, do you want to hear the whole story?" Gabriel took the seat.

"I'm all ears."

"Since this concerns all of you, you can both stay," Gabriel looked at Malachi and Nyleena.

"Good, I have a lot of questions," Nyleena stated.

"Let me do my bit then you can ask any questions that haven't been cleared up." Gabriel got comfortable in his chair and took out an electronic cigarette.

He offered me a drag. I took it. I puffed off of it, but it wasn't as satisfying as a real cigarette. It would do while I was stuck in a hospital bed. There was some irritation on the part of doctors that I had been admitted a day earlier with hypothermia and now for multiple wounds that had needed stitches. So they were pretty determined to either keep me in a hospital bed or in a rubber room. The hospital bed seemed like the better alternative.

"It would appear that the moment the doctors told Jessica and her family that her brother wasn't going to wake up she began plotting revenge. Including marrying one of his doctors to get access to money. It just turned out to be a fluke that it was Al Welbourne and therefore, her half-brother. However, she also knew he probably wouldn't turn her in for identity theft when their marriage was annulled." Gabriel took another drag off his electronic cigarette.

302

"Sorry, does that work?" I asked him.

"For me, no, I still smoke and chew, but this keeps me from smoking two and half packs a day." Gabriel frowned at me. "Can I finish now?"

"Yeah, sorry," I muttered as he blew out water vapor.

"Ok, so using his credit cards she tracks you down when the story about Gerard Hawkins breaks. She heads to Washington and audits a couple of classes. While there, she also gets involved with the Seattle fringe groups and collects a small following. She tells them that she is the incarnation of Lilith and they believe her because she has that kind of charisma. She's as kooky as you," Gabriel gave me a pointed look.

I smiled back at him. Nyleena raised her hand. He turned his attention to her. She lowered it.

"She's plotting revenge against Ace in the beginning, then Al needs a date for a family wedding. He had been accepted by his newly found father. He shows up with Nyleena. At this point, her focus shifts, after all, while Ace could have stopped the beating, it was Nyleena that got her brother's attention. She comes back to Kansas City and orders the Maidens, some Scavenger's Daughters, two Brazen Bulls, a breast ripper, head cages, and creepier, something that is being examined by Dr. Samuels because he's never seen anything like it."

"What?" I asked.

"It's sort of like a rack, but as the handle cranks and the limbs stretch, spikes come out of the wood." Gabriel informed me.

"That is something new." I frowned.

"Yeah, so she sees Nyleena and Al and threatens Al. She's going to tell Nyleena about their marriage unless he cooperates. He agrees. He lets her keep his credit cards and gives her a debit card. He also steals a copy of your thesis and gets pictures of three plates from your book on torture when Nyleena has it in her custody."

"Which is why they only had the three to go off of," I sighed.

"That would be correct," Gabriel put away the annoying cigarette machine.

"What about her followers?" Nyleena asked.

"She's brilliant; she's been keeping them hopped up on LSD and PCP. Turns out that when you are the drug dealer, making the drug yourself, you can keep a following of wayward young adults. They all had petty records, most of them were run-aways, they were just searching for a leader. Jessica Thompson filled the bill."

"How very Manson-esque," Malachi finally commented.

"Precisely, she got a cult together using drugs and charisma and got them to kill for her. That's why the first set of victims were sexually assaulted. After she found out, she killed one of them to get the others to keep their hands to themselves. One thing Ace was right about though, she kept her victims in Hanging Coffins. She also kept them drugged. It appears that she was psychologically torturing them for the three days. According to Lucas, keeping them high on a hallucinogen was a good way to torture them."

"How'd they pick them?" Malachi asked.

"Jessica gave a description; women between 5'6" and 5'9," size eight or smaller, with dark hair and blue eyes. They trolled shopping areas looking for targets. When they found one, they would follow her and get her habits down. Then when they had the perfect ten and Ace was in town, they would kidnap them. They also had three back-ups for each killing, in case something went wrong. It turns out that Nyleena keeps a very detailed copy of your schedule, which is how they always knew where you were going to be. From there it was pretty easy; they rented a U-Haul to move the Maidens and impaling stakes. I was working with the theory that the Maidens would be incredibly heavy, turns out they aren't..."

"They are hollow," I interrupted. "Most people think they weigh tons, they don't, two strong men and a dolly would easily move one. If you remember, Lucas managed to wrestle one of them on his own when we were in the morgue."

"I hadn't thought of that." Gabriel frowned. "They used horses for the drawing and quartering and cleaned up afterwards. Hence no manure or hoof prints."

"Why my ex?" Malachi asked solemnly.

"Because she sort of fit what Jessica remembered about Nyleena and Aislinn. Humans are terrible witnesses, always have been. Even seeing her the second time, didn't help her. She could get dark hair and light eyes, but she couldn't remember her exact height or weight. When I asked, she referred to Nyleena as a model. Tall, leggy, with dark hair and light colored eyes, she couldn't remember details like how dark her hair was or her exact eye color. So she guessed her eyes were blue and her hair was dark brown. Your ex was just a victim as it turns out. Jessica was unaware you two had history. She couldn't remember much about you at all. When I asked her to describe the man involved, she said he was tall and thin. Nothing about hair or eyes, it seems that you didn't leave an impression. Even after we showed her a picture of you, she couldn't identify you. Your lack of contact over the last two years with Ace was probably a good thing."

"Then you don't know Malachi, it's dangerous to stalk him," I giggled and shot Malachi a look.

"Yes, neither does she; that was the crux of the problem." Gabriel told me. "She couldn't target Malachi because she couldn't remember him. Besides, she blamed her own gender not Malachi for her brother's condition."

"Great," I sat back in the bed and looked at the ceiling.

"What?" Gabriel asked.

"We have the who, what, where, when and why and most of it was thanks to my pseudo-serial killing stalker."

vocab

"Point taken." Gabriel sat down. "Do you think this is going to be a problem?"

"My pseudo-serial killing stalker?" I looked at him.

"Yes."

"Who knows." I shrugged at him.

"Ok, we'll work with it as it crops up. If it becomes a serious problem, we will focus all our energy on catching him. Something I don't think he wants." Gabriel patted my leg.

"Thanks, boss," I said to him. "Hey, how'd the police get there when they did? I don't remember a call being made."

"I'm tagged," Gabriel rolled up the sleeve of his shirt and showed me a scar. "I have a GPS implant. Michael couldn't get a fix on it when we were in the bull, but once we were free, it started transmitting again. You and Lucas both get out tomorrow. I have some things to take care of and then I'll be heading home."

"Where is home?" I asked him.

"As of yesterday, Kansas City, Missouri. Before that, a motel wherever I was stationed." He winked and walked out.

"'We're going to go as well." Nyleena told me.

"Fine. Whatever. I see how it is. You're just going to leave me on my own, in this hell hole."

metaphor
character change

"I'm sure you'll find a way to entertain yourself. Besides, visiting hours are ending," she kissed my cheek. Malachi kissed my forehead. I watched them both leave.

Then I yanked the wire off my heart monitor.

Yeah, I could entertain myself.

Ahh!!!

Epilogue

There was a moving van outside the Federal Guard Apartments. My meager belongings were being shoved into it with about as much care as someone discarding oyster shells. Nyleena was standing next to me. The day was busy and almost over.

I picked up my cane. They were moving me to my new house. It was conveniently located two houses down from Lucas. Xavier was my next door neighbor. Malachi was about a block away.

"Ready?" Nyleena handed me the keys to my car.

"Ready." I told her.

We drove in silence. The GPS occasionally telling me where to turn. It took about thirty minutes to get out of the city and into Blue Springs.

The FG Neighborhood was built out here. As we approached, I was reminded of the Fortress. There were guard towers. There was a white, concrete fence completely surrounding it. It was at least twelve foot tall. The brochure told me it was reinforced concrete.

We stopped at a gatehouse. I showed him my credentials. Nyleena showed hers. There was some talking amongst the three men in the house. Finally, one of them handed me a map.

"Dr. Cain, you're expected. The moving van should be here any minute. It's a pleasure to meet you. I'm Captain Yosh; if you need anything tonight, just give me a call."

"Thank you, Captain," I said. He opened the first gate. I slid my car into the space. The gate closed behind me and a second gate opened. I entered the neighborhood.

I found the street, ironically named "Stonemason Dr," Nyleena gave a short bark of laughter as she looked at it. I smiled and turned right.

"Look they named the street after you," Nyleena gave another quick bark of laughter.

"No, after you. I changed my last name, yours is the one that means stonemason."

My house was the fourth one down the street, on the left. It was a two story house. Not a split level. It had a fortified basement with a panic room. I wasn't sure what I would do with the panic room, but the basement was a good idea in Missouri.

We parked in the drive. Nyleena hit the button, revealing the garage. There was no door leading from the garage to the house. I didn't pull in.

"Expecting to need to make a getaway?" She asked as I hesitated.

"No," I sighed and slid the car into the garage.

The living room was white. The kitchen was white. The bathroom was white. The hallways were white. I frowned as we went room to room only to discover more white.

"I think I'll have a friend of mine come decorate," Nyleena said.

"I was told to leave it, it would be decorated to my tastes shortly," I repeated Xavier's words.

"We are going to be late to Lucas's if we don't hurry."

She led me outside. I limped along behind her. We crossed the street as Xavier exited his house. We waited for him on the porch.

"Michael's already here." Xavier said.

I didn't have anything to say to that, so I rang the doorbell. A small man, wearing glasses and a flamboyant dress shirt, looking every bit like Elton John, opened the door for us. It was eye-bleedingly bright yellow, but it worked for him. He stuck out his hand.

"Ace and Nyleena?" He asked us consecutively.

"Yep," I answered, realizing I was right.

"I'm Trevor. Is your house white?" He asked.

"Horrifyingly white." I agreed.

"Ok, well the next time you go out on a case, I'll get in there and get it done. Now come off the porch, we'll talk about it inside." He didn't come across as being flaming, but something told me that he probably was.

"Lucas, the others have arrived," Trevor said it in a sing-song voice. I decided I was probably going to like him.

"Great, come on in, guys!" Lucas shouted from the living room.

"It's great to meet you," I said to Trevor as we followed him to the living room.

It was very tastefully decorated. Photos of Lucas and Trevor on the walls. Photos of what I could only assume were their families also decorated the walls and mantel and shelves.

"Ace, you've met Trevor. Expect him to be annoying the next couple of days or so. He'll be determined to get to know you and then decorate your house accordingly." Lucas put an arm around the smaller man and smiled at him. I envied the secret held in that smile.

"As long as I don't have to decorate it, he can be my shadow," I smiled at them. The tension drained from the room.

"I'm also a professional chef; feel free to join us for dinner any night. I stopped working a couple of years ago, but I love to cook. The more the merrier and you are a lot prettier company than Xavier." Trevor told me.

"Thank you," I smiled wider and grinned at Xavier.

"Yeah, yeah, I need to shave and I need to pay more attention to my clothes and this and that, yadda yadda yadda."

"We've been working on him for years, but I think he is a lost cause. You on the other hand have lots of potential. I'll make sure you get a more manageable hairstyle and if you need anything for your wardrobe, I'm your guy."

"Trevor is our personal shopper, chef, interior designer and friend," Michael said.

"Awesome. I hate to cook, shop, or decorate!" I told him. "The hair may be an issue though. I keep this style because it requires a brush and a ponytail."

"Understandable, but when you have dates and things, feel free to come over or call me. I help with clothes, make-up and hair."

"I haven't been on a date in years, Trevor. Sorry."

"Damn, I finally get a girl and she's more disastrous than you guys." Trevor joked.

"She's not a Barbie," Lucas mockingly scolded.

"I don't want a Barbie, they have no character and they can't stand upright," Trevor told him.

"Trust me, if I ever have a date, you'll get a call," I told him. "Since I haven't done my hair or make-up since I was an undergrad, I wouldn't have a clue what to do with either now."

"Oh goody," Trevor clapped his hands. "Dinner is served."

About the Author

Hadena James began writing at the age of eight. As a teenager, she had several short stories published in literary magazines. She completed writing her first novel at the age of 17. Hadena graduated from the University of Missouri with a degree in European History with minors in German and Russian studies. She has always wanted to be a writer so she also took several classes in creative writing.

When she isn't busy writing or running her business, Hadena enjoys playing in a steel-tip dart league. She also loves to travel throughout North America and Europe. Her favorite cities are Chicago, Illinois and Berlin, Germany. She is an avid reader; reading everything from the classics like Jane Austen to modern writers like Terry Pratchett. One of her all-time favorite books is "Good Omens" by Neil Gaimen and Terry Pratchett. She writes all of her books while listening to music and the bands tend to get "honorable mentions" within the pages.

www.facebook.com/hadenajames
@hadenajames
http://hadenajames.wordpress.com

CPSIA information can be obtained at www.ICGtesting.com
Printed in the USA
LVOW07s0033191015

458789LV00023B/402/P